I0536791

To my loving family, who supported me throughout all the long days and nights I spent writing, and
their unwavering faith in me as a storyteller.

Table of Contents

ROBERT KAUFFMAN

THE GUARDIANS OF OLYMPUS

1

THE RISE OF OLYMPUS

PANDA BOOKS PRESS

Copyright © 2016 by Panda Books Press Inc.

All rights reserved.

No part of this publication may be reproduced, distributed, or trans-
mitted in any form or by any means, including information storage
and retrieval systems, photocopying, recording, or other electronic
or mechanical methods, without the prior written permission of the
author. Except in the case of brief quotations embodied in critical
reviews and certain other noncommercial uses permitted by copyright law.

This book is a work of fiction. Names, characters, places, and inci-
dents either are products of the author's imagination or are used
fictitiously. Any resemblance to actual persons, living or dead,
events, or locales is entirely coincidental.

For permission requests, email: Contact@PandaBooksPress.com

ISBN 978-0-9907329-0-7

ONE

MY VACATION GOES
HORRIBLY WRONG

"**D**avis, come on, we don't want to be late for our flight!" yelled Mom.

Her voice jarred me from my thoughts as I carelessly tucked the last of my belongings into my suitcase. You see, we were heading on this family trip to Paris, France. The trip had been planned for months, and it was hard to believe summer vacation was already here.

I had just finished packing my stuff, well everything except my favorite outfit that I was already wearing. It's just this ripped up pair of blue jeans, a denim shirt, and my red and white tennis shoes. Before leaving my room, I massaged some mousse into my medium length brown hair and picked up my suitcase. I tried to pack light, but it felt like I was hefting around a bowling ball.

On my way downstairs, a thumping sound caught my attention; it was coming from my parents' room. I burst in, only to find Dad struggling with getting his suitcase down. There was so much stuff packed on top of it that it looked like he was playing Jenga. He was wearing a silver gray Armani suit, a black silk tie, and Rolex watch. Half the time he doesn't even dress that sharp for the office. His salt and pepper hair was sloppy like he ran his fingers through it. He didn't appear to be very enthused, but he was a manly, rugged type guy and very tough to read. No doubt he would pass for the tall, dark and handsome stereotype.

"Are you excited about the trip?" I asked.

The question brought a spark to Dad's chestnut brown eyes, pulling his train of thought off of what he was doing.

"These are some of the highlights I want to see," he said, flipping open a travel brochure showing me pictures of places we would visit.

They were sites like Versailles, the Louvre, Notre Dame and the Left Bank.

But I managed to draw out my father's hidden zeal when I asked, "So, Dad, what are you looking forward to the most in Paris?"

Dad brightened, saying, "I hear the food is great."

"Yeah. What else?"

"Well," he added, "there's always the nightclubs like Moulin Rouge."

"Is that romantic?" I said warily.

Dad scratched his chin.

"Hmm. Maybe not. Maybe that nightlife scene wouldn't be so hot for your mom. She's into romantic walks along the Seine, small cafes. Stuff like that."

"If I were you, I'd make sure she got it."

Dad grinned back. "You're a smart young man, Davis, wise beyond your years."

Mom called for us again, "Ryan, Davis don't forget we are on a tight timeline."

"We will be down in a sec, Ashley, Davis is helping me get a few things."

As I contributed to carrying out our luggage, I could feel a chilly breeze blowing in from the north. I guess this was starting to be "the norm" with the unusual weather patterns here in Pennsylvania, the sky was a pale shade of pink with a few smoky cumulus clouds whisking by as the sun sank beneath the horizon. We were way over packed. The white Cadillac Escalade had been stacked to the roof.

It was obvious how excited Mom was about the trip. She was almost bubbling over with joy. Besides that, I can't remember the last time I saw her dressed up this beautiful. She looked like she'd walked right off of a runway, she was all dolled up like a movie star, and wearing a silver laced dress, which complimented her honey blonde hair that was both wavy and curly. Other people traveled internationally in Bermuda shorts and sandals. Not my parents.

I fueled their enthusiasm by adding my own to it and asking questions. "Mom, what is the Left Bank?"

With a silly grin, she'd answered in a pseudo-French accent, saying, "La vie en rue, cheri."

"Yeah, right, Mom. Like you know what that means. It's something about the street of life, right?"

Mom smiled.

"No, honey, it's simply the Bohemian part of Paris. You know arts, music. L'amour," Mom said, drawing the word out and giggling.

Dad managed to agree with her. "I could not say it better myself; you're spot on, darling."

I found this surprising because he is one of those people that stays totally focused on whatever he is doing. Yet he still voiced his opinion.

Departure went smoothly, and I have to admit I can't remember the last time I saw my dad with a clean shave. It was just too weird.

I haven't flown that much. Once to my grandparents' ranch in Arizona and once to a wedding in Florida. So while I didn't love it, I didn't hate it either. The takeoff was kind of exciting. After all the waiting in the terminal, all the delays on the tarmac and all the taxiing and waiting in line, the final roar of four powerful jet engines, the breathtaking race down the runway and reaching a speed of over a hundred miles an hour. The liftoff. And then Mother Earth diminished to patches of earth stretching out like a patchwork quilt far below us. I didn't know it at the time, but this would be the last time I ever saw my parents.

Everything seemed perfectly normal as the aircraft gained altitude. There was the usual stirring in the cabin as the flight attendants went about their routine work. Except for perhaps an occasional cough from one of the passengers, people mostly just engaged in quiet conversation or rested as the long flight began. An hour or so later, I looked out the window realizing just how high the plane had climbed, far below the jet's wing, city lights were glimmering in every direction, cutting through the darkness of night.

For the first time in a long time, I was excited to be going to a strange place where no one knew me. I figured, after all, Paris is the city of love, so I'd have no problem hooking up with some hot French babes! About an hour into the flight my daydreams came crashing down on me, when a flight attendant startled me with an announcement, "Ladies and gentlemen, the Captain has turned on the fasten seatbelt sign." We are now crossing a zone of turbulence. Please return to your seats and keep your seat belts fastened. Thank you."

Mom pursed her lips, as the color in her face faded to a nauseous, flushed complexion.

"This is normal. Nothing to be alarmed about," she said.

Dad chimed in, "Yeah, I fly all the time and this is quite common."

I honestly was not the least bit nervous, but I was concerned for Mom, I think she was reassuring herself more than me. I was anticipating that she could hurl at any moment. You see she has had a fear of heights, since like forever; it started when she was a little girl and fell out of a tree. So no doubt this turbulence was not in her best interest.

The aircraft bucked around for a bit, and then the end of the silence came like a thunderbolt – accompanied by sheer horror when the jet veered into a dive, and our oxygen masks dropped down. There is nothing more terrifying than an aircraft falling thousands of feet in just seconds, it's like riding a roller coaster into a brick wall. Dad quickly put on his mask, Mom helped me put on my mask before she attached her own. I took several deep breaths getting used to the mask.

Dad took charge of the situation. "Davis, Ashley, assume the bracing position. Lean forward, put your hands on top of your head and then place your elbows against your thighs. Ensure you have your feet flat on the floor."

My heart was beating out of my chest, the minutes seemed to drag on forever as I waited to hear something gets announced, but all I heard was the creaks and groans of the aircraft, it sounded like it was tearing apart at the seams. I looked over at Mom and Dad. I couldn't help but wonder if this would be our last moments together.

"Everything will be fine, I'm sure the pilots are working on stabilizing the situation, just try to remain calm," Dad insisted.

Mom looked over at me her gaze lingered for a moment and then her focus shifted to Dad.

"I love you guys, you are both my world, and I'm so proud and blessed for you both being part of my life if we don't make it just know that I love you."

"Don't talk like that, Mom, everything is going to be fine, right, Dad?"

The hurt in mom's voice surprised me, so I looked over at Dad, and he looked me deep in the eyes, it was like I was peering into his soul, he firmly gripped my shoulder. His thoughts were audible; we were in a heap of trouble.

The pilot's voice came back over the speakers, this time, it was trembling, "Brace, brace, brace, brace!"

It happened so fast. A blinding light illuminated the entire cabin; I could see the terror in the panic-stricken passengers' eyes. Mom and Dad wrapped their arms around me. Flames erupted, igniting everyone a few rows ahead of us on fire.

Freaking out I pulled off my face mask, it felt suffocating. The acrid stench of smoke filling the cabin was overwhelming; I held my shirt over my face struggling to breathe. The cabin became steaming hot. My mind raced a mile a minute, but there was no escaping this, the anguished screams of people dying all around me drove home the reality of it. The uproar of the passengers made it clear that we were doomed. I took one last look into my mother's big emerald green eyes, then I slammed into the seat in front of me, my body went limp as the Atlantic Ocean swallowed up the aircraft, leaving me unconscious.

TWO

A DOLPHIN SAVES ME

At first, it felt like I was having a lucid dream, I could feel myself being pulled, belly up through a body of water. Opening my eyes, I saw a million stars peppering the night sky, I was still in shock from the plane crash and had no idea where I was or who or what was pulling me. With little thought I stretched an arm over my head, feeling around for what was tugging at me. My hand was greeted by a wet, smooth and slippery rubber surface, which I soon realized belonged to a living creature as it stretched and contracted with each movement.

Whatever was pulling me, did not leave me feeling threatened; in fact, at some point, I passed out from my dwindling condition.

***

The morning sun warmed my face. Eyes still closed, I was dreading what damage my body sustained from the crash. I breathed in the strong aroma of salt water, which I could almost taste. My ears honed in on the sound of what I immediately recognized as seagulls. Whatever was pulling me was no longer here, I could sense that my body was on a solid surface and no longer in motion.

First I wiggled my toes, they seemed to work, I could feel the surf licking at my feet. Then I closed my hands, I felt a wet sandy texture that affirmed I was on a beach. I took a deep breath and then opened my eyes, the sunlight was so intense that I couldn't help but squint. So far everything felt fine, and there was no obvious pain.

Without any thought, I routinely went to shield my eyes from the sun with my right hand, which is my dominant hand but was greeted by a snapping sound that sent pain shooting throughout my entire body. Once the initial shock wore off, I pushed through the pain enough to sit up. My body was mangled, I looked like a victim straight out of a slasher flick. There was flesh hanging off my right arm, I could see the exposed bone. With my good arm, I lifted my shirt up, my stomach was severely bruised. Both pants legs had blood stains. I could feel an excruciating pain when I slowly hiked up my left pants leg and could see that the bone had punctured through the flesh, my leg was apparently broken. My other pant leg was blood-soaked, and I could feel my earlobes getting hot, then a nauseous feeling washed over me. I was dreading what my other leg was going to look like since there was like a hundred times more blood on this side. To my surprise, my leg was fine upon inspecting it, and I realized that the blood must have been from one of my other injuries. Or worse it could belong to my parents, I quickly shook that image out of my head, I didn't want to think of them being hurt.

There was no way I was moving, I scanned the beach for any signs of life, the ocean stretched out as far as the eye could see in front of me, the aqua blue body of water seamlessly met a cloudless sky on the horizon. Behind me was a dense tropical looking forest that halted at a sheer rock face that seemed to run the length of the island. My body was too banged up to search for help, so I went with plan B. I screamed for all I was worth, "Help, somebody help me—Mom, Dad anybody! Please HELP!"

I screamed until my throat was raw before I finally gave up. There was now little doubt that either I was on a deserted island or that I was too far from civilization for anyone to hear my screams. My mouth felt dry like sandpaper, and I was having hunger pangs and worse yet I was left without any shade, and my skin was beginning to stinging from the blistering hot mid-morning sun. The hours passed, and I watched the sun sink into the horizon. As twilight set in the island became blanketed in shadow, I hesitantly embraced the unwelcoming realization that I'd be spending the night here and not in a hospital, which I was severely needing.

As the hours passed by, I caught myself shivering uncontrollably; I was wet, cold and feeling weak. I tried so hard to focus on staying awake, but at some point, I lost the battle. That night I had the strangest dream that I was helplessly sinking into the depths of the ocean, the weight of the freezing cold sea was bearing down on me, forcing me deeper into the dark and unknown abyss below. Looking up, I could see flames licking at the surface. The orange glow emitted from the inferno above brought into focus silhouettes of lifeless bodies and floating debris. I could vaguely make out chunks of jet and random stuff, which I assumed to be luggage from passengers' sinking all around me.

I had a hopeless feeling like I just knew there was no coming back from this. I was no longer fighting, but accepting the inevitable, and coming to terms with that realization. At that very moment a large, fish-like creature circled me. Oh great, now I'm going to end up as fish food, I thought to myself. The creature approached me, and I could clearly make out its sea green eyes, as if they were glowing underwater, it was a dolphin. We stared into one another's eyes, its eyes were sad like it had an understanding of my current situation.

Then I was torn from my dream, awaken by a strange, but familiar sound.

"eeeeeeik eeik eeeek."

After a moment of listening, I honed in on the sound and spotted a dolphin splashing just off the coastline. Then it disappeared back into the sea, and I never saw or heard it again, the remainder of the time that I was stuck on the island.

That morning, I lay around feeling helpless and pitying myself. My only solitude from the pain was my brief thoughts of the dolphin. I could not help but wonder if it did save my life. Was my dream actually a memory that was forever burned into my mind? Everything felt like a dream at this point, and I kept hoping I would wake up from this horrific nightmare and be back home, safely in my bed, but unfortunately I knew that was just wishful thinking.

The sun climbed higher in the sky, my best guess was that it was high noon. It was torture, being in an endless body of water and not being able to drink any of it. My mouth was painfully dry, and my lips already started to crack and burn. Scanning the horizon, I saw no sign of ships or aircraft in the area and began to accept that the only way I was ever getting off of this island was by my own doing, or I would die here… all alone.

After a few deep breaths, a decision was made. I was going to fight, there was no way that I was dying here. I had to beat this and make it back home. I clamped down hard with my teeth anticipating the pain and slowly removed my shirt, I needed to use it as a tourniquet. It was torture getting the shirt off of my mangled arm. No matter how careful I was, it was impossible not to inflict pain on myself. After finally getting my shirt off, I could for the first time, see the full extent of damage that I sustained. It was no pretty sight.

The hanging chunk of flesh seemed to have somehow fused back to the wound, and the wound was now covered over by a big scab, and the surrounding skin was now turning red, I feared it was getting infected. I took a deep breath, focusing on what I knew needed to be done. This was survival, and I had to clean this wound. I submerged my arm in the salt water, and gently brushed my fingers over the wound. The pain was unbearable, but I pushed through it, I knew my life depended on me getting my wounds cleaned out.

I gently wrapped my right arm with my shirt, every wrap was excruciating, and I could feel sweat beading on my forehead and back from the pain. Using my left hand and teeth together, I managed to tie off the tourniquet. Next, I removed my belt and pulled my pants down, slowing I inched them toward my ankles. Oddly, my bone was no longer protruding through my leg, and it too was now scabbed over. I thoroughly washed my injured leg, the pain was just as bad, if not worse than my arm. I wrapped the belt around my wound on my leg and made it taught. I scanned the horizon once more, in hopes of a boat or plane but still saw an endless ocean. So, I started to army crawl using my left arm and right leg to propel me forward. It was an agonizing crawl and my energy felt totally drained, but the thought of being back home with my parents gave me the strength to push onward.

After hours of crawling at a snail's pace, I barely covered much distance. I kept to the coastline in hopes of finding someone or being spotted. As the sun once again sank below the horizon, my hopes of being saved started to diminish. Maybe I was really going to die here. I tried to shake the thought of leaving everyone I knew behind, without ever getting the chance to say goodbye, or to drive a car, or do a million other things typical fifteen-year-olds look forward to doing. The more I thought about everything I would be giving up, the stronger my desire became to beat this and get off this rock. I pushed forward, crawling throughout the entire night.

When dawn broke, I saw luggage and wreckage washing in and out with the foaming white surf, there were dozens of suitcases clumped along the beach, just a few hundred feet in front of me. Despite how much my free hand hurt and the rest of my body hurt, I mustered up enough willpower to move forward, I was sliced and banged up from pulling myself forward, over sharp and jagged rocks, my exposed flesh felt like raw hamburger. I could only hope there were other survivors, or food and drink inside the suitcases and dry, warm clothing.

It didn't feel like it took me very long to reach the bags, then again this was the first time in three days I felt a glimmer of hope like I might be rescued after all. I looked around and again saw no sign of life, outside of a couple of seagull's squawking at once another, fighting over some peanuts that washed ashore. It felt like Christmas morning, as I rummaged through the suitcases, looking for food, drink, matches, medicine and dry clothes. I scored a fair amount of food and drink and found a new set of clothes and silver Zippo lighter with the letters LM engraved on it. Most of the clothing was soaking wet, but fortunately for me, one suitcase seemed to keep its contents dry. The clothes looked like they belong to an older gentleman and were nothing I would normally be caught dead in. But today, these were the most fabulous clothes, and I was excited to get them on.

After feasting on a bunch of snack foods like beef jerky, chips and candy, and chugging a bunch of Soda, I felt satisfied. Now I needed a fire, to make me more visible and it also offered the benefit of keeping me warm throughout the night if I was still stranded here at nightfall. I also found a white shirt and a chestnut walking cane and made myself a rescue flag that I could hold up and wave around for help if I spotted a boat or plane. The remainder of the day I worked on emptying the contents of all the suitcases and spreading the clothes out to dry so I could burn them and collect anything that could be used for survival.

As twilight washed over the island, I began to stack clothing, suitcases, magazines and anything else that was burnable into a heaping pile, and then I used the Zippo to ignite it. Once the fire took, I started inching away from it.

As night settled in, the insects serenaded the night, and the light from the fire made my stay a bit more enjoyable, as I watch the glowing embers from the magazines and newspaper float off into the night sky, it offered a false sense of security, which I was happy to have. It made me feel that I had a much higher chance of being rescued, and it warded off any potential predators. I ate a pouch of Sunflower seeds and washed them down with a bottle of spring water.

I tossed a few more clothes and suitcases onto the fire and crawled into the remaining pile of clothing to get some sleep. I lay there restless, thinking about the crash, reliving the events over and over. What was that blinding white light? It made the front of the jet ignite in flames. Was it the engines exploding? Would that look like a spotlight? Then my train of thought switched back to the dolphin, did it actually rescue me? At some point, I fell asleep.

The following morning, I woke up to the whump-whump-whump-whump sound of a helicopter. My fire was barely burning, frantically I tossed clothes on it and anything flammable I could get my hands on, then I picked up my rescue flag and waved it high over my head. The helicopter came into sight and passed me, my heart sank, I screamed at the top of my lungs, "HELP, PLEASE HELP ME!" a moment later the helicopter circled back making two passes over me, I knew I was spotted; it was the best feeling ever. I was going home.

THREE

I MAKE THE NEWS

A glance around told me I was in a hospital, but I had no memory of arriving and no clue what hospital I would be at. The last thing that I could remember was getting loaded into a rescue chopper, on top of a gurney. If this was not a hospital could I be dead, was that a possibility? Leaning forward sent my pain receptors into overload. To say I hurt everywhere would be a gross understatement, but this helped reassure me that I was still alive.

So when I complained to the first person in hospital dress I saw, I was relieved when they flipped some gadget attached to my arm. And a blessed relief replaced the pain.

A half hour or so later the pain had diminished, but I still had no idea how long I had been here, when I got here, or even what day it was.

My distress was relieved so I asked the nurse who had arrived to check my monitors, "Where am I?"

She came close enough for me to read her nametag, but it was blurry. I thought it read Angel. As I tried to discern it through my drug-induced haze, I said, "Angel? Your name is Angel? Am I in heaven?"

"No, Davis. You're in the ER at Mercy Hospital."

"Mercy…? Where…?" I said.

"Mercy Hospital, Holbrook, Long Island."

"Long…?"

"Long Island, New York." She said.

"But I was on my way to Paris with my parents…"

"Hush up now. The doctor will be along in a while to answer all your questions."

About an hour or so later a gray-haired doctor in a white lab coat stood over me. I didn't need him for any details because it all came back to me. The details were so vivid; my heart was pumping so fast that I could hear it, as I flashed back.

The horror on my parents' faces, the horrible gut twisting sensation of an aircraft in a fatal dive and then that white light, as blinding as a spotlight followed by flames and the tumult of passengers reeling in pain.

When I tried to turn my head to sob in semi-private, I realized that there was a neck brace around my neck and I couldn't move. This added to my building paranoia.

"Hello, Mr. Finch, I'm Dr. Nelson," he said glimpsing at his chart.

"After running a battery of tests, there appears to be nothing wrong with you. In fact, not even a scratch. You are one lucky kid, to survive something like that... I'd say you have someone looking out for you, like a guardian angel!"

"So my legs and arms are not broken?"

"Not at all, son, they are perfectly fine."

Luck? I didn't feel so lucky. More like dazed and confused, it felt so real. How could I imagine all the damage done to my body? Also, why didn't I fight with Mom and Dad about going to Paris? Disney World in Florida, to name just one place, would have been much more exciting anyway. If we'd gone there instead, none of us would have been part of the crash.

"So, my neck's not broken or anything?" I asked.

"Nope, the neck brace is just standard protocol to stabilize the victim, for when we suspect a patient may have sustained trauma to the neck or head."

"How long have I been in the hospital?"

"You arrived last night, so about a day, at most," Dr. Nelson replied.

I looked into the doctor's dark blue eyes.

"Are Mom and Dad Ok? And the rest of the people, did most of them make it out of the wreck?" I blurted.

I could hear the regret in his voice.

"I'm sorry, son... so sorry. You're the only survivor."

"An NTSB agent is waiting to speak with you, I'll be sending her back now that you're awake," Dr. Nelson said glancing at his charts.

My heart sank, how was it possible to survive a crash when both of your parents die right beside you, and everyone else on the jet. My guilt was boiling like a volcano about to erupt. I could feel a familiar sting in my eyes as they pooled with tears. This was no doubt the worst day of my life.

A female agent approached my bedside. The agent's dark black hair was up in a bun, and it bounced as she walked. A sleek black pistol holstered to her side caught my attention.

"Hello Davis, I'm agent Snyder with the National Transportation Safety Board. I'm here to take your statement," she took out a pen and paper. "Please take your time; I need you to capture every moment down to the smallest detail, about what happened on Flight 381 from the time you boarded, until the time it went down."

I went over the entire event as best I could, it was not easy. I tried to focus my attention on the yellow wording on her sleeve that read "NTSB," trying to hide my tears, I'm pretty sure that this was the most I had ever cried. I felt so empty and resentful.

Turns out they suspected a terrorist attack, and that there were 300 passengers aboard the jet, including myself. This made me feel so hurt and torn; the guilt that was weighing on me for being alive was immense. I almost wished that I had died alongside everyone else. It just seemed so much simpler that way. What was so special about me that I was spared and nobody else? What really bugged me was my memory of being mangled, it felt way too real to just shrug it off.

The next morning, I woke up to a newspaper sitting on a tray with my breakfast. The front-page headline blared: "Teenage Boy, Sole Survivor of Flight 381!

A survivor of the North Atlantic plane crash is now called "The world's luckiest boy" after being found alive and well a week after the European-bound jet went down. It was previously thought that all 300 passengers died in the wreck. The death toll has now been changed to 299 after identifying Davis Finch, who was listed as a passenger aboard the ill-fated Flight 381.

A freak accident in the North Atlantic led to his discovery when Captain Carter Miller and his crew were nearly capsized after a blue whale crashed into their ship. Scientists speculate the whale's internal navigation was to blame.

The whale left the engine room of the "Fleeting Hope" flooded and Captain Miller was forced to radio for help. A rescue helicopter was dispatched to the location and spotted a few pieces of wreckage on a nearby uncharted island, where they later found the 15-year-old boy—"

Enraged, I tore the paper in half without reading another word.

FOUR

A NEW START

After three days at Mercy, I was excited to be getting released today. I would not miss the sterile world of the hospital with all the white, the antiseptic smells and the strangers in hospital garb. I was more or less stuck here until they got hold of my guardian, who is Aunt Lisa, my Mom's sister.

I thought about the trip and a lot of questions popped up. Along with a lot of guilt. I didn't know if this guilt was the inevitability of being the only survivor to a major tragedy or something deeper, but whatever it was it wouldn't let go of me.

What if my parents had picked a different destination? Obviously, we would have been on a different flight. Why had they picked Paris? When I thought about it, Paris was kind of a romantic destination, the idealized escape of many middle-aged people with romantic fantasies. It was hardly the dream trip for a 15-year-old.

Was that my parents? Secret romantics? I had never noticed if they had that tendency. Growing up as a typical kid I didn't pay attention to them more than my parent-child relationship required.

But they had planned it as a family vacation even waiting until school got out to do it. So their plan had been for us all to go.

Aside from the guilt trip, I was on, other questions haunted me. Like what are the odds of a whale swimming into a ship? If not for that freak accident, I'd still be stranded on that godforsaken island; I honestly had never heard of anything like it. The odds had to be astronomical, and my injuries just seemed to magically heal overnight. There was no way I imagined them, the pain was burnt into my skull. Pain like that you don't just forget, you take it to the grave. And the blinding white light, that was definitely surreal. Was it possibly, something from the nether world?

That too was strange because I wasn't particularly mystical or even interested in the 'beyond.' Well, no more than any other kid my age. Sure, when I was a little younger my friends and I used to talk about death and what it was like to be dead. But it was strictly Halloween kind of talk. Stuff kids talked about after a scary movie. We had seen "Ghost" and thought it was cool the way dead people didn't leave the earth but remained as spirits to influence the lives of their loved ones and others. I wondered where my parents were in the universe. The old church teachings of heaven and hell came into play, but I couldn't imagine them as anyplace but heaven. That is if they were anyplace.

The more I thought about it though I seemed to get more in touch with my mystical side, that is, the other side. The light had to be some type of portal or symbol or even a guide. Of that I was sure. I was also certain it was no fantasy and that I might have had an out of body experience. Still, there were so many questions. The one time I brought up the white light with one of the nurses, she said something about making an appointment with a psychiatrist so I quickly dropped it. Next time I saw her I lied and told her that I was sure now, it was a dream. I didn't want to say or do anything that would prolong my stay in the hospital, and sure enough, the issue just faded away.

Aunt Lisa finally arrived to pick me up. Her face was pale and full of concern. On the way out to her vehicle, a slew of reporters surrounded us, snapping pictures and focusing their camcorders. Their microphones felt invasive as they pressed them into my face, asking me a flurry of questions.

"Is it true the plane was the target of a terrorist attack?" shouted one reporter.

"Can you tell us what it was like when the plane was going down?" asked another one.

"Is there anything you would like to say to the families of the people on board Flight 381, being the only survivor?" came yet another question.

I stood there nearly petrified, shielding my face with my hands.

"Back off!" screamed a familiar voice.

"Do you people not have a heart? My nephew has just been through a traumatic event and lost his parents. He does not need this," Aunt Lisa scolded them, shoving one of the reporter's camcorders away from us.

We made a dash for the car and backed away as the reporters swarmed in for a closer shot. I honestly hated being the focus of this pack of media jackals. It felt like I didn't deserve such recognition; after all, it's not like I was a hero and saved the day!

On the car ride home, I rolled down my window and the fresh air circulated through the car, permeating it with a welcoming smell of fresh cut grass and apples. Aunt Lisa lived in apple country, and you can't go more than a few miles in any direction without seeing orchards.

"Thanks for that, back there..." I said.

"I'm sure you would have done the same for me."

I could feel the tension building inside the small Ford Taurus as Aunt Lisa skipped through the radio stations; she appeared to be tense, and very fidgety.

"Would you like to talk about the..." I said then found myself pausing before I could finish the sentence.

"We do need to talk, Davis... we have to decide something crucial."

"And that would be?" I said.

I couldn't help but wonder what could be so important; my mind was whirring in a million directions. Up until now, I'd never given any consideration to what my future had in store for me, once I left the hospital.

What she said next tied my stomach in knots.

"I really have no experience at being a mom, and this is all so sudden. But I do want you to come live with me. My sis and your father had appointed me your guardian after all."

I huffed, "So you're stuck with me then, I get it!"

"No, no sweetie… I didn't mean it like that. I'm trying to say this is going to be new for the both of us. You know? Like a new beginning."

I could sense her sadness, though she tried to conceal it as she reasoned with me. But no matter how she tried to make it sound, I knew the truth. This was no new start. It was my only option if I didn't want to end up living in a foster home. But nothing could change my sad reality. Life as I'd known it had ended forever.

FIVE

THE FUNERAL

Time was going by so fast, the accident happened a little over a week ago, and here I was still dwelling on the same questions. I innately knew that this type of obsession wasn't healthy and I should forget it (not my parents) and get on with my life. As Aunt Lisa had told me, it was going to be a new beginning for her and for me.

These were my thoughts during the long, lonely days after being released from the hospital. I had to ask myself how was this much different than the hospital? It was the same dull routine, except this was a routine that led nowhere. At least in the hospital, there was the goal of getting out. What was my purpose living out a boring life at Aunt Lisa's? The only thing I had to look forward to was school in the fall.

Any other year I would have been excited about going back to see my friends, but this was the least of my cares at the moment.

Aunt Lisa took me shopping to get a suit for the funeral; I was really not looking forward to it. But at the same time, I had hoped that I might feel some sort of closure and be able to get my obsession with what happened under control before I ended up in the loony bin wearing a straightjacket!

The days leading up to my parents' funeral were chaotic, to say the least. I'd been to a couple of funerals before, but nothing prepares you for the moment you have to put both of your parents in some deep dingy hole, in the middle of an ancient looking cemetery.

The funeral was minuscule and wet from the rain. A few relatives made appearances. Many of them I did not recognize. I was the youngest of the pallbearers. Most of them were my grandparent's neighbors, or from the church, my parents and I used to attend. Despite my fears, the service went smoothly. I did my best to focus on the task at hand, trying really hard not to screw things up. My heart was beating uncontrollably; the weight of the coffin was mine to bear, it made my stomach turn in knots wondering which of my parents lay inside. I spotted my Aunt Lisa amongst the sparse crowd, tears streaked down her face she held a tissue in her hand, offering me an obviously fake but encouraging smile.

We carefully placed the caskets over the freshly dug graves. The priest opened the coffins and began reading from his bible. His voice continued in a low tone. The words seemed to string together in a way that was foreign to me.

My mind could not wrap around the reading but lingered on the past.

My heart sank when I finally saw my mom and dad; it was the first time I laid eyes on them since the plane ride. They didn't look like the same people, they seemed bloated, and their skin tones were off. I was told they both drowned, which was far from comforting. The thought of my parents fighting for air their last moments on Earth weighed heavy on my emotions. I clasped my hands in front of me and lowered my head to say some final words in silence.

I couldn't bear looking at them a moment longer, if not for the rain my tears would have been really obvious. Aunt Lisa was right beside me; she looked very conservative in a somber sort of way. She was wearing a long black dress, a black satin-laced veil that masked her face, and she held open a black umbrella sheltering her frame as rain beaded and pooled together near the top before trickling down the sides.

Everything about the funeral felt wrong, it felt like I had been robbed like my parents got the short end of the stick. They looked too young to be stuffed into two identical black walnut coffins.

The gray sky, billowing black clouds, and light rain seemed almost fitting for the occasion. It looked as dreary as everyone's mood. After lowering my parents into the ground I was ready to get out of the cemetery, I was not feeling festive. I wanted no part in feasting after the funeral.

I seriously lost my appetite, and I couldn't picture Mom or Dad being offended if I didn't eat right after seeing them dead.

After the service, Aunt Lisa insisted that we go to a nearby church hall for the wake. The guests filed into a big cafeteria-like room in the church basement. A brunch buffet had been set up along one wall, with fresh fruit, croissants, and pastries. Another table presented coffee, juice and a pitcher of water. A few cookies and confections had been spread in yet another location, drawing the interest of a couple of small children who were among the group.

My Aunt Lisa picked at a few pastries, but didn't eat; I could tell that she was just as torn up inside like me. We took a seat at one of the tables, away from most of the other mourners. My aunt greeted a few of the family members she recognized, and I offered a hello when appropriate.

A lot of strange people that I never met previously offered sympathetic words and condolences about my parents. I secretly wished that they would stop. I understood that they meant well, but it rehashed memories of the things I was trying to not think about.

Finally, the gathering began to thin out.

"Davis, how about we head back home. I have a long day ahead of me tomorrow."

"I can't wait to get out of here!"

Getting out of here was a huge relief. I was happy that I got through it all without breaking down, and the suggestion of going home was a welcoming thought.

"We just have to find your grandfather." Aunt Lisa murmured.

I located an older man speaking to the priest and instantly knew it was grandpa; he was wearing a worn dress suit that probably was popular in the 40's. He ended the conversation, immediately turning his attention on me.

"Davis!"

Grandpa had a twinkle of sadness in his eyes. He gave me a firm handshake.

"Sorry for your loss my boy, wish we were getting together on happier terms."

"Hi, grandpa!"

I was glad to see my grandfather. He always had a very kind way about him that brightened my mood, but I was too overwhelmed with grief to enjoy his company.

"I know this wasn't easy for you, to be up in front of all those people," Grandpa said.

"No, it was ok, grandpa."

"Good." His grandfather turned to Aunt Lisa. "Thank you so much for bringing him, Lisa."

He gave her a hug.

"It was no problem, Mr. Finch, you know I…"

"Please, call me Jonathan!" He smiled; Aunt Lisa returned the gesture before starting again.

"Jonathan…you know I would never have let Davis miss this. I am so sorry for your loss." Aunt Lisa said.

"My dear, I am old. I miss my son dearly, and the world will not be the same without him. However, it is something we all must endure." His voice cracked slightly but still he remained steadfast in his convictions. "One day I will be with him again. Until then, I will continue to be strong." He immediately changed the subject.

"Davis, it has been so long since you came to the ranch. Perhaps one day you and your aunt could pay me a visit?"

He rested his hand on my shoulder.

"Sure, Grandpa."

The thought of taking a trip to the ranch again sounded like a good distraction. I could still remember certain parts of it very well, especially the old barn. I used to spend hours playing in the hay, petting the horses and looking for mice in the old building. It felt like centuries had passed since I last visited the ranch.

"Wonderful."

My grandfather laughed. He steadied his gaze on me and then on Aunt Lisa, "I suppose you have a long drive ahead of you. I will not keep you any longer than I already have. It was wonderful seeing you both."

"You as well, Jonathan… have a safe trip home." Aunt Lisa said.

I gave grandpa a hug and said goodbye.

I couldn't wait to get back to Aunt Lisa's, once inside the car I secured my seatbelt, loosened my tie and unbuttoned the top buttons of my dress shirt.

"I can't wait to get out of these clothes!" I said.

Aunt Lisa muttered, tugging at her stockings. "There, that looks good."

The drive home seemed so long. Aunt Lisa put on the radio, I figured she was not in the mood to talk. So I reclined in my seat, thinking about all the fun I had at my Grandparent's ranch.

***

The following day I found myself sitting in my room gazing listlessly out the window. It was a bright sunny day with a dark blue, cloudless sky. I was trying to keep a positive outlook, but the funeral weighed on my emotions like a bar of lead. I focused my eyes on two gray squirrels bouncing about and playing tag in the backyard; if not for watching them I would have never noticed Alicia Thomas next door.

She went inside the front door of a medium size log cabin, it was the only log cabin on the entire dead-end street. She had a white tank top, black shorts, and her golden mane was tied back in a ponytail. Alicia had been my secret dream girl from the very first time I laid eyes on her, never in a million years would I have guessed she lived next door to my Aunt. I had never had enough courage to get into a lengthy conversation with her yet the few times

I could remember spending any time with her I had been enchanted, totally completely captivated.

Our only real connection had been school. Although I was thrilled to learn that Alicia lived right next door, it brought back a kind of hopeless longing.

Alicia was one of the most popular girls at Mill Creek, the type of girl who would never consider an average schmuck like me. The kind of girl I'm talking about, stunning looks, perfect grades, and an active social life, I'm sure you know the type...

I watched her for several days, trying to build up my courage. Mostly in her yard, which was a large tract studded with ancient oak. The trees blocked my view of her activities sometimes, and that was kind of frustrating. Alicia was part of the gymnastics team in school and would practice her routine that was a mixture of bending, stretching and acrobatics. She was fun to watch. I honestly never knew anyone who could move with such grace. It was obvious how serious she was about the sport, with all the hours of practice she put in every week.

I never would have planned it the way it happened. I just wasn't ready yet. I feared I would swallow my tongue trying to talk to her. But -- thankfully -- Alicia broke the ice. When I opened the front door one day to get the mail there, she was. Right in front of me.

"Oh," Alicia said, surprised. "Davis! We have your mail."

Alicia handed me a couple of letters. I hardly looked at them when I took them. She said, "I had no idea you lived here. Is Lisa a relative?"

I froze. The silence was loud. Finally, I reacted to her shuffling feet and said, "Oh yeah. My Aunt Lisa," I managed to blurt.

"I see. Look Davis, I heard about…about your parents."

It was like she couldn't get it out. Then she took a deep breath. "I read about the terrible plane accident in the local papers. Again, I'm so, so sorry."

"Thanks. I…"

"It must have been so hard for you. I—I can't even imagine." There was another silence, this one even more awkward.

She said, "You do know who I am? Alicia Thomas?"

"Yeah. Of course," I managed to say.

We haven't actually said two words to each other since the ninth grade.

"Davis, I've been thinking about you, but since school is the only place I see you, there was nothing I could do."

I was happy that she even remembered me. But I thought that she was just acting polite, and it was all about my parents. This was all right, but I would have liked it to be a little bit about me too. Still, I appreciated her giving me any thought.

When a new silence between us became unbearable, Alicia turned to leave. I mumbled a goodbye.

When she got to the porch steps, she turned and said, "Davis…if you need anything…or even just to talk. Please call me. We're in the book. Ok?"

"Thanks," I said, hoping my voice didn't betray how elated I was by her attention.

I lazed around on the sofa in the living room most of the evening, my mind focused on two things, Alicia, and going back to my old house in the morning to collect some belongings. I can't quite describe what I was feeling on an emotional level, something along the lines of getting run over by a stampede of bulls while crawling belly down over a layer of hot coals? Yet Alicia brought back a flicker of hope that was previously extinguished.

SIX

A DAY TO REMEMBER

Aunt Lisa and I made the trip back to my old house, something I had been dreading. We had to pick up the rest of my things. When we turned into the driveway, I could feel a wave of memories wash over me, like when I was younger and drew colorful creatures on the driveway with sidewalk chalk that would linger on for days and how Dad and I use to toss the ball in the backyard every summer. I spent my whole life living in this one place, and now it felt alien to me. The grass around the house was overgrown, a sign that the property had been vacant, and the flower garden that lined the white picket fence bordering the yard was clumped with weeds.

The architecture of the house closely resembled that of a vintage home during the Victorian era; it was encased in a gray stone exterior. I stepped inside, and it felt lifeless, cold and ominous like a museum. A layer of dust had gathered over the cherry wood, spiral staircase, and the other wooden furniture. Soon I knew newcomers would be exploring my family's old house. The thought irritated me. They would poke and prod, examining its worthiness. Eventually, someone would take an interest and make it theirs. The mental image of strangers in my home and enjoying the place deepened my sadness.

I gathered my things in my bedroom. I stuffed my PlayStation 4 into one of the duffel bags, packing up controllers and games as well. In my old life I took pride in owning a video game collection, but now I just carelessly tossed everything in my bag.

The duffel bags filled quickly. When they were ready, I hefted them over my shoulder and headed to the car. The hardest part was reminding myself that Mom and Dad were not ever coming back home… I swear that I could almost feel my Dad working in his study and my Mom looking out the window while admiring her flower garden, sitting in her favorite chair in the kitchen. Shaking the feeling was hard.

I walked through the house looking for any trinkets or mementos that would help me remember my parents. Aunt Lisa left me alone. I could read her facial expressions and body language it was obvious she wanted me to do this alone; she must have felt I needed this time to myself. I found my father's old collection of baseball cards and a small golden locket that had been in my mother's family, an heirloom. It had an intricate relief design that swirled around the center. One side hung a little crooked when the locket was opened. But it still remained securely closed when shut.

On my rounds through the house, I noticed Aunt Lisa sitting on the old orange floral print couch in the living room. She was paging through my Mom and Dad's wedding album that sat on the coffee table. Aunt Lisa must have caught a glimpse of me out of the corner of her eye.

"Davis come sit down, I could use some company," she said.

I sat down on the sofa beside her. It felt so comfortable, like sitting on a heaping pile of feathers. Odd how you take things for granted, I never once thought of the sofa as comfortable the entire time we owned it, up until now.

I could sense my aunt was holding back bottled up emotions as her gaze lingered on each picture. I'm sure she was trying to be strong for me, and I appreciated it.

There was my mother, Ashley looking beautiful as she always did. Her white gown was elegant, with spaghetti straps and a wide ballroom skirt embroidered with dainty white flowers and pearls. The excitement of that day had now evolved into a world of grief.

I had the distinct feeling that something was finished forever and something new was about to start.

***

The following morning, I was greeted with a nice spread, Aunt Lisa had awakened early to make me a surprise breakfast. I could tell from the bags under her eyes that it had been a sleepless night for her. From the best I could gather, she was haunted by the recent tragedy and my future.

"Good morning, Aunt Lisa," I said.

"Good morning, Davis, I whipped up some breakfast for us," she said with a warm smile.

The food was already on the table, but I wasn't used to sitting down to a hot breakfast. My parents were always busy, so my idea of breakfast was a cold bowl of cereal.

"I wasn't sure what you'd like," she said, "so I made you eggs and pancakes."

The distinct smell of hot oil and eggs lingered in the air. Half asleep I poked at the food on the plate, shoveling a few bites into my mouth. I felt a bit rude and ungrateful for not finishing my plate but how I felt was almost impenetrable.

After breakfast I felt like a robot as I prepared to go outside and see if I saw any sign of Alicia next door; there wasn't any. While waiting outside, I noticed even the smallest little thing triggered memories of my parents and set me into tears, I knew deep down that it be a long time before I'd start to feel normal. Sick of feeling down, I finally got the guts to accept Alicia's offer, I went back inside, got out the phone book, and flipped it open to the T's. I skimmed through the White Pages under the name Thomas, until I spotted one with a similar address to my aunt. "Bingo," I said aloud, nervously I picked up the cordless phone and poked in the numbers.

On the third ring, a familiar voice answered.

"Hello, this is the Thomas residence."

I could feel my palms sweating as I gripped the phone. "Uhhhh, hi," I stammered.

"Is that you, Davis?" she said.

"Yeah Hi, this is Alicia Thomas, right?"

"Yeah, I'm like totally surprised you called," she said.

Surprised? What did she mean by that? After all, she did offer for me to call her. I felt all choked up. Did I misconstrue her offer, was the offer phony and just a way of saying sorry in a nice way because she pitied me? Thank God she responded before I slammed the phone down on the receiver.

"Davis, hello, you still there?"

"Yeah I'm still here," I said, my heart still pounding.

"I meant I was like just holding the phone, getting ready to call you. That's why I am surprised that you called. Weird, huh? Like we must be on the same wavelength or something."

I felt an immense relief; if you clocked my heart, it had to be doing at least 140 mph! The phone call lasted for a good twenty minutes, and we shared some laughs, reminiscing about how I stuck crayons up my nose back in kindergarten, yeah I really did that... long story. I generally never talk this much, but with Alicia, I can't seem to stop. After a bunch of mostly lame jokes and trying to not sound too much like a dork, she asked me to hang out with her that afternoon at one o'clock.

To say I was ecstatic would be a horrible understatement. I was smiling so much that my cheeks were hurting. I spent the last three hours getting ready, rehearsing lines, and stuff to talk about. Aunt Lisa noticed my smile. "I can't remember the last time I saw you smile that much, what got into you, mister?"

"I'm hanging out with Alicia in about two hours."

"It shows… She is a sweet girl. She helps me with my garage sale every year, I hope the two of you have fun," Aunt Lisa said.

Without another word, she went back to her morning routine around the house. She always did her cleaning in the morning, and then she would head off to work at noon. She was the branch manager at the local bank, Milbank, a silly name. But also fitting since we live in the big city "Mill Creek."

I listened to the ticking sound of Aunt Lisa's grand-father clock as I paced the dining room floor, glancing up from time to time at the hour hands, which seemed to be taking forever. After what felt like an eternity I finally heard the dong, dong, dong sound of the grandfather clock. I'm pretty sure I floated out the door, but maybe it was just a chronic case of jitters and butterflies in my stomach. Right on time, Alicia was already outside waiting for me, and she looked even more stunning than normal.

Alicia smiled at me, she looked breathtaking in her blue dress that stopped a few inches above her knees. The front was not very revealing, but it hinted toward naughty. It had a double strap design showing skin in all the right places. She had on high heels with black Roman style straps that wrapped around her ankles, straightened long blonde hair, pink lipstick, and black eyeliner surrounding those intense blue eyes.

"You look beautiful…" I said, trying to keep from drooling.

"Awe thanks, you look good yourself," she said.

Alicia reached into her pocket and pulled something out. Talk about a blast from the past, she held up two old sock puppets that our class made back in the third grade.

"Remember these, Davis?" Alicia said blushing.

"Oh my God, I can't believe you still have them. You like totally rocked in that play in third grade," I said.

The rest of the day went by so fast, Alicia and I completely hit it off, and we both were disappointed when we heard her mom calling over the wooden slat fence for her to come home for dinner. Up until today I never would have imagined Alicia, and I having a conversation, let alone spending hours together just chilling and talking about old times.

"Well… I guess it's time for me to go home… I had fun, Davis, we should do this more often."

"Maybe tomorrow we can meet at the same time?" I said, I hoped I wasn't blushing.

"Sounds good, I'll see you then," Alicia said biting her lip.

She walked away and looked back over her shoulder. With an uncoordinated wave and big smile, I sent her off. I felt like a big lumbering oaf watching her walk away until she disappeared out of sight.

SEVEN

FACE OF A STRANGER

The days, weeks and months flew by; Alicia and I were now inseparable. Our days revolved around one another. Aunt Lisa, she was my new best friend, and living next door to Alicia was comparable to all the good stuff I'd ever heard about Heaven. But there was still the nagging obsession in the back of my mind, with why I survived. No matter how hard I tried to shake it and move on with my life, I was not tuff enough. One thing became apparent, I needed answers if I was ever going to have a chance at a normal life ever again. Looking back, I wish I had clung onto every moment. Life as I knew it, was about to do a complete one-eighty.

I couldn't help but giggle to myself, as I watched Aunt Lisa; she was leaning against the kitchen counter, fixated on her cell phone. She typed furiously, her tongue peeking out from the side of her mouth. Her lips were curled in a partial smile, and her brow was furrowed as her slender fingers hit each button. I saw her texting coworkers and the few friends she kept in touch with every now and again. But, she had always been very casual about it and never looked so intent.

I stared at her for several seconds, thinking she would notice me giggling. It was apparent she had no idea I was here. A few locks of her silky hair slid down around her face. Her fingers suddenly stopped as she hit one final button and looked up from her cell phone.

"Oh!" She appeared startled." I didn't hear you, Davis." She quickly tucked the cell phone into the pocket of her denim jeans.

Aunt Lisa's cat Caesar trundled into the kitchen, stopping to lean against my leg. I reached down and gently stroked his silky head. The cat nudged its head into my pant leg, narrowing his eyes and lowering his ears. Satisfied with the attention, he continued into the kitchen, scanning the backyard as he pressed his nose against the sliding glass door. A few dried smear marks indicated this was a favored spot for Caesar.

"I didn't mean to interrupt," I said, trying to measure my Aunt's reaction.

"You weren't interrupting anything." She responded quickly.

I walked over to the sliding door, parting it enough for Caesar to slip out. I couldn't help but feel suspicious of my aunt, she was acting strangely.

"Will you be going to see Alicia later?" Aunt Lisa asked.

I could feel my cheeks getting warm.

"I don't know."

I grabbed a bright red apple from the bowl of fruit that Aunt Lisa always had on the kitchen table, I took a bite, and it was sweet and juicy.

"You probably should, I bet she would love to see you!"

I shrugged.

Caesar returned to the sliding door, and I left him back inside. A moment later the cordless house phone rang, breaking the awkward silence. Aunt Lisa hurried to answer it.

"Hello? How are you, Alicia? I'm good, thank you! Why yes of course he is. One second, I will go get him." She spoke into the receiver, covering it with her hand and holding it out for me.

"It's Alicia for you." She whispered.

I stood up, taking the phone. I knew something was up, so I kept giving my aunt an awkward stare. But for the life of me, I couldn't figure it out. She was defiantly up to something that much I was sure of.

"Hello, Alicia."

"Hi, Davis!" A cheerful voice exclaimed. "I was wondering if you were busy today?"

Like seriously, every time I hear Alicia's voice I get butterflies in my stomach, she has that kind of effect on me.

"Me? No. I don't do much on Saturdays."

"Great! Well, I was going to see if you would like to go to lunch, maybe? My mom was going to go shopping at the mall, and she said she could drop us off someplace and pick us up when she was done. She is even letting me drive!"

"Cool! I didn't know you had your permit?"

"Yup just got it a few days ago, but don't worry my dad has been teaching me for a while. I promise I won't drive fast or anything." Alicia giggled.

I'd never tell Alicia, but I was secretly jealous that she was driving before me, but then again she was a few months older than me, so I guess it made sense.

"Well—congratulations!" I said.

"Thanks! So um, how about I pick you up in fifteen minutes or so?"

"Sure, alright."

This was the first real date I've ever been invited to, and I already felt nervous.

"Ok, see ya then!"

"See ya!" I said.

Walking back into the kitchen, I saw Aunt Lisa emptying the dishwasher.

"Er...Aunt Lisa? Is it alright if I go to lunch with Alicia this afternoon?"

"Of course."

Her voice sounded muffled because she crawled halfway into the cabinet under the counter. She was clanking the stoneware and ceramic dishes as she worked. After getting all of her mixing bowls properly stacked, she stood up again.

"Did you know she was going to call?" I said.

"Me? How would I know when your girlfriend is going to call and ask you to go out, I'm not a psychic?" she said, looking guilty.

I tried to spell out that Alicia was only a friend, but Aunt Lisa refused to listen.

"Here, take this."

She fished a wad of dollars out of her pocket, handing them to me.

"That should cover it I think."

I looked down at the wrinkled bills in my hand and counted them. It was thirty dollars, I never expected my aunt to give me any money, especially this much. Like five or ten bucks, sure but thirty?

"I can't take your —."

Aunt Lisa interrupted, "No no—It's not a gift. You earned it by helping me around the house. So consider it your paycheck. Maybe sometime soon we will discuss an allowance. For now, you have somewhere to be, so get going!"

There was no point arguing with Aunt Lisa, once she sets her mind on something forget it—so I decided to go get dressed for my date. I picked out a clean pair of blue jeans and a green polo shirt to wear. I had just enough time to get dressed and run a comb through my hair before the doorbell rang.

I could faintly hear my aunt speaking, so I figured it must be Alicia.

Before Aunt Lisa could finish her sentence, I was already downstairs and standing in the entryway.

"Hi!" I said.

It occurred to me that I had no idea what else to say, I suppose this is what stage fright must feel like, but I had only an audience of one. A second of awkward silence had passed before Aunt Lisa ushered us out.

"Go have fun you two!" She said, shutting the door behind us.

I climbed into the back seat of Alicia's mom's car. I had no idea what to say to the woman. She was very friendly and outspoken, she asked me a flurry of questions from how I was doing, to how my aunt was doing financially. Some of the questions seemed a bit intrusive, but I was trying to get Alicia's mom's approval. I had no idea how much she knew about my past. However, I did notice that she seemed to avoid mentioning my parents.

Honestly, I was terrified of saying the wrong thing with Alicia's mother in the car. As it was, I was surprised she allowed her daughter to spend time with me. I assumed her mom knew about my brush with death and the loss of my parents, I'm sure I had juvenile delinquent stamped on my forehead. Maybe she didn't know, or Alicia came up with something that sounded better. If so, the last thing I wanted to do was contradict whatever Alicia had told her. I was thankful to be isolated in the back seat while Alicia drove and her mother sat beside her.

Alicia suggested we eat in the mall food court, and I agreed. Where we went did not matter to me. I was willing to go anyplace she suggested.

We made our way into the mall, finally parting with Mrs. Thomas. She agreed to call Alicia's cell phone when it was time for us to go.

We zigzagged through the densely packed crowd of people, ordering greasy burgers and fries before finding a seat, we managed to find a table that overlooked the first floor and escalators. It was hardly a romantic setting, but none of that mattered to me, I was excited to be on an actual date with my dream girl.

"Your mom seems nice."

I was secretly, hoping a compliment might work in my favor. I also hoped that if Alicia had told her mom something about me, she would share it now.

"Yea, she's alright," Alicia said, popping a fry in her mouth.

"I, uh hope she didn't mind bringing me?"

"Nope, I asked her. Trust me she would have said no if it was a problem." Alicia laughed, rolling her eyes.

I nodded, taking a bite of my burger.

Alicia was not offering any information, and I had to know. So, I finally decided to come out and ask.

"Does she know about me?" I said, locking eyes with Alicia.

"Oh, you mean, about the accident?"

I nodded.

"Well, it is hard to not know about it." She muttered.

Her expression changed. She looked concerned like maybe she upset me or something.

"I mean, it is no big deal. I talked to her about it. I told her that you are a nice guy and been through a lot... and our now living with your aunt."

Feeling some stress roll off of my shoulders, I took another bite of my burger. I was not sure what to make of that, but at least Alicia did not outright lie for me.

As we sat, enjoying our noisy meal, I felt more at ease. Alicia was excited to be going back to school soon, and told me about the friends she missed at Mill Creek. Most of the names she mentioned I did not know.

"So, what do you like to do?" Alicia inquired.

"I read a lot I guess," I said, feeling like the dullest person alive.

"Cool, what do you read?"

A small group of teenagers caught my attention on the lower floor. A few faces seemed familiar. They disappeared further down the corridor. I was delighted that they did not stop by the food court because I wanted to bond with Alicia one on one.

"Um, fantasy mostly or anything about Greek mythology. The occasional mystery is good too, though."

"I like fantasy. Well, fantasy movies I guess. I don't read much." She said, taking a sip of cola.

Alicia was fun to talk to; I was no longer drawing blanks the words seemed to be pouring out of my mouth the more we spoke. I loved spending time with her and found her company invigorating. And best of all, she seemed to be enjoying my company as well. The time passed quickly, and I figured Mrs. Thomas would soon be returning. There was something I needed to ask Alicia in private, and time was ticking, so I went for it before my opportunity passed.

"So, um, we are friends, right?" I asked.

"Yea?" Alicia put her cup down, leaning forward slightly.

Her eyes no longer wandered, I had her full attention.

"Well, are we...just friends then?"

"I'm not really sure." Alicia laughed. "Are you asking if we are just friends or if we can be more than just friends?"

I smiled, "I like you, Alicia."

Before she could respond, I stretch my arm across the table, offering her my hand. For a brief moment, I was terrified that Alicia would not reciprocate.

"I like you too, Davis."

She gently placed her hand on mine.

"Well, why don't we be more than just friends then?"

Somehow I found the courage to ask—otherwise I would not be going steady with the girl of my dreams.

"Ok!" Alicia smiled wide, taking my hand in both of hers. "I would like that very much." She whispered.

I leaned closer to the small bistro table. Alicia did the same, closing the short gap between us. Before our lips could touch, her cell phone rang out, breaking the moment. I sat back, feeling as though I had just been caught doing something wrong. A few patrons at a nearby table turned at the sound of the phone but immediately went back to their meals.

Although the moment had been broken, I could not believe how well the date had gone. We were officially a couple now. The girl I've secretly had a crush on apparently felt the same about me.

"Well, looks like my mom is done and we are to meet at the car."

Alicia sounded a little exasperated by her mother's unintentional intrusion.

We cleaned up our trays and walked hand in hand through the mall. I wondered if Alicia would hear about it if other students from Mill Creek saw us together. She did not appear concerned, so I pushed the thought out of my mind.

The ride home was a little less tense for me. I had some idea about what Alicia's mother knew, and even more importantly, I had finally found the courage to pursue the girl of my dreams. It felt like time was standing still. I still could not believe we actually had the conversation, and it went so well despite any interruptions.

Alicia dropped me off at my house; I could tell she was anxious to get in as much driving time as possible. I said goodbye to Alicia and her mother and watched her pull into her driveway, my thoughts lingered on our almost kiss. I couldn't help but picture how amazing it would have been. I caught myself daydreaming and started toward the door.

"So how did it go?"

Aunt Lisa was waiting for me on the other side of the door. I noticed she was taking her shoes off as if she too had just returned home.

"Well—," She said.

I smiled.

"Good or very good?"

"Magnificent."

"Ah, I see." She grinned. "Don't worry, I won't ask for any details. Alicia certainly seems like a nice girl for you."

My cheeks seriously hurt from smiling so much, Alicia washed away all the bad feelings I've been bottling up, allowing me to feel like myself again. I took a seat in the living room, and Caesar jumped up beside me, laying half in my lap, half on the couch, purring. I gently petted the cat, thinking back on the events of the afternoon. I could not remember the last time I felt this happy.

Aunt Lisa came in with a cup of hot green tea, sipping at it as she sat in the nearby recliner.

"So, I believe someone's birthday is coming up next month?"

I had completely forgotten about my own birthday, and to some degree, I forgot about it intentionally. This would be my first birthday without my parents. The thought of them not being here for my birthday really dampened my previous excitement; the thought was too painful to bear. Aunt Lisa must have picked up on the change in my mood because her tone softened.

"What do you want for your birthday?"

I shrugged.

The things I wanted were impossible to have. Aunt Lisa decided to change the subject entirely.

"I saw Alicia was driving, did she get her license?"

"Not yet, just her permit."

"How do you feel about driving? I mean, do you feel you are ready to give it a try?"

I thought about it. I did start learning late, my parents did talk to me about getting my permit a few times before everything happened. Honestly, I had not even considered actually trying again.

"You don't have to do it. I mean, I am not telling you to. But if you feel ready, I will look into classes or teach you myself if you prefer. You could maybe try to get a part time job and buy your own car eventually?"

"I don't know, I guess I could."

I had not really thought about it. It was something that most boys my age were already doing. Most ordinary teens that is.

It hit me that for the first time since the death of my parents, I was starting to feel like a part of the world again like I had a place. It felt like the pieces of my life had been tossed about and were now finding their way back together. I could once again look forward to the things that most teenagers my age looked forward to. There were so many things that I pushed aside to deal with the emotions that consumed me, after my parent's death.

"Why don't you think about it for a while? I don't mind driving you places, Davis. However, I want you to be independent. And you can't really do that if you don't start to learn these sorts of things." She continued sipping.

Caesar rolled onto his back, his legs splayed as he begged for a belly rub. I absently obliged. My mind was overwhelmed. My first girlfriend, talking about driving and remembering my birthday all in a single day.

"Maybe I could start to learn," I said.

"You sure?" Aunt Lisa eyed me over her cup.

"Yes. I am sure I want to try. You are right, I have to be independent. I can't expect to live my life like this forever."

"Let's not rush things, though. Ok? Take it slow and one step at a time. I only want to help you, Davis, I don't want to push you into something too quickly."

"I know," I said, offering her a smile.

Aunt Lisa appeared visibly relieved.

"Good."

Aunt Lisa reclined in her seat, glancing up at the wall clock that hung across the room.

"I don't suppose Romeo could help me get dinner started?" She said, grinning mischievously.

I tossed a couch pillow at her. Caesar immediately noticed the object flying across the room and pounced on it.

"Oh alright, Caesar! I won't throw things anymore. I know you don't allow it."

"You told Alicia she would have some competition with that cat, right?" Aunt Lisa said, snickering to herself.

She headed for the kitchen with her tea.

"Are you kidding me? Once she gets to know Caesar, I will be the one competing." I moved to the carpet, enticing the cat to play with a ball of yarn from his vast collection of toys.

"He does have an addicting personality, doesn't he?" Aunt Lisa said, pulling ingredients from the fridge.

I entertained the cat for a few minutes before getting up off the floor.

"Alright, Caesar. We have to help Aunt Lisa out, or we won't be eating."

The cat meowed happily before pawing at the discarded ball of yarn and pounced on top of it a few times. When he earned no response, he settled down on the sofa.

Aunt Lisa kept staring at me and smiling, my best guess is she too noticed that I was starting to belong.

Deep down I wished my parents could be around to meet Alicia and see me grow up, I was dreading how I might feel on my birthday. But I also knew that I had my Aunt, and Alicia and both of them loved me. I decided to push the thought of my parents not being around out of my mind for now, and focus on my happiness.

***

The time had finally arrived; it was the first day back to Mill Creek High School. Alicia and I were juniors this year, which was exciting. My Aunt gave us a lift to school that morning, Alicia and I held hands in the backseat our fingers laced together as Aunt Lisa chauffeured us to our destination. Passing the large brick sign that read "Welcome to Mill Creek High School" felt kind of welcoming.

Aunt Lisa tapped her French manicured fingernails nervously on the steering wheel as she pulled up to the entrance. I could sense that she was concerned about me returning to school after all that I had been through.

"Have a good first day you two and Alicia… Promise you will keep an eye on Davis for me?"

Alicia nodded.

"Sure thing, Miss Jones," Alicia said.

My cheeks felt a bit warm, I was severely embarrassed, Aunt Lisa might as well pulled out some naked baby pictures of me from her wallet, I doubt it would have felt much different.

"Don't worry about me, I'm in good company," I said glancing at Alicia.

Here I was arriving at my old school, with one of the most popular girls, I had a huge self-esteem boost going on. We walked toward the large red brick building, it had a flagpole in the blacktopped parking lot, and the flag was flapping around carelessly in the morning breeze. The parking lot was filled with cars belonging to students and teachers, and a few yellow buses lined the side of the building.

We walked through the double glass doors, entering a noisy river of youth; everyone was talking and giggling, catching up on their summer break. This was the best I felt about myself in such a long time, my appearance changed considerably over the summer, and I now looked like one of the popular kids. Alicia picked out a fresh hair style for me, it was shorter than normal, but then again it was time for a change. So I was open to trying new things. I was wearing a red muscle shirt, and some loose fitting blue jeans with the knees purposely torn out, it was a popular trend. Alicia's friends surrounded us like a swarm of killer bees.

"So, I see you picked up a new boy toy this summer," Becky Smith snickered, as she stared me down with her beady little eyes.

Carry Myers chided, "I'm sure he is just new to the school or a relative, right Alicia?"

"Umm, like his name is Davis… we are not related, and he has been going to school with us since like Kindergarten. Maybe if you all paid more attention to something besides your powdering mirrors, you would recognize him," Alicia huffed, then she grabbed my hand and stomped off, me trailing behind at arms-length.

I was insulted that they thought I was new to the school, or just a relative like I had never existed… that got my blood boiling. But I kept my cool because I knew for a fact this year was going to be my turning point, and I would be more than just "That Guy." People would remember my name.

And boy was I right, but it didn't happen quite the way I had pictured it. You see shortly after I had arrived at school, this oversized teen that must have been related to Paul Bunyan started to give me a hard time. But Alicia told him to back off, and being one of the most popular girls in the school she seemed to have some influence (not that I was proud of my girlfriend fighting my battles, but at the same time I didn't really want Alicia to witness me getting pulverized).

My morning was starting to turn out like an episode of the Twilight Zone, it turns out Alicia, and I had the same homeroom, Room 203. English and homeroom were the only classes Alicia, and I shared together, but in any case, I wouldn't be part of the school system long enough to really enjoy it.

We were a few minutes early, and I noticed some familiar faces following me as I walked into the classroom. Alicia settled into a desk in the front row that was open, beside two of her girlfriends.

I moved silently to a rear desk. The back corner seat had been taken, so I settled for the next one over.

As I took my seat, I noticed a couple of new girls stopped their conversation and glanced at me. One girl turned and said something inaudible. They both giggled, deviously looking at me. I did my best to ignore it even though I was certain the laughter was for me and derisive.

The teacher, a woman in her forties with close-cropped dark hair stepped before the class. "Welcome back, everyone. I am Mrs. Arkwright. I hope you all had an enjoyable summer!"

The students fell silent, focusing on Mrs. Arkwright's hourglass frame, as she paced back and forth, ratcheting her gaze from face to face with a pleasant smile. She wore a conservative skirt and blouse. A brilliant glass medallion dangled from a cord around her neck.

"I see many familiar faces," she said scanning the room until her gaze lingered on me. "And," she added, "a few new ones."

One of the girls who had noticed me began to giggle again as she responded to her friend's whispered comments.

"Hannah! That's not a great way to start off the new school year," Mrs. Arkwright scolded, crossing her arms. As all eyes focused on her, Hannah blushed, quickly shutting her mouth. It was clear Mrs. Arkwright meant business. She got that point across well.

The students paged through their new learning material, checking the signatures on the inside cover for names they knew. I merely tucked each away, completely disinterested.

"Move it!" a voice suddenly grumbled.

I turned to find the tall, steroid dude glaring at me. I said nothing and pretended not to hear him. Finally, he settled in another seat behind me. Like why did he have it in for me? The only reasonable explanation I could come up with was Alicia and I being a couple. All of the jocks would probably have a bone to pick with me at one point or another.

I heard the bell clang and waited for the other kids to leave. Alicia walked out with the two girls she'd sat down beside. They were whispering something to one another. I felt disappointed that she didn't wait for me, but I suppose that goes with dating someone so popular. The rest of the day went relatively good. I caught myself daydreaming during class a few times and sketching "Alicia + Davis" inside of a heart in my notebook.

Right before lunch my dream of having a perfect school year came crashing down on me. You see, there I was minding my own business, a few students were stowing away their belongings inside of the lockers beside me. I was tinkering with my combination lock trying to remember if it was one or two turns left when I was rudely interrupted by the same jerk from this morning, and he appeared to be a grinning idiot. Beside me, the rows of lockers now looked more like the bars of a prison as he closed in on me. I did what anyone in my situation would have done.

"Umm excuse me… this is like my personal space you are invading…"

Then one of the weirdest things happened, the guy started sniffing me, like I wasn't already freaked out enough having a guy that looked like a professional wrestler in my face, like seriously what did his parents feed him? I can only image how much their grocery bill was feeding this guy! I tried to move, but there were literally only inches between us.

"Look, this is not cool, what is your problem, man?" I said.

His blonde hair draped down over his eyes, he seriously reminded me of a refrigerator with limbs. He said, "You have no right being here, Greek!" What the heck was he talking about? The last time I checked, I was American.

"Umm if this is some racial thing, I'm American so you can back off!" I said.

He said something in a language that sounded vaguely familiar to me; I swear he spoke of a prophecy, and Lord Hades biggest fear had come to pass, and I definitely didn't like the part about him tearing out my heart and dragging my soul back to his master...

He grabbed me by my face with one of his oversized hands, like my head was a basketball and pinned the back of my head to the locker. His palm was pressed tightly over my mouth; all I could manage to get out was a weak squeaking sound. I helplessly looked out the spaces between his fingers and saw my friend Jake Miller staring at me (he was a big guy and one of the best wrestlers at Millcreek), he rushed over and grabbed the dudes arm, trying to free me. I struggled with his fingers trying to pry myself fee, but he had the grip of a vice.

The boy grumbled, "Mortals use to worship Polybotes, now you attack me, BE GONE MORTAL!" he shouted, flinging Jake across the halfway like he was a sack of potatoes. A circle of students started to crowd around and chant "Fight, fight, fight..." and a few other kids were crouched down checking on Jake. After surviving on the island and recently getting my life somewhat back there was no way this guy was going to take it all from me, I fought too hard to keep alive this long. I started to elbow him in his ribs, each blow felt harder, like my adrenaline was giving me superhuman strength or something, on my fourth blow he let a gut-wrenching roar and lost his grip on me.

What was up with this freak…I did not want to fight him. So I ran down the congested hallway filled with students heading to and from classes, trying my best not to plow down any kids as I weaved in between them, before running into the Boy's Room. Looking around I decided to form a plan of action, without much thought I locked myself inside a stall and lifted my feet up off of the floor, so they were not visible underneath the door.

I heard the restroom door open and close, it felt like a nightmare, and it was now becoming seriously scary. It was obviously the oversized freak because I could hear sniffing sounds like some sort of wild boar. I tried really hard not to breathe, so he would not hear me. But he must have had a really keen sense of smell because I heard him outside the door sniffing and then the door rattled and ripped off of its hinges. Right before my eyes the guy started to morph into a giant, his arms, legs and torso stretched and grew, then his skull seemed to dislocate under his flesh, as his head became larger stretching his skin. His skin became ashen and lost its original rosy complexion. Also, his fingernails grew like talons from his fingertips, they looked yellow and crusty like he had a case of extreme nail fungus. There was no longer a large teenage boy in front of me, I was now staring down a lumbering giant, with its back pressed tight against the ceiling, wearing nothing but a loincloth, twenty feet tall and weighing a couple of tons. I could feel the heat radiating from its sour smelling breath, as it washes over me. There was no logical explanation for a guy shape shifting into a giant, or why a giant was now in the boy's restroom. I'm not sure what happened exactly, but for some reason, my body kicked into hyper mode like I had some sort of battle reflex preprogrammed into my DNA.

Polybotes struck its fist down at me, but I pulled away quickly, as though I had been snake bit.

"Do not resist little one, Polybotes shows you mercy, I smash you quick, hurt only little."

"Umm, think I'll pass…but thanks!" I shouted.

Polybotes narrowed his eyes at me. Leaning forward he leveled its most intimidating glare. I moved to turn around, anxious to get out of this situation but saw no possible escape.

My silence must have been intimidating in its own way. He lurched forward trying to pummel me to the floor with both fists balled like hammers. But I quickly rolled out of the way. I saw in my peripheral vision another fist crashing down with tremendous force, but again I dodged.

His fist splintered the tile floor like tissue paper. There was no way I was letting his fist connect with me if I had any say in the matter. I'm not sure what I was thinking, maybe I had a death wish, so I balled my fist. There was so much pent-up anger boiling inside me, from losing my parents, almost dying on a deserted island and now this, I had enough.

After sizing up Polybotes, I felt that I had a good chance at victory since the ceiling crippled his movement. I charged at his ankle like a cheetah and pinned his leg against the brick wall in front of me, I slammed his foot into the wall with so much momentum, that the tiles cracked. Polybotes groaned, so I now knew that he could be injured. Here I was fighting a giant, I was always a pacifist, so I had no experience at brawling. Polybotes's hand closed in on me, I could see the shock in his big brown, softball-sized eyes as I rolled out of the way and his hand clamped nothing but air. He knocked down one of the mirrors, and it shattered on the floor. I saw a large piece of glass and immediately knew what I had to do. I ran between his legs and rolled on my shoulder to avoid his massive hands swatting at me like an annoying insect.

"Stay still godling, Lord Hades pulls Polybotes from Tartarus to make sure prophecy no mess up and Olympian's stay trapped for good."

"Thanks, but no thanks," I said, quickly scaling his leg, making my way up the shirt on his back like a rope ladder, he roared in frustration, smashing his body into walls like an angry bull, trying to knock me off or crush me. It was like riding an oversized bucking bull in a rodeo, but I managed to hang on. Once I reached his neck, I reached around and sliced his throat with the chunk of glass ripping his flesh wide open all the way across. A river of golden ichor spilled onto the floor, and he screamed in agony, cupping his wound in his hand, but his skin somehow magically meshed back together just as fast.

"You win this time demigod, but next time on battlefield when Polybotes in real form, you no so lucky!" he explained.

My head was swimming with confusion, like what could he possibly look like in his actual form; I already met two versions of this guy, and each was scarier than the last, I couldn't begin to picture him any more horrific than he currently was. And what battlefield was he talking about? And why would I be there? Before I had a chance to ask him some questions he exploded, leaving me unconscious on the bathroom floor. When I came to a teacher was standing over me, he grabbed me by the arm and pulled me to my feet. When I looked back the restroom was destroyed, the walls and floor were scorched like a bomb had detonated. It was as though the entire event was just a hallucination. No giant, no kid the size of vending machine. My mind was having problems digesting the scenario before me, was I losing my mind? Did all the stress finally catch up with me, and cause me to blow a gasket? Did I set off an explosion somehow?

While I was being escorted to the principal's office from the restroom, my reflection in the mirror caught my attention. It was not my own. I stared back. Was this really me? The mirrored version of myself seemed hollow, like an empty shell. I did not recognize the young man looking back at me. I watched as the image morphed into my parents in the mirror, smiling back at me. It sent a shiver down my spine.

Now a thought came to mind, taunting me. The boy I saw in the mirror was a complete stranger. I recognized my face, but the dark brown eyes seemed soulless. The teacher gave me a tug, snapping me back to reality.

Once at the principal's office I sat down on the chair right inside the door and glanced around the room. There was no sign of the principal, other than a nameplate engraved Mr. Gardner. The room was a small square cubical, with a green leafy plant in an orange pot to my left, a large map of the United States on the wall behind the principal's desk, and a cup filled with pencils beside a globe of the world atop the desk.

After a lengthy wait, I heard the office doorknob turn, and it slowly creaked open. I was surprised when I saw Aunt Lisa and Mr. Gardner trailing behind her. There was no doubt. I was in major trouble. The look on both of their faces was loud and clear.

Aunt Lisa breathed heavy, heaving her shoulders up and down then she said, "Davis! What were you thinking? Do you have any idea the trouble you have caused?"

"I got attacked in the hallway and ran into the Boy's Room, I…I just went inside the restroom and got knocked unconscious."

Aunt Lisa glared at the principal. "Did you see him set off an explosive or not? If I find out you have no proof, and my nephew is innocent, there will be hell to pay!"

"Well, he was the only one in the restroom... Mr. Shultz, one of our teachers, found Davis, after hearing the explosion, he was out cold on the floor," said Mr. Gardner.

"Davis come on, you are done at this school! You could have been killed... And as far as I am concerned, they have no proof you did anything wrong, the last I checked victims get cared for, not further victimized. You don't need this with all you've been through!" Aunt Lisa snapped.

We walked out the door and never looked back. The cops never came looking for me or contacted us. Maybe the school was scared of my Aunt Lisa suing them and never reported I was there? Either way, life as I knew it was never going to be the same. I was now on my way down a path that had no positive ending. My destiny was now in my own hands, and I needed to know why I survived the crash and what battle Polybotes was referring to!

EIGHT

I HEAD OUT WEST

While being upset and confused something began evolving very clearly. And that was I didn't want to live with this guilt any longer, I needed some answers. After all, nothing had changed no matter how hard I tried to let go of the past. Things were now getting worse! Like the fight at school with Polybotes and me being mangled with broken bones on the island, I knew there was no way they could both be a hallucination. Did I really have anything to do with the explosion? The decision was made. I was going to run away!

My first impulse was to thrill at the idea of a great adventure before me. I didn't have a picture of me on a freight train with a stick and a handkerchief full of my valuables over my shoulder, but it was still an intriguing prospect.

Then the reality of it all hit me. There was Alicia and Aunt Lisa. There was no doubt that I'd be lost without seeing Alicia every day and my Aunt didn't deserve all the anxiety such a thing would cause. But I knew I had to do it.

Alicia met me that night, after dinner, and when I sat down on the porch beside her, I almost changed my mind. I stroked my fingers through Alicia's long, silky hair thinking how to break the news.

"Oh my God, Davis did you get hurt? Please tell me you had nothing to do with the explosion? There are rumors of you purposely setting off a homemade pipe bomb." Alicia stammered.

"I'm fine…I'd never do anything that could injure anyone, you know me better than that right?" I asked.

"I'm so glad that you're safe, I was so worried… I never doubted you, not even for a moment, I defended you at school. Everyone talks about it, like everyone at school talks about you every chance they get. I would say you're like the coolest kid ever to go to Mill Creek after that incident!"

"This isn't really how I wanted to be remembered my freshman year, but I guess it's better than not being remembered at all!" I said.

"I'm sorry about my friends Davis… that was horrible of them not to remember you. I can't imagine how bad that must have felt for you since we all have been going to school together since kindergarten."

"Don't sweat it, kind of goes with being me. I never really been the social type, I keep to myself… I just feel like I don't fit in or belong… if that makes any sense?"

"I don't get it personally, but... I do find it attractive; it makes you seem so mysterious. Will you be coming back to school anytime soon?" Alicia said.

"I doubt Aunt Lisa would let me, even if I could... Besides, there is something I have meant to tell you."

Alicia suddenly seemed troubled. "Is everything all right?" She said.

"I need answers... I have this obsession with why I'm alive. I think maybe the explosion at school, might possibly be related somehow. I don't think I'm crazy, but I do need help," I said.

"I'm here for you Davis, like anything I can do to help... just say it, and I'll make it happen."

I nodded and said, "Promise me you will be here for me when I get back? I need to go see someone; I know deep down they can help... But I have to run away, I know Aunt Lisa won't understand what I'm going through and I don't expect her to, she has done enough for me."

Alicia tried everything in her power to convince me that I had other options. But I wouldn't accept another solution. I promised I'd be back. This wouldn't be permanent. When she looked up at my inane jabbering her big blue eyes were full of concern. I told her, "I'm just going for a while. I'll be back. I promise."

"I promise too, Davis. That I'll be here waiting for you... But I don't want you to go, just know that, okay?" she said.

I looked deep into her soulful eyes.

"Where are you going?" Alicia said.

"Well…uh, I get along great with my grandparents. So, I'm heading to their ranch in Arizona. I'll leave Aunt Lisa a detailed note explaining it all so she won't worry about me. Of course, I won't tell her I'm practically broke, and my travel mode is going to have to be kind of creative."

"Davis, promise me you will be careful, Ok?" She reached into her pocket and pulled out some wadded up cash. "It's not much, but I want you to have it!"

I tried to refuse because I hate feeling pitied, but she would not take no for an answer. "It will make me feel better if you take it," she said.

I tucked the money into my pocket, finding the words to say good-bye was unbearable, but I managed to force the phrase out. Our hands and gazes lingered for what felt an eternity. And then there was silence. She was gone.

Before leaving, I wrote a note to Aunt Lisa. I couldn't act like we were more to each other than we were; yet I wanted her to know that I would miss her (she felt more like a big sister than a mother figure). I even implied that I wished she would visit me. I gave no timetable as to when I would arrive at my grandparent's or return.

This got me checking the rail and bus schedules and fares. When I compared it to my available funds, there was just enough money for me to travel from here to Cleveland,

Ohio, and be able to eat. After that, it was my thumb and the open road.

My backpack over my shoulder, I walked to the bus depot and bought a ticket for Cleveland. If I was careful, I'd be able to eat till then and a little more.

As the big Greyhound's diesel engine revved up and rumbled my spirits did a quick soar. I knew it was a temporary adrenaline rush. I made myself comfortable and settled down for the long ride ahead.

I thought I would sleep a lot, but my mind whirred out of control like a supercomputer processing millions of thoughts per second.

At the Cleveland bus stop, I was confronted with the reality of what I was doing. I was broken and hungry. There was a Burger King at the bus stop, so that was my first stop. I needed time to think.

As I sat munching my burger and fries, I noticed a Help Wanted sign posted. When I was through I asked for the manager. A tall, skinny, bald headed guy who looked strained and frustrated approached me with an application in hand. "Did you just get off a bus? I see you have a backpack."

Thinking quick I said, "No, I just go visit my grandparents overnight on Mondays."

His eyes narrowed like he was making up his mind if he believed me or not. "Kids," he sighed. "They're my problem. Never show up when they are supposed to. Guess who has to cover?" he asked rhetorically. "Okay, I'm stuck. I'll take a chance on you. Can you start now?"

"Sure," I said.

Soon I was wearing a headset, taking orders and any job that needed doing from dropping French fries into the fryolator to pouring soda and coffee. I also enjoyed eating dinner and snacks on the house. By my shift's end, I knew I had no place to stay, so I made myself at home in the bus station waiting room in a chair with a small TV hanging on the wall, in front of me.

The later it got the more unsavory the place became. After midnight it hosted an assortment of shady types, ranging from homeless beggars to other runaways like me, to pimps and worse.

In the middle of the night, I was dozing off when a cop tapped my foot. "You okay, Sonny?"

"Oh yeah," I said. "Waiting for a bus."

He eyed me and moved on. I went back to sleep thinking about how comfortable I was getting at telling lies.

I worked at the Burger King for two more nights. I got an advance on my pay and rented a ten-dollar room at the YMCA on the next block.

By week's end and payday, I knew I had to move on. I felt bad about quitting my job at the drop of a dime since the manager had put his trust in me. So I did the only decent thing that came to my mind, I left him a nice note telling him I had a family emergency and would not be able to work for him any longer and thanked him for the job.

I figured I had enough money to get me to Oklahoma City. And a little more. So far things were going well. Evidently, Aunt Lisa didn't put the cops on my trail, and I'm sure she notified my grandparents that I was on my way. I could only wonder or more to the point hope that Alicia would actually wait for me. I'm pretty confident, what I felt for her was love.

But as the bus rolled over the flat endless wheat fields of Kansas and the plains of waving grass of Oklahoma I began to get concerned about my future luck. Once in Oklahoma City, it quickly became apparent that no convenient jobs were waiting for me. I needed to be creative if I was going to earn money, or I had to find another means of travel.

I wandered the city for an hour finally finding a shady bench in a public park to rest. And think. I gazed up at an equestrian statue of some hero on a prancing horse and began thinking about Arizona and the West. I was anxious to get there now, but I seemed to be at the end of the road as well as my wit's end.

NINE

I BEFRIEND A
RUNAWAY

I never realized how difficult it was to kill time when you have nothing to do. I wandered the city aimlessly for what seemed like many hours but when I checked only an hour had passed.

I found another park bench, I felt weary and defeated. Was going home an option? I suppose so. I could get out on the road and put my thumb out. But, if I did that I might as well head west. I wasn't at all sure what to do. My great adventure seemed to be falling apart already. And I wasn't even halfway to my destination.

But right now, I was hungry and broke. I noticed a girl on the next bench over. She seemed to be fishing in the waste barrel beside her. I only looked at her for a second, before turning my head. But I saw her opening a McDonald's bag. When I leveled my eyes at her, she was munching French fries.

I must have been staring, and she snapped, "Find your own."

I didn't know how to react. I was embarrassed but most of all I was starving. Taking her advice, I checked out the next barrel. Sure enough, there was a pizza box. It seemed to hold something. There was a half-eaten slice of cheese pizza and some fries. Thankfully, the barrel was relatively clean. Besides, I was starving. Wolfing down the half-eaten slice of pizza and the fries, I went looking in the other barrels. I found a piece of a soft pretzel and an untouched chicken wing. And my hunger was satisfied.

The girl was still on the bench. She was rummaging through her backpack looking for something. When she caught me peeking at her, she turned and gave me an angry stare.

"I'm looking for my bus ticket if it's any of your business."

She said it kind of rude, so I didn't answer her. I wasn't yet ready to head for the Interstate because I hadn't really decided which way to go.

Next time I looked she was staring at me, I accidently made eye contact with her and locked onto her intense emerald green eyes that reminded me of my mothers, like I never actually met too many girls that had green eyes, it had to be pretty unique. I turned away embarrassed for showing my interest. She was actually pretty in a rough kind of way. She wore torn jeans, and I surmised not the stylish kind of torn jeans, and a denim jacket. Her backpack looked like Army surplus.

"Where you heading?" she eventually asked in a more civil tone.

"Dunno," I said. "I just don't know."

"Don't have bus fare, huh?" she said.

I looked at her and evenly said, "No."

"Why not get yourself a squeegee and a bucket?" she suggested. I guess I looked so dumbfounded she had to grin. "Don't know what I'm talkin' about, huh?"

I shrugged.

C'mon, use mine. I do not need it," she said as she took a squeegee broken down into two parts from her backpack.

She headed to the nearby street corner. At the corner, she said, "You're gonna need some water. Get some from that McDonalds," she said pointing.

Armed with the water and brush, she led me to the street corner. Two street people were dashing to the cars stopped at the red light and quickly washing windshields during the stop. She looked at me and said, "Go ahead."

I did. At the next red light. The first two people ignored me and drove off, but the third handed me a dollar. Within the next hour, I had seven more paying customers, and some gave me more.

She had been sitting on the park bench watching me. When I approached her, she said, "Still short, huh. Where you going?"

I said, "West. Arizona."

She said, "Are you willing to do this again in Amarillo?"

"Sure," I said. "Why?"

"'Cause I'll lend you the difference if you pay me back in Amarillo."

"That'd be cool. I'm Davis by the way."

"You can call me Kelly," she said.

Next thing I knew we were sitting together on the next westbound Greyhound. I was doing it. I was still heading west. One way or another.

Kelly didn't talk much before dozing off. She was snoring softly as the flat plains of Oklahoma rolled by the window. She had dark hair and a rosy complexion with a splash of freckles across the bridge of her nose and her cheeks.

She slept through the first rest stop but was awake for the next. By now, I had a real need to stretch my legs. She got off with me and went to the Ladies Room.

I was hungry again and was wondering about asking her for a further loan and also thinking I might be pushing my luck with her.

When she came out, she must have seen my hungry, for-lorn kind of look and said, "I'm starving too, but I'm broke."

That made me kind of wonder. Had she given me her last dollar?

She sat down at a table, and I naturally followed her. She said, "We're gonna have a hobo lunch."

For the second or third time now I had to give her my dumb look. She just grinned. "I have enough for a cup of coffee. Here," she said handing me a dollar and change. "Get it and ask for crackers."

I did. Back at the table she took the crackers and made several sandwiches out of them with the nearby ketchup. Kelly ate her crackers with a half-cup of coffee and gave me the rest. It wasn't great, but it killed the grumbling in my stomach.

We hit Amarillo at three in the morning. She said, "Nothing to do but sack out here at the bus station till it's light. Then we can go to work."

We went through the same routine and that night we were again back aboard a bus bound for Albuquerque. But we had new seats, and they weren't together. Kelly was sitting at the very back of the bus in the fourth-row seat next to the bathroom, and I was a couple of seats ahead in an aisle seat.

When I came out of the bathroom, I saw her struggling with a guy who had his hand over her mouth and was forcing himself on her. There was nobody else in the back seat, and most of the people on the bus were sleeping.

I got close enough to make sure that what I was seeing was correct. Unfortunately, it was. I was scared to death, stuff like this only happened in movies, not all that long ago. The guy looked like he could kill me but I couldn't let him molest her. So I took a deep breath, clenched my fists.

… But before I could do anything I saw her flash her other hand over his face, spread her fingers, and the guy seemed to fall unconscious. I looked at her, speechless.

"What had happened?" I said.

She whispered, "He decided to go to sleep and leave me alone."

"But…?"

"Don't ask," Kelly said. "If you're around long enough I may tell you."

We found two seats together and left the guy sleeping in the back. I kept glancing back at him, but she immediately dozed off to that soft snoring she did. Getting rest turned into a daunting task, I tried to fall asleep, but every time I did I was haunted by a reoccurring dream about the plane crash that woke me up, ever since that dreadful day. I'm sure the survivor's guilt ate at my subconscious… I hated the fact that I was still alive.

She woke up just before Albuquerque and said, "So, why are you on the road anyway?"

I said, "Looking for answers," and waited for her response. But she didn't question me. I thought that was strange but said nothing further.

At Albuquerque, her assailant was still sleeping. I cast a wary glance his way as we slung our backpacks and stepped off the bus into the brightest sunshine I had ever seen.

When I came back from the restroom, she was gone. I saw her walking towards the street and wondered if I should go with her. But maybe she didn't want me tagging along? I took a chance and hurried after her.

She seemed surprised. "What are you doing?" she said.

"Are you gonna wash windshields?"

"I dunno. I thought I'd look around. I might want to stay here for a while," she said.

I was again at a loss. Without Kelly, would I be stuck in Albuquerque? I'd like to think some of her street smarts rubbed off on me, but to be honest, she was the only reason I'd made it this far. She started off. I didn't follow until she looked back over her shoulder and said, "You can come if you want. But I'm not heading anyplace in particular."

Without hesitation I accepted her offer, I really didn't want to see where the path of me being on my own would lead, I figured worst case, we could earn some money together. That would buy me some time, and if I were lucky we'd make enough cash to cover fare for at least a few cities or even a state or two at best. The thought of me taking a leap of faith and having to travel once again on my own was nerve-racking, to say the least!

We both stopped at the sign in the restaurant window that said Help Wanted. They needed waiters and dishwashers. Maybe we'd get lucky.

TEN

I FIND MY SPECIAL TALENT

Three days later we still had not connected with a job, and the "hobo dinners" weren't cutting it. The first three fast food managers looked at us like we were sewer rats. One even told us so. I guess my lack of hygiene was starting to catch up with me, the thought of a hot bath was tantalizing!

So we took to the streets with our squeegees and managed to make enough for a fast food meal. I didn't want to look like a starved rat when I arrived at the ranch, but I might have no choice.

Sleeping accommodations were turning out to be a problem. It was raining in the high country, and a park bench was an uncomfortable perch in the rain. It didn't let up, and we were getting more and more miserable. We had spent the last night under a big oak, with newspapers for cover. So we started looking for something else.

The next afternoon, we were hanging out near a storage shed company. We were soggy and miserable, having only managed to dry out some at the bus station. When they closed the storage place, we hopped the fence, and I tried my hand at lock picking.

I don't know why but I had a feeling I could pick a lock and get into a storage bin for the night. I had never done it before, and that's what made it odd that I thought I could do it.

I looked over at Kelly. "Do you have anything tiny that I could use for a lockpick?" I asked.

She fished around in her pockets but produced nothing substantial. Then the bobby pin in her hair caught my eye.

"May I borrow that bobby pin for a few?" I said pointing to her hair.

"I forgot that even existed, it's been so long since I had a chance to do my hair," Kelly admitted.

When I fitted the bobby pin into the lock it felt hopeless, I seriously had no idea what I was doing. I hoped I wasn't blushing because this felt idiotic of me, maybe my math skills weren't the best, but I'm pretty sure picking zero locks in the past gave me exactly zero skill at lock picking.

"Think it will take long Davis?" Kelly asked.

"I don't know how long it will take—."

All of a sudden a weird tingling sensation washed over me and all the hairs on my arms and neck stood up. I took a step back, and arch's of electricity exploded out of my hands, sending the bobby pin and the red door on the storage unit flying through the air and slamming against the back wall.

Kelly gawked at me. "You never told me you could do that?"

"Umm... How about you tell me how you did that Vulcan touch thing with your hand back on the bus, and I'll tell you how I blew the door off," I said.

I honestly had no clue how I did it. It was a new feeling like I had unlocked some sort of ability. My fingers felt energized and tingled when I held my pointer fingers side by side bolts of electricity jumped between them.

"Ok, you win! It's sort of like a sleeper hold, but I used the energy from my body to interrupt the flow of energy to the neural network of his brain," she explained.

"Is it like using your chi, stun-gunning him? Like a kung-fu master?"

"Maybe, I'm not too familiar with kung-fu, but I told you my secret, so it's only fair that you share yours," she said.

"Don't get upset, but I really don't know how I shot lightning from my hands. It kind of felt natural to me, like I'd done it before. But I never did it before today," I told her in all honesty.

She looked slyly at me and shot me a glance that was somewhere between 'yeah right,' and 'what else aren't you telling me about yourself.'

As far as her own secrets I didn't want to probe her anymore, but it looked like I aroused some curiosity about myself. I think she thought I was kind of noisy as it was. But I couldn't help myself. She was so darn mysterious.

That night we were sitting in the shed snacking on coffee and pastries. It was our third night in the dull, colorless little place. Conversation was our only entertainment. Our only light was a decorative candle we had bought. The good thing about it was it was scented with cinnamon and reminded me of my destination, the ranch, and Grandma's apple pies. I asked, "Have you decided where you're going?"

She hesitated, thinking a while. "I need someplace warm where I can sleep out without needing a room."

"Couldn't you just get a job?"

She gazed at me for a moment. "I really don't want to work that hard. I'm not out here on my own to find a career. I'm looking for things."

"What things?"

She grinned a rare gesture. "Somehow I knew you'd ask that. I'm afraid with me you're not going to get many answers. I don't have any. Not yet, anyway."

I felt a little guilty; the mystery thing with Kelly was really attractive, not only that, but she also radiated an inner innocence. I'd only been gone for a short while, and I found myself staring at her, every time she spoke I caught myself daydreaming about kissing her soft lips. I never thought freckles were cute, but on her they were hot.

She gazed at me for a while. "You're really shocked at someone like me, aren't you?"

She had hit on the truth, but I wasn't sure how to answer without offending her. She was like my crutch. I didn't know where I'd be so far without her.

Then I finally replied. "Yeah," I said. "But there is nothing wrong with that. You make life exciting, you are like a free spirit, I'd wager you enjoy life more than most ever will in a lifetime and that's really cool in my book."

She kind of smiled (at least that's what I think it was) and said, "I believe that you've run up against your first real free spirit."

I said, "That's cool."

"I guess the word, 'Cool' is really popular where you live; where is that anyway?" she said.

I felt a little dumb. I knew I wasn't as worldly as her. I said, "Yeah. That's what they all say. All the time, back in Pennsylvania."

She looked at me and concentrated, her green eyes studying me, then finally she said, "I see it now, I thought your accent was Dutch."

The moment was starting to feel awkward, but I still managed to ask, "Where are you from? And do you have any idea where you're headed yet?"

"Like I said before, I'm like a closed book… But if you stick around long enough I might spill. As for where I am headed, I was thinking along the lines of San Diego. It's warm there all the time. I think I'll head that way."

I didn't say anything. Oddly enough I was already getting a feeling of loss.

She seemed to be making all our decisions. I just realized that I had been following her agenda.

***

Next afternoon Kelly ran up to an old lady walking her poodle at the park, calling her grandma. She wrapped her arms around her like she was giving her a hug. But I saw what she was really doing, as her hands went to work inside her purse. She pick-pocketed the old lady and ran back over to me.

She said, "Don't look at me like I'm a bad person, Davis! This is survival, and it's not like I took all of her money, I left about half in her wallet."

"I'm not judging, so don't worry about it. I understand that we are trying to survive. The only thing I'm wondering is are you going by way of Flagstaff by chance?"

She thought a moment. "I'm not up on my geography, but I do think that Phoenix would be closer to San Diego. Why you getting off at Flagstaff?"

"My grandfather's ranch is just northeast of Sedona."

"Sedona?" Her eyebrows arched almost imperceptibly.

I nodded.

"That the place where they got those spiritual things going on?" she said.

I cocked my head, confused by the comment. "Spiritual things?"

"Yeah, spiritual things that sometimes transpose into physical things," she said.

I thought about that for a minute.

"Like you being a human stun gun?" I said.

"Yeah. Something like that." She paused. "Yeah, they got some famous red rocks, they call, let me think… Cathedral Rock and I think Red Rock. They got something they call… Uh, let me think… Oh yeah, vortexes."

"Say what?" I said.

"Vortexes. Got something to do with a whirling, a coming together of different energy levels and different spiritual planes," she said.

"Never heard Granddad talk of it."

She was quiet for a while. Finally, she said, "I guess I could go with you as far as Flagstaff anyway. Can't make much difference in my trip."

I don't know what came over me. I planted a kiss right on her lips. It lasted close to a minute before she pushed me away.

"Look, Davis, I'm flattered that you think of me that way…" said Kelly.

"But…?" I said, feeling dumb and disappointed already.

"There are things about me… It's not you, Davis; I felt something special when we kissed, that's why I didn't stop it right away. But… I don't know if being more than friends is a good idea, at least not yet."

"So it's just bad timing then on my part and not because you think I'm a freak from what happened back at the storage unit?" I said, feeling a flicker of hope.

"Yeah, that sounds right…" she said.

I never knew how lonely a person could be traveling to strange places. I wasn't a baby or anything like that, but it was better to be with someone than be alone. At least at this point. Thinking of Kelly and me as a couple gave me a more positive outlook.

We got a bus and were on our way. Our tickets were for Flagstaff. The last leg of my trip.

It was pretty country.

As we climbed out of the desert with its mesquite, rolling sagebrush cactus and wildflowers the landscape changed. Somewhere along the way, I saw a sign saying the elevation was six thousand something feet. It was still dry and desert like, but it was probably what I had heard Grandpa call "high desert." Lots of unusual rock formation, buttes and sawtooth mountains. I had never seen such blue skies every day as there were here in the Southwest. And it was Indian country. Signs of it were everywhere. Not the Indians selling trinkets kind of sign but the look of the people with their swarthy suntanned faces and ten gallon Stetsons. Not Fancy Dan clothes, but working kind of cowboy clothes.

Flagstaff was pretty, green and mountainous. When we got off the bus, an awkwardness came between us. We knew that this was going to be the end of our relationship, our friendship.

We were having lunch at the local Taco Bell, and we were both quiet. Finally, she turned to me. "Your route is right out there," she said pointing. "Route 89 to Sedona."

I said nothing but was feeling sad. It's not like we had been friends for a long time. But I was still feeling the effects of the kiss we'd shared, and I couldn't help but wonder if she was feeling the same. I kind of felt she would be well suited in Sedona, since she was into that paranormal kind of stuff. We ate slow, knowing we would be parting.

Back out on the road, she said, "It's just a short hike to town from here. But you're going in the other direction, so I guess we'll say goodbye." We just stood there. Time stood still. Suddenly she lurched at me and planted a kiss on my lips, biting her bottom lip as she pulled away. "I'm going to miss you, like who is going to pick locks for me now? Oh yeah and try not to forget some of the survival stuff you learned from me. Might help you out somewhere."

With that, she swung her pack carelessly over one shoulder and started out towards town.

Maybe it was an irresistible impulse or whatever but I called out, "Hey, Kelly?"

She turned.

The words stuck in my throat. She waited. I got them out. "You... could come with me to the ranch. You know... until you figure out where you really want to go— I'd like to share with you why I actually came out here, if you're interested I mean."

She said nothing but did shift her feet. I saw what for her passed as a smile, more like a little smirk. "Vortexes, huh? Sounds interesting."

A few minutes later we were hiking along the road, our thumbs out, Sedona bound.

ELEVEN

I GET A DOG

We walked together toward the center of town and the highway at the far end; one gentleman slowed down but sped back up as soon as he saw me with Kelly. So far, we had no luck with hitchhiking. I felt kind of bad like I was slowing Kelly down. Yet without looking at each other, we seemed to sense each other's contentment at the decision to stick together for a while.

The Arizona sun took its toll on us, and we had to stop to rest on a bench in front of a Waffles pancake house. The small town looked straight out of the 50's, it was lined with small little shops on both sides of the street and a handful of people were walking down the sidewalks on either side. One little boy was carrying a red balloon, holding an older ladies hand whom I assumed to be his mother, they just walked into a barber shop on the corner. It was midday, and I could hear my stomach rumble. Kelly grinned and said, "I'm starving too. That pancake house sure looks good.

The aroma out here is mouthwatering. Reminds me of my grandmother's famous Belgian waffles. How much money do you have?"

I checked. "Four fifty."

"Good. We have enough. You game?" she said.

There was no need to ask me twice.

Inside it was a world of glass and imitation leather, a cool, dark cavern and relief from the blazing sun. The sweet scent of the food inside was even more tantalizing, a little bit greasy for my tastes but I was so hungry I didn't mind. The waitress, a middle-aged gum popper gave us a double take. I guess I wasn't always conscious of our shabby appearance after all this time on the road.

The pancakes were excellent, and when we were finished, we didn't want to move. I was taking another sip of coffee when a glance over Kelly's shoulder riveted my eyes. I felt my jaw slacken. He had just left the line at the cashier station, and I couldn't really get a better look. My God! I must be hallucinating. Was that Polybotes?

Kelly too seemed to be reacting to this apparition. In fact, she appeared to be genuinely startled.

It looked like she was getting ready to make a run for it. As bad as I wanted to question her, I just left it alone. If anything were up, she wouldn't tell me anyway, just the type of person she was. We both kept our eyes glued to the stranger, luckily he did not stay long.

The Waffle house had a small gift shop inside, I found a postcard that I thought Alicia would love, after all, it felt like forever since we parted. I dug around in my pocket, only producing some linen. I simply had to have the post-card, like there was no choice in me walking away without it. In my mind stealing was not an option, so I spoke with the cashier.

She was an overweight, middle-aged woman, with curly red hair; I glanced down at her nametag and said, "Hey Becky, would it be possible for a credit line for a postcard and a postage stamp? I really would like to contact my fam-ily, it's been weeks since we last spoke and it would make them happy knowing I'm Ok."

She eyed me for a moment trying to decide if I was kidding or not. Before she finally said, "Sorry son, I can't help you. My boss would fire me if he found out I gave you items on store credit."

Before I could say another word, someone tapped me on the shoulder. When I turned around it was a man in his late twenties, possibly early thirties. He handed me a five-dollar bill. "There you go, kid, I was once walking in your shoes. Don't worry about paying me back, but promise, when you have five extra bucks and see someone in need, you to return the favor."

"Thanks, mister, I'll be sure to help someone first chance I get!"

I purchased the postcard, which read: "Greetings from Flagstaff, Arizona" in big bold bubble lettering. It had silhouetted cowboys atop their horses on the bottom and at the top of the card was a horse trotting down an old desert trail, pulling a covered wagon, with the Rocky Mountains in the distance.

"Is it possible to buy a single stamp?" I asked the woman at the register.

"I only sell books of stamps, but you can get singles at any post office," she said.

Back at the bench recuperating from the huge, satisfying meal our attention was drawn to a small black and white mutt, it appeared to be a dachshund mix.

She was hungry, as she kept sniffing, but at a distance. Every once in a while, she would stop smelling the air and gaze at us. I pulled a piece of beef jerky I had been saving from my backpack and held it out to her. When I put my hand out to urge her forward, she came so far and then, frightened, scampered away.

Finally, she gathered enough courage to snatch the jerky from my hand. Up close she was mangy and appeared to be battle scarred. Probably earned by fighting for her place at the garbage pail.

Suddenly she leaped up between Kelly and I and settled in, her face on my lap. Kelly grinned. "Not very choosy is she?"

The quiet moments that followed put me back on what I had seen. I asked Kelly, "Did you recognize somebody back there?"

She turned to me, a strange look on her face, but said nothing.

"I mean back there at the Waffles house?"

She hesitated. "Well…some guy seemed to be checking me out, but I've never seen him before. Who would I know out here in Arizona?"

"Yeah," I said, "I know what you mean." But honestly, she wasn't very convincing. It all seemed to fit into the outright strangeness of Kelly.

When we got over being lazy, we headed for the highway. The mutt tagged along right behind us. When I raised my voice and said, "Go on, Waffles. You can't come with us," she stopped momentarily. Then she gave us what was probably a brilliant look for a dog and when we went on she happily followed.

I stopped outside of a post office. "Do you have a pen by chance, Kelly?" I asked.

She reached into her backpack and handed me a gray Bic. "You writing home?"

"I'm writing Alicia," I said. "I bought a postcard for her back at the Waffle House."

"How? I thought we spent all our money?" she said.

"A guy overheard my conversation with the cashier and gave me five bucks," I explained.

"Well… Thanks for telling me… It is nice to know we have some extra money!" Kelly said in a sarcastic tone.

"You're right… I should have told you about the extra cash," I said.

"So who is this Alicia girl, a friend or something?" I noticed a slight change in her tone of voice.

"Well… She is my girlfriend back home," I said.

"I get it, you're a player. Well, you're not going to be playing me, Davis. I was actually considering us you know?" she said.

"Look it's not like that, Kelly. Before I met you, Alicia was my world. Now it's like I have no idea how I should be feeling. I felt things with you that I never felt with her! There is real chemistry between us, which I never shared with Alicia," I stammered. "The only reason I'm even writing her is to let her know I'm still alive, she knew my plan to hitchhike to my grandparents' ranch. I owe it to her, to let her know I'm still alive."

Kelly seemed to relax after I explained it more, if I didn't know any better, I'd say she was jealous of Alicia. I wrote a brief and quirky message to Alicia:

"Hey babe,

I Just wanted to let you know I'm still kicking! I've met some interesting people along the way and ran into some scary stuff. But I'm doing fine, and just wanted to let you know I'm almost to the ranch. I should reach Sedona in the next day or so! This trip is taking way longer than I anticipated… can you believe it's been two weeks already since we last spoke? Anyway, I hope you are holding to your promise and please let Aunt Lisa know I'm fine.

Love Ya,

Davis"

I walked into the post office and bought a stamp and mailed the postcard, it felt great to send word back home. It also made me feel slightly homesick for the first time since I'd hit the road. But I had Kelly to lean on, so I knew without a doubt we would make it to my grandparents.

The road seemed never ending like we had been walking in slow motion. The entire day got digested before my eyes, and by the time we had arrived at the highway, twilight had already set in. There was little traffic on the Interstate, and we were tired so we didn't spend much time trying to thumb rides. We hiked into the desert, far enough away to avoid attention and set up our camp behind a couple of giant Saguaro cactus. I made a campfire, and we sat around it toasting a couple of day old hotdogs for our meal. Day old or not they tasted like a gourmet dinner to us. Waffles snuggled in between us, trying to secure her portion of the feast. I finally spilled everything that had been bottling up inside to Kelly over dinner. From the strange white light during the plane crash, how I was the only survivor out of the three-hundred, how a green eyed dolphin saved me, how I magically healed while stranded on the beach and all the way up to the part when I blew the door off of the storage unit.

Kelly nodded.

"Makes sense…" Kelly said.

"What does?"

"Everything you just said. I think our meeting was no accident. I can't tell you anymore than that for now. You will just have to trust me on this. But when the time is right, we will talk more."

I was use to Kelly's half ended answers by now and figured it just meant I got to spend more time with her, not that I'm complaining… Like what guy wouldn't want to be traveling with a hot, mysterious chick with cool powers.

The next morning, we lost a couple of rides because Waffles wouldn't leave and tried to get in the stopped car for us. I guess we could have forced her out, but neither of us had the heart to do it. So when a farmer in a pickup came along, he had no objection to all of us riding in the back.

By nightfall, we figured we were only a day or so from Sedona. We didn't bother looking for a place to sleep in the little burg where the farmer had dropped us off but again made camp in the desert.

There were no hot dogs tonight, and we had to make do with a couple of candy bars we had bought along the way. At bedtime, Waffles settled down between us. I felt and heard her get up in the night. Probably has to pee, I thought. Then I listened to an awful screech. Waffles was in trouble! As we got up wiping the sleep from our eyes, she came limping back into camp a few minutes later. She was bleeding.

"Must have run into a coyote or something," I murmured.

Kelly cooed to her, "Come here, girl. Let me see what that bad coyote did to you."

She wasn't hesitant as she waddled over to us. I took out my flashlight since the campfire was only embers by now. There was a gash in her upper hindquarters and what looked like a bite mark to her upper haunches. Kelly dug her fingers into Waffles' wound as she tried to squirm away, emitting a pitiful little whimper.

"What are you doing? You're hurting her!" I protested.

"Trust me, okay? I know what I'm doing!" said Kelly.

If I were not there, I wouldn't believe what I was seeing. The wound started closing around Kelly's fingers. As the wound got smaller, Kelly removed another finger, until no fingers were left in the wound. It had sealed as if Waffles had never been injured!

Waffles pounced up on Kelly, licking her face repetitively with what I could only guess to be gratitude.

Kelly giggled, "See, momma won't let nothing bad happen to you, Wawa."

"Since when do you call her Wawa? And how in the heck did you do that?" I said, feeling a bit flabbergasted.

"She told me that she liked Wawa better than Waffles when we were connected. Like I said before, Davis, you won't get many answers from me. Just know you're in good hands."

"Connected? So you can stun gun, read minds and heal… Are you even human?" I said.

"Look Davis, I don't feel like explaining myself, at least not yet. I have the feeling that secrets run deep in the both of us. I've felt some things with you that I only ever read about when we kissed. Maybe at the ranch, we can talk more. But for now, let's keep focused on the task at hand," she insisted.

I let it drop, and we settled back down for the night… Wawa or Waffles as I liked to call her really seemed to take to Kelly. She curled up on top of her belly. I couldn't help but wonder if Kelly was like an angel or something, there was little doubt she had powers that could pass as divine.

***

At first glance, Sedona looked like any other mid-sized Arizona town. Low Adobe looking buildings with red Spanish tile roofs. Clean streets baking in the morning sun, and desert and mountain in the distance. I know now why they call this Red Rock country. Red rock monoliths dot the outskirts. A local pointed out a couple to us. There was Cathedral, Coffeepot and Thunder Mountains.

I called Grandpa who didn't seem too surprised to hear from me, I guess Aunt Lisa contacted them by now. He said he would pick us up in an hour or so. We settled down at a shopping complex called Tlaquepaque Arts and Crafts Village. It was built as a Mexican village.

If it weren't for the signs advertising Meditation Centers, psychics and posh resorts it would have been any other Arizona resort town.

Kelly said, "Too bad."

"What is?" I asked. Waffles looked up at her too as if to say 'what's too bad?'

"This place truly has special powers and spirituality that is found nowhere else. Spirituality shouldn't be canned and sold like any other product. But as soon as the Wall Street types get wind of it—they commercialize to the point where it seems like just any other tourist trap designed to grab as many dollars as possible."

I had no comment. Kelly always seemed deeper than I ever could be.

I was ecstatic when Grandpa pulled up in his old, blue, beaten up Ford pickup truck. A short drive later we were all sitting down to one of Grandma's spectacular Western ranch breakfasts. It wasn't just your usual ham and eggs, but a veritable feast of beef enchiladas in sauce, corn bread, and rather than ham and eggs, steak and eggs with home fries to boot. It didn't come any too soon. Grandma must have seen that we looked half starved. Even Waffles was treated to steak ends, potatoes and corn bread. She wolfed it down almost as voraciously as we did.

We found ourselves napping that afternoon. I had expected a whole barrage of questions from Grandpa, but he saw how worn out we were and let us sleep, both of us on different couches in the living room. The theme of the room was Western from the sandstone walls to the wall length rock fireplace with the long horn cow horns over it. We might have been in the Old West of Louis Lamour.

Later that evening, we were feeling pretty good. After another huge Grandma-style dinner, we settled on the front porch. The sun was about to set, and the desert glowed purple and pink with multiple colors in between. The air was soft, but with no breeze stirring.

After some general conversation about our reason for being there, Grandpa's gaze leveled on me. He said, "I've got some important stuff to tell you, son, it might very well be the key to your future."

I remained silent.

I stared at my grandfather. He was looking somehow a lot older than when I had seen him recently at the funeral. There seemed to be more wrinkles and a general weariness about him that I hadn't noticed before.

"I'm listening, Grandpa…" I said.

TWELVE

I COMBINE TWO
CRESCENT MOONS

Kelly and I were together as Grandpa began to talk. I had braced myself for a lecture about my irresponsible behavior in leaving home the way I did. I didn't have a good answer ready nor was I expecting any adult to understand. Heck, I didn't even completely understand it myself.

Was it all about the plane crash? I know that my life has evolved into something unexplainable, since that day. I'd battled a giant that destroyed the entire boys' bathroom at school, shot lightning from my hands and now my best friend was a girl that is possibly angelic. Something weird was no doubt happening in my life and for the life of me, I could not connect the dots, to see the bigger picture.

Grandpa made only one more quick reference to the situation back home. "Evidently you worried some friends back East. There is relief now that they know where you are and that you are safe."

He leveled his gaze at me and shot Kelly a quick glance. "Son, I have some things to tell you that most would consider very personal."

At first, I did not get my Grandpa's point. Then I realized that to Grandpa, Kelly was a stranger, so I turned to her and tried to find the right words. After a brief pause, I changed my mind. "Gramps, Kelly and I have been through a lot together. I trust her. I hope you don't mind if she stays."

Kelly seemed pleased.

Grandpa settled back in his chair. "No, I don't mind. I myself value loyalty. You, young people, should understand it too. I don't know much about this girl nor do I think you do either Davis since you just met, but as for myself I hope to get to know her better."

Kelly cut in. "And vice versa, Grandpa. I've been rootless for a long time and freedom, and the open road isn't all it's cracked up to be. Family is what it's all about."

Grandpa smiled, shook out his pipe and tamped in some fresh tobacco. "So how did you two youngins meet anyway?"

I could feel my cheeks warming up, and as I glanced over at Kelly for approval, she nodded. "Well... I noticed Kelly eating some fast food out of a trashcan, and she was a bit rude at first, thinking I was trying to steal her meal. But it turned out after we both ate some trash food that we got along rather well."

"Well, that is a story to tell your kids someday. It's not quite fine dining like most young couples do when they court one another. Can't say it sounds all that romantic, but it's hard to judge, being I wasn't there," he said.

Kelly and I both chuckled a bit.

"Like I said this is personal, Davis, I'm not sure what all you shared with Kelly. But I do know you loved your parents very much and that you miss them. We all do. But Davis, I have to explain the circumstances of your birth and knowing you I know it will not make one bit of difference in your feelings for them."

Now he had my full attention.

He lit up his pipe. "Davis, I'm getting old and my time is limited, so I'll get right to the point. You were adopted out of an orphanage. Unfortunately, now you find yourself an orphan once again."

I was shocked, but when I thought about it, it was not as overwhelming as the feeling of losing my parents. After Grandpa had given me time to digest that, he reached over and patted my arm. "It's only an accident of birth, son, you guys were a loving family and that's what matters, not your biological roots."

Kelly and I managed to exchange a quick glance. Grandpa said, "So in keeping with getting right to the point I have something here I have been directed to give you." He reached into his inside vest pocket. "I am to give you this upon the death of your parents." He dangled the object in front of him. It appeared to be a locket. My eyes transfixed on it, and it seemed to hypnotize me as I stared at it. He opened it. It had a bright red gem attached. A crescent moon shaped gold frame with strange symbols had been set around the gem. Grandpa handed it to me. The first thing that struck me was the strange, yet oddly familiar symbols. It was something I couldn't explain because it was a most ambivalent feeling. Strange, yet familiar. Why familiar? Something in the far recesses of my mind told me the symbols were something I knew about. Somehow.

When I turned to Kelly, I found that something about the locket had agitated her. She looked restless and nervous and lost the eye lock we'd had had on each other. If I didn't know better, I would say the look she gave me was one of suspicion. I thought I heard her murmur something but did not question her in front of Grandpa.

The old man said, "I know I've given you a lot to absorb so that's all I want to talk about right now."

I nodded to him, and Kelly and I both seemed to simultaneously head to the door.

The afternoon sun blinded us, and it took a few moments to adjust to the bright light. Kelly was acting odd. My first instinct in the house had been right. Something was wrong.

I glanced at the amulet in my hand and kind of hoped for something to come to me about it. I was holding it up to the sunlight, maybe looking for divine guidance as to how or what I was supposed to feel about it when Kelly suddenly snatched the amulet away from me and held it up to her own locket. They were counterparts, only hers was green. The two half crescents matched up and locked to make a full circle. Once the lockets were married, a bright blinding light exploded out of the crystals. I felt like I was picked up in a tornado and whirled into another dimension. It was terrifying yet breathtaking. That's when I started catching glimpses of scenes. I saw my birth parents; it was two enormous, ancient looking men, not your average Joe, mother, and father deal, they radiated power. The younger of the two touched a trident to the others hand, rivulets of golden blood spilled into the sea, lightning spider-webbed through the night sky, then the younger one holding the weapon pricked his own hand, and the waves swelled as his blood foamed against the sea. Don't ask me how, but I instinctively knew it was them. It made no sense at the time, but I swore I was witnessing my own birth. I had quick glimpses into my past, which intriguingly didn't seem to be taking place on this earth. While absolutely nothing was clear, I had certain impulses that had something to do with my purpose in life. Some great thing I was going to do or was expected to do. As I said, it was not at all clear, more feelings than images. The problem was there were so many of them, yet they were not lucid or projected logically enough for me to see what was happening.

When I was suddenly plopped back into the reality of today and Grandpa's ranch, I must have looked stunned. Kelly said, "What happened? What did you see? What did you learn?"

I just stared at her. I had no answers.

When I was completely lucid again, I turned to Kelly. "Where did you get the amulet? It obviously has some kind of strange powers."

She turned away and said nothing.

I kept insisting, and she finally turned to me. "It's hard to explain but believe me it is safer for you not to have it. Actually, I've been searching for the other half, that's the whole reason I was on the road in the first place. Weird how it turned up at your grandpa's." She paused. I waited. "It's not time to explain everything to you yet," she said.

I was so confused. Nothing that she was saying was making a whole lot of sense, and I wasn't going to give up on my demand for her to give me back the amulet. Or at least my half of it. Eventually. But first I needed to clear my head. "Can we saddle up a couple of horses and ride out to the river. I remember where it is from my last visit. I really need to get thinking straight again."

We saddled a little paint for her and a palomino mare for me. The horses were smaller than stallions and mares and just right for our pre-adult heights.

Maybe it was something about the smooth gait of horse-back riding that tended to sooth my frayed nerves. Waffles who had been a bit bored found something to do. Waffles chased after and insisted on coming with us.

By the time we arrived at what I had remembered as a river, which now seemed no more than a fast running creek, I felt much calmer. We drank from the stream. It was fresh and cold, Waffles, right beside us lapping hard.

We tied our mounts up in the shade and in range of grazing. I took Kelly by the hand, and we headed for the burbling creek and plopped ourselves down on the grassy bank. The sawtooth red mountains in the distance loomed hazy in the midday sun.

She lay back with a long blade of grass in her mouth and gazed at the passing clouds. We were silent. Then I said, "I don't really know what that was all about but I did get some distinct feelings."

She gazed over at me. "Like what?"

"Mostly I felt like there was something I had to do or was expected to do. Something important. And I had a glimpse of my birth parents, there were two guys, I must have seen it wrong, but I had a distinctive feeling that I was being born. Something was special about them, the guy holding the trident drew blood from both his and the older, gray haired man's hand, as their blood spilled, the older one appeared to command the lightning in the sky, and the other made the sea swell."

Kelly chewed her blade of grass for a minute. "Two guys, with abilities that's an impressive vision and you felt like this was your birth—" She went back to thinking. "Do you believe that all of this has anything to do with what happened to your parents?" she asked.

"Yes, I do."

She seemed surprised by the quickness of my answer. "Interesting, so a blinding white light was the cause of the crash?" Kelly said.

"Yeah," is all I could say.

"Has anything else happened that seemed out of the ordinary?" Kelly asked.

"Well... back at the Waffle House, I swore that was Polybotes that we both saw."

I looked her deep in the eyes, waiting for her to laugh at me. But she never did. It almost seemed like she was expecting me to bring this up, it felt splendid getting this off my chest. Besides, Kelly was the queen of weird, so I felt pretty safe talking about not so common topics.

Her eyes widened, "Look, Davis, don't judge me Ok? You're right that was Polybotes... but I do not want to talk about it."

It was hard getting answers from Kelly, but at least she confirmed that I did actually see Polybotes back at the Waffle House. Was nice hearing confirmation that I wasn't crazy. Kelly got silent, and after a while, we saddled up and headed back to the ranch. Kelly was silent for nearly a mile.

"Davis, I know you're looking for answers… And you know I got them. And I thank you for not pushing me to talk." Kelly said.

I nodded.

Once back at the ranch, we put the horses back in their stalls, I was getting re-accustomed to modern day luxuries, such as abundant food and proper hygiene. It was pure bliss after roughing it two weeks cross-country. We were living like guests on a dude ranch going for rides, having cookouts at night. Taking part in some of the farm work. And Kelly and I were getting closer by the day.

That's when Alicia showed up. I have to say I had no idea at all that she would follow me out here – and it was stunning to see how Kelly's jaw dropped at the sight of the cute girl from back home.

We had met her cab out in front of the ranch house. When she got out, she threw herself into my arms, and I got the feeling that my troubles had just begun.

After the greeting, I of course had to introduce her to Kelly without giving any real details of how and why we seemed to be together. The girls almost immediately launched into a thorough female appraisal of each other, eyes lingering on one another's seemingly best features. I was shocked; Alicia was the last person I expected to get out of that cab.

While she was in my arms, her head and hair buried in my shoulder, she murmured, "That was a terrible, terrible thing you did, scaring your Aunt like that and me too. You should have stayed home as I suggested."

I pulled my head back and looked at her. "Did you receive my postcard?"

"Yes, I got it a few days ago and hopped a plane out to Arizona, then I called a cab from the airport, and now I'm here." I smiled. "I take it you kept your promise?"

"Yes, but how on earth did you manage it?"

"That is a long story. And where Kelly comes in. We came out here together."

I immediately realized my mistake. I knowingly had brought another girl into the picture. Now I had to explain her and not make it seem like we were a couple in any way. Although I guess, we actually were. In fact, we had shared some intimate moments together.

Alicia cocked her head and tugged a strand of hair behind her ear. "You mean you guys traveled together out here?" I could see her head processing that information and conjuring up all kinds of things, most of which never happened.

Her eyes locked on Kelly seeming to give her another, even more thorough evaluation and when she was through there was fire in her eyes.

Alicia glowered at me. "Do you have someplace for me to stay? I won't stay long. I'll be out of your way soon."

"Hey, wait a minute. You're letting your imagination go wild." She only gripped her backpack and said, "Just show me where I can get some sleep. Please."

It was the last word that let me know how she felt. After I had shown her the guest room, I returned to join Kelly outside. Kelly was standing on the porch one hip loosely against the porch rail. "She's pissed in case you don't know it."

I shrugged it off. "Nah. She's just tired. She didn't expect anybody like you."

Kelly simply said, "No. She's pissed."

THIRTEEN

I TAKE A MIDNIGHT STROLL

I woke up early. Trying my best to be quiet, I crept downstairs. There was no doubt that I was swimming in the deep end and could use some solid advice from an outsider, like Aunt Lisa. Besides, after seeing Alicia, it made me miss my aunt even more.

Once inside the living room, I picked up the handset of an old black rotary phone that looked like it belonged to Alexander Graham Bell himself. It felt like I stepped back in time as I pressed my index finger down on each number of the telephone dial, spinning the clear plastic dial to each digit. It was neat watching the dial reset as it rotated counter-clockwise making a clickety-clack sound.

A few short rings later, a familiar voice answered, "Hello."

"Aunt Lisa, it's me…" I said.

"Davis… My God I was so worried about you. Did Alicia make it out safe?" she said.

"Yeah, that's part of the reason I'm calling you."

"Is something wrong?" she asked.

I gathered my thoughts for a moment, "Well… I ran into a girl named Kelly along the way cross-country, she's about my age, and I brought her to the ranch with me. I'm not going to lie we are both attracted to each other, and things have been leaning toward us being a couple. Well, that was until Alicia showed up, now it seems I'm in a mess. She reminded me of all the strong feelings I had for her, the moment I held her in my arms. I don't know what to do…" I said.

"Whoa… Sounds like you had a busy few weeks. Well, before I go giving advice, I want to make one thing clear, Davis. You could have come to me; I would have paid your way to your grandparents after all, that is how Alicia got there…" she said.

I felt a bit shocked at what she said, so I'd done all this, and I never had to? Maybe Aunt Lisa was a lot cooler than I originally thought. "So you're saying I hitchhiked all this way for nothing?" I said.

"No not for nothing, but it could have been much simpler. After all, it sounds like you met someone on your journey and I'm sure you got to see life from a different perspective. I know I did when I ran away from home."

"You ran away from home?" I said.

"Yeah, but that is a story for another day. I'm happy to hear you're doing fine and that Alicia has arrived. As for your problems, you're not married, so I would suggest that you treat them both as friends and figure things out. I'm sure if you told them how you feel they would understand, Alicia is no doubt very mature for her age," she said.

We caught up a bit, and I told her all about my big adventure out West, minus the supernatural stuff, and she seemed to be hanging onto my every word, provoking me to spill the little details. I heard some stirring upstairs, so I cut the conversation short with Aunt Lisa and promised to keep in touch.

Breakfast felt a bit awkward, Alicia and Kelly were sitting on opposite ends of the table. But thankfully Grandma kept the conversation flowing in a peaceful manner, between the five of us. Then the topic changed to something a bit more intriguing, and Grandpa chimed in, "I've had an archeologist friend at the local university check out the necklace awhile back, and he had told me that he could not translate the inscription. It appeared to have come from a long dead language. So my guess is that the necklace is very ancient."

Grandpa tugged at his short, white beard very concentrated. "Davis, if you wanted to learn more about your birth parents, you need to be careful not to lose the necklace because I'd wager it holds many secrets," he said.

My Gramps was not very cryptic, so I took his advice to heart. I caught Kelly rolling her eyes in my peripherals, let's face it, the answer, at least to the necklace mystery lay with her. I would have to convince her to tell me. I suppose I could demand she tell me, but I knew enough about her to know she wouldn't. As for Alicia. Another problem.

Yesterday I was a mere high school kid, a bit shy and not what you'd call a ladies' man, but this morning -- amazingly enough -- I was a guy with women trouble!

I walked out onto the patio to get some fresh air and think how to get Kelly to spill the beans about the necklace and get my half of it back. While sipping my coffee, Alicia found me. I tried to seem cheerful, yet I had no idea how to provide the answers she wanted, without offending her, I said, "Good morning. How did you like breakfast?"

"Good morning, Davis. Your grandma makes the most fabulous ranch breakfast. Not that I've ever had a ranch breakfast before."

Good. She was cheerful. However, if I thought that she was going to pass over the Kelly thing I was wrong. I had a feeling that the question was on the tip of her tongue. "So who is this chick, Kelly and what's your interest in her?" she asked.

I was surprised I didn't start off with a stammer. Instead, I said rather coolly, "I met Kelly on the road. She had some survival skills that she shared with me, and if it weren't for her, I wouldn't have made it here." I paused to check the reaction. Getting none I went on. "Not that I wouldn't actually have done it, but I would have had to turn myself in and go back home. And I didn't want to do that."

"Why did you come here?" she asked. "You never did explain."

I chose my words carefully. "Okay here comes the spooky part. At least some of it. I don't know why I came here, but it's like something was drawing me here. I sure don't have all the answers yet, but I found out yesterday that some of the answers lay with Kelly."

"Well you took a while getting here," she said, sounding a bit annoyed, "but what is it with you and this girl?"

I tried for my most sincere voice. I looked her straight in the eye and said, "I don't have any feelings for Kelly other than being grateful for her help."

Alicia was quiet, thoughtful. Then she said, "Why is it that I don't feel that way?"

"I don't know, Alicia. All I know how to do is tell the truth. And that is the truth," I said.

Alicia kind of cocked her head as if she was wondering whether or not to believe me. A few months ago I didn't have a girlfriend. Now I had two girls in my life, and I was under suspicion like I was some kind of Casanova.

I took Alicia's hand and said, "I'm going to talk to Kelly soon, and I hope to get some answers."

Immediately there was the squinting of the eyes that could only suggest suspicion. "You're going to be alone with her when you try to find out?"

Now was the time to stammer. "I…I guess so. Why is that important? Most people don't speak in confidence with an audience. Especially about what I have to find out from her. I'll tell you about that later. For now, just know she knows something, and I intend to see what it is."

Alicia didn't seem convinced, but I was heartened by the kiss she planted on my lips. "Do the right thing," she said.

At that moment I was determined to do it.

I slipped a note under Kelly's door because I didn't want to ask her at dinner. The letter asked her to meet me in the barn at midnight.

When I crept out to the barn early in the morning, everybody else had already gone to sleep and Kelly was already waiting outside. I had rehearsed what I would say multiple times. I had made up my mind to appeal to her sense of fairness, and I hoped to throw in a little charm. I only hoped that doing so wouldn't have me making any unrealistic promises to her I couldn't keep.

I saw her shadow as I approached. We went into the barn.

"I like how your hair looks in ponytails," I said.

"Thanks Davis, but I'm sure you didn't ask me out here to compliment my hair," she said.

"I called you out here to ask about the necklace. Grandpa made it clear that it has something to do with my family," I said.

Kelly smirked. "It's nothing to do with your family, it might have belonged to them. But there are no answers you will find written on it. The symbols are a warning… That's all you will get out of me, so let's drop it," she said.

No matter how hard I tried to reason with her, she was unmovable, sticking to her story that it would be dangerous for me to know. My hands clenched and unclenched in frustration. A cuss word hung back from the edge of my tongue. I said, "Look, if you can't be more upfront with me, then at least return what is mine. You owe me that much if nothing else."

Kelly stomped her foot. Her chest heaved, and she lit into me. "Owe you!?" she snapped. "You have some nerve throwing around bold claims like that. If not for me, you would never have made it this far."

She did have a point as I well knew. Still, part of me persisted.

I tried a different approach. I said, "Just give it to me. After I find what the symbols mean, you can have it back, if it means that much to you!"

I was met with silence. I was gearing up for another round when the horses began to stamp restlessly. "What's wrong with them?" I wondered aloud. They kept it up, getting more restless, whinnying and neighing.

Then I saw him. My eyes bugged out of my head. Kelly looked at me. Probably wondering what had spooked me. He was an odd little creature and seemed like a drunken elf. He was about two feet high, with a ray like tail, long boney feet, a pot-belly and a quirky smile. Long rabbit like ears drooped down and a little patch of hair stuck up like an island on the top of his head. He wore a mischievous grin that was at once silly and charming but looked very out of place in a barn. He said, "She can't hear or see me. But we need to talk." His voice was a cross between Alvin the Chipmunk and Elmer Fudd.

I took a deep breath and said, "Kelly, do you see it too?"

"I'm not sure what you're gawking at," she said.

"Doubt if you would believe me if I told ya."

The creature blinked out of sight and then was at my feet.

He said, "Master called Oogle Doogle?"

"Oogle, what?" I said.

"Master did call with amulet. Yes?"

"Who are you talking to?" Kelly demanded.

"Master speak with Oogle." He turned to Kelly. "Shush now, Annunaki traitor your ancestors done enough damage! Give back what is Master's." With a snap of his finger, Kelly was pushed against the wall and silenced, and the necklace around her neck was now dangling around mine.

I gasped. "How did you…?"

"Time for that later, let Oogle help Master remember."

"What is this all about?" I said.

"Master, you either be a savior or the cause of much doom. Lord Hades is raising an army to take over Earth, its inhabitants are heading for much trouble, Master is the only one with the power to fix," Oogle said.

"What? I'm only a high school kid." None of this was making any sense to me – especially considering the bizarre messenger! "You make it sound like I have to be Alexander the Great, or Caesar or something."

"This is truth. You are going to have to be smart and make some smart decisions." Oogle said.

"Say again?" I said.

"Oogle not tell master lie, in thirteen days' time, Lord Hades will unleash the KERES, wicked female spirits that will ravage, disease and destroy humanity. Once every 3,600 years, the veil wears thin, and they stir, becoming restless. Gods of Olympus do not stop them this time... Maybe Oogle not say enough. But if this too much for you now—," he explained, with what I may have only imagined was a tinge of condescension in his voice.

Oogle continued, "I leave master now—just know Oogle, not dream or imagination. I am as real as reality. Oogle contact master when more ready to accept status and responsibility!"

With a touch of his elongated finger, memories started to flood my mind's eye. It was the same memories from when Kelly put the two crescent pieces of the necklace together, this time they were a bit less jumbled and made a clear picture. Still, it was too fast to catch the entire thing. One thing I did see clearly was a really young boy, my best guess is he was around the age of three walking out of the surf and onto a beach, Oogle was standing on his shoulder. I had an uneasy feeling that the boy in the vision was me.

"Whoa... That don't get any less weird the second time around," I said aloud. "Like is that real? Everything I saw? And some of the things I saw I can't quite recall. Is that normal?"

He spoke. "Master supposed to have necklace on at all time. This why you have problems remembering. Inter-dimensional travel is dangerous on mind; amulet keeps memories safe. In time you will have memories back, Oogle helps fill in blanks for now."

"Is Kelly okay?" I said.

"Yes, she is fine. Oogle makes her sleep, but master need find better companion, this one ancestors was cause of you losing your family."

With another snap of the tiny imp's fingers, Kelly was set free of her trance and looked really bloodthirsty which I found to be quite attractive in an odd sort of way.

"What the hell just happened?" she snapped.

"I honestly don't know!" I replied.

I glanced around looking for the little creature. He was gone, and I was left there with one pissed off chick, the horses, the mule and a couple of goats wondering if I had just stepped into some kind of crazy Disney World portal. I shook my head several times to see if I was dreaming. But everything was there. The barn. The smell of the animals. The crickets and insects of the night. All as real as real could be.

FOURTEEN

I MEET A CHIMERA

There was little doubt Kelly was furious for answers, with her flared nostrils and piercing glare. But we finally hit a checkmate, and I intended to leverage the information I had obtained from Oogle. I was determined to get to the bottom of this mystery once and for all, regardless of the repercussions. I was sick of feeling crazy, and I needed to get some solid answers.

"Kelly, we need to be more upfront with one another. Like starting with some basics. For starters, after nearly three weeks I don't even know your last name? And that is entirely unrelated to anything supernatural," I said, closing the barn door behind me.

Kelly and I strolled toward the house. She remained silent for a bit and then shouted rather loudly, "My last name, you seriously think this is the appropriate time to be asking me, my last name?"

She paced back and forth a moment, my guess was that she was processing everything, then finally she said, "But I assume your last name is Finch, like the songbird? I figured that much out on my own without being intrusive… After all, that's what is painted on your grandparents; mailbox—."

She stopped for a moment dangling her arms as she said, "I suppose if it's really that appropriate my full name is Kelly Elizabeth Ridinger!"

When we got to the porch I was about to say something when Alicia appeared at the screen door, Kelly had probably woken up everyone in the whole house with her obnoxiously loud demeanor. Uh oh. This is going to have to be explained. I knew that Kelly wanted to talk about what had happened, but this wasn't going to be the time for it.

When Alicia spoke, her tone was dripping with sarcasm. She sounded ticked off. "Having a moonlight stroll?" She wisecracked.

"No," I said. "I was just asking Kelly some questions about her roots," I shrugged. "Was nothing bad, honest."

Alicia fixed a laser gaze on me. She seemed to be trying to figure out whether to believe me or not when Kelly announced, "I'm going to bed," and hurried off.

Now Alicia and I were alone. I took her hand, and we began to stroll aimlessly out to the empty corral. I hung my arms over the top rail, took a deep breath and looked up at the desert sky. It was ablaze with stars. We rubbernecked for a while, both of us touched by the magic of the universe. The silence was awkward and palpable. Finally, Alicia spoke. "I gotta tell you, Davis, I'm beginning to feel like a fool."

"Why?" I said hoping I sounded sincere.

"Let's face it, how needy do I look. I chased you out here only to find you swooning over a girl you just met."

I sighed, knowing she was right. "I know it might seem that way, Alicia, but that's not true. I don't have anything going with Kelly. I would hope you'd know that but if I have to convince you I will. I hope we can get to the point where we will just trust each other and not worry about it."

She now sighed. "Sounds nice."

I planted a kiss on her lips, it felt great... sending tingles down my spine. She pulled me in closer; I could feel her slightly chilled hand make its way up my shirt, stopping on my bare chest. I wanted to make out with Alicia and going past second base would be a dream come true... but this didn't feel right. The timing was off, and I was feeling so damn confused. So, I back away.

I took a deep breath and said, "We can't, not tonight. It just doesn't feel right, and I want it to be special for you, your first time."

"It's okay Davis, I get it," Alicia said.

I just hoped to get off the hook on this drama, but no matter what I did I only seemed to dig myself a deeper hole. We headed for the house, though, still hand in hand but I could sense a difference in her touch.

The next morning, I got up early hoping to catch Kelly alone to talk to her. She was already in the kitchen drinking coffee. "Morning," I said, pouring myself a cup.

As I stood by the sink drinking it, I was worried about another "gotcha' moment with Alicia. Yet I needed to talk to Kelly. I motioned her to the den where we sat in separate chairs facing each other. It would sink me to get caught somewhere alone with her again.

I said, "Please talk low, but we gotta get some things straightened out."

"Couldn't agree more," she intoned. "So let's start with what happened back in the barn last night. You saw something, and somehow I was put out of the picture for a while. I had the feeling that I'd been asleep. So yeah I agree that we need to shine some light on things. With some reservations."

"Look, I'm done beating around the bush, it appears we both want some questions answered... But frankly if you expect me to tell you anything, then you're telling me what the necklace inscription means, you said it was a warning," I explained sternly. "And what reservations?"

She looked away, over my head. She was somewhere else. "Look, Davis... I think I get you... But I don't want to burden you if I am wrong, Okay? As far as reservations, I mean we both are holding stuff back, it's more than obvious..."

I did a double take. "At this point, I could care less if you're wrong, Kelly... I need to know what the heck is going on with my life... I'm not an idiot nor am I holding anything back! I can tell something weird is happening, so if that's what you're talking about."

After a brief silence, Kelly said, "The necklace, reads of a prophecy." She reached for the amulet and noticed it was not around her neck. "I take it, the necklace was stolen from me while I was out too?"

"Sort of, but not by me," I said.

I pulled the necklace out from beneath the scruff of my shirt; Kelly leaned in closer to read the inscription.

She murmured, "Fine, you win!" As she tugged at the chain, it tore at the hair on the back of my neck. Then she cited, "A child conceived of blood and foam, Shall walk this path by choice alone, His weakness is a friend that's foe—," she muttered. "There seems to be another half, but it's missing."

"Yeah, well that didn't help much... Think you can fill in the blanks a tad?"

She chewed on her lower lip. "I don't know much about the inscription," she promised. "It's time for you to hold up your end of the deal... I did as you requested, now tell me the truth, Davis, what did you see last night? And what happened to me?"

"A tiny creature appeared, he said only I was able to see or hear him, and he kept insisting I was its master. He called you an anti-something traitor, and then he put you in a trance-like a master magician and then you floated across the barn... My only guess is he was levitating you like Yoda, from Star Wars," I said.

She thought about what I had said. "Hmm, sounds like an imp or possibly a trickster."

We were still sitting in chairs facing each other. She leaned over and took my hand. "Maybe it's just not the right time to tell everything we know, but we can make one firm commitment."

"Which is?" I said.

"That we are not doing or are going to do anything that would hurt each other. We were friends on the road. I liked that. Now there are all these suspicions about each other and Alicia. I don't like her being here it makes me feel so uneasy."

About then Grandma came down and started rattling pots and pans in the kitchen, and the delicious aroma of griddle cakes filled the house. Grandpa and Alicia arrived downstairs by the time breakfast was ready. We all sat down together to a traditional ranch breakfast.

After the girls had helped Grandma clean up the breakfast dishes, Grandma announced, "I'm going into town to run some errands and could use some help. I'd appreciate it if the two of you would come along," she said leveling her gaze on both Alicia and Kelly.

"Sure thing, let me grab my purse, and I'll be ready," Alicia said.

"Count me in, I'd love to help in any way possible. After all, it's the least I can do, considering all your hospitality," Kelly admitted.

Grandma gave Grandpa a hug and a kiss goodbye and then she said, "Now stay out of trouble boys and be sure to get the chores done, no slacken just cause I'm not about to keep you on your toes… Will be back in a couple of hours."

I followed Grandpa out to the barn where he said he had some haying to do. It was a beautiful morning in the high desert country. The sun was bright and the morning air was still crisp. I went along and grabbed a pitchfork to help.

As we were heaving hay from one pile to another, I asked Grandpa, "What was I like as a child? And do you know much about my adoption?"

"Well," Grandpa said, as he heaved a forkful of hay. "You were a lovable little bugger. You appealed to your parents. But you had problems. Couldn't or wouldn't talk. You had been abandoned and appeared to be about eight. As I said, you appealed to them, and they wanted very much to help you get back into the world."

"So," I said, "I don't really know how old I am."

"Right. But before they adopted you they came to see you several times and were able to connect with you. They sensed you were intelligent but besides that they wanted you very much. They made arrangements to adopt you. Then their task was to get you to talk. Both of them worked very hard at that, spending a lot of time with you. That was good in a couple of ways. It got you talking again, and it helped you all to bond and become a family. They found out how intelligent you were by the questions that you asked."

"Like what?" I asked.

He grinned before answering. "Like where the Earth was located in the universe. The distance to the nearest star. The volume of water on our planet. The genetic makeup of humans. It was quite remarkable. Amazingly astute questions for a little kid."

"If I was already eight years old did I talk about my life before I was adopted?" I asked. It was more than a little perplexed hearing all of this for the first time. "I don't remember anything," I said.

Grandpa pushed back his cowboy hat and wiped his brow. "When they finally got you talking, you didn't talk about anything that had happened to you before the adoption. So for all intents and purposes your life started then," he said.

Things were beginning to settle. A lot of questions were being answered.

"Now that I answered your questions, I think it only fair, you answer one for me. son… What's all this lollygagging with them girls? You been playing both them lovely ladies something fierce, hate to see any young hearts get broken," he said.

For the first time in a while I found myself tongue tied. "I… I don't want to play games with either of them. Before coming out here, Alicia was the center of my universe. Now I feel like I'm being tugged in two different directions…" I said.

Sitting down on a bale of hay, I felt so nervous I caught myself chewing the sides of my fingers, which broke my deep concentration.

"Well, Kelly is equally amazing, and we connect at a level I never experienced with Alicia. But at the same time, I experience feelings with Alicia that I don't with Kelly… It's so damn confusing, Grandpa. I'm scared that if I pick one, I'll lose my friendship with the other or something worse might come about while they are both together and I lose both of them," I said.

"Well son, can't say I ever had that type of woman troubles. But that's what you're gone get if you keep things going the way they be. That's a whole world of hurt cooking up to a boil, I suggest you figure something out to defuse things a bit, take the pot off of the open flame before it blows its top," he said.

"Thanks for the advice, Grandpa, I'll see what I can figure out."

When Grandma and the girls got back, I had an idea. As a sort of peace offering and for Alicia to realize that I wasn't interested in Kelly romantically I suggested we mount up and head out for a ride. I had the little creek Kelly and I had gone to in mind.

I could see both of them hesitate. They barely seemed to tolerate one another, but maybe my insistent, cheerful attitude made up their minds.

Kelly and I picked out the little paint and palomino from the other day. I chose a little sorrel for Alicia. We mounted up and with each packing a little snack we rode for the high country. The water was rushing over sandstone rocks and looked so appealing we decided that we would take a dip. Although it wasn't really deep enough for swimming, we were hot from the blazing desert sun. So we stripped down to our skivvies and jumped in the water.

We frolicked like three little kids splashing one another and sitting on the creek bed and letting the rushing water be our private bubble bath. Every once in a while, one of us would splash the other, and the war would start again.

We were refreshed when we left and headed back to the ranch. Even if we weren't the best of friends, we were on better terms than before.

As we rode up to the corral to put the horses up and rub them down, my horse became agitated, something startled him. My first thought was a coyote, I kept my eyes peeled and then I caught sight of a young man working on the corral rails. It looked like he was repairing them. As we rode the horses began to whinny, so I motioned for the girls to stop, and his features became clear my heart thudded to the pit of my stomach. Was it.....? Oh my God.

"Is that Polybotes?" I muttered to the girls.

"What? Poly who?" Alicia asked.

"That bully from school," I said.

Kelly said, "Davis, that's impossible. It's my father."

Alicia looked at us as though we'd lost our minds. "You're both seeing things," she hissed. "It's that bitch Sandy Keohane who beat me out for the cheerleading squad."

I said, "Okay, everybody calm down. Something's going on that none of us understand." I leveled my gaze at Kelly. "Or do we, Kelly?"

Kelly gave me a weird look. Then she closed her eyes and began chanting. Alicia and I just watched her, our mount's reins in our hands.

Kelly was obviously not among us but in a far off distant place. She continued to chant in a language I couldn't hope to understand. It sounded like those TV preachers that spoke in "tongues." It was very weird. Both Alicia and I had our eyes glued to her. When she stopped, we followed her gaze to where the guy from school (or at least that was who he looked like to me) had been standing. He was gone. In fact, no human being was there, rather the strangest of strange animals began roaming the corral. Oh my God, what the heck is it? It seems to have parts of different animals!

Recognition suddenly flashed across Alicia's face. "This is not possible," she said, awestruck. "Davis, remember Homer's description in the Illiad, from Mr. Merrill's Ancient History class last year, about the Chimera? I think that's what we are looking at..."

I kept staring, even as we all backed up a few more steps. "yeah—sort of," I said.

"A Chimera has the body of a lion with a tail that ends in a snake's head and the head of a goat rising up from her back in the center of her spine. They're extremely dangerous."

As if I couldn't figure that part out for myself!

We had almost stopped breathing as we watched this strange monster roam the corral. Then in a flash, it was gone. Vanished into thin air.

Somewhere a hawk overhead called to his mate, as if all were perfectly normal. Well, at least his world hadn't turned completely upside down.

FIFTEEN

FROZEN IN TIME

We were in the meadow beyond the corral moving slowly and silently (well, as silent as you can possibly be riding three horses) toward the house. The air was humid, and the heat of the sun was stinging my skin. None of us knew what to expect besides possibly Kelly, but she was keeping to herself. I'm not sure what the others were thinking about, but I had plenty boiling in my head. What was a Chimera doing at my grandparents' ranch? Were my grandparents in any danger or even us for that matter? I couldn't help but feel a little guilty; after all, I've become a magnet to monsters lately. To date, I've encountered a shape-shifter, Kelly whom I assume an angel, Oogle Doogle some sort of imp or trickster, and now a Chimera. Either I was crazy, or the normal life I once knew was forever gone.

I went over every event that led up to the present over and over, desperately seeking clues to put it all into context, but it seemed so confusing. Yet I knew deep down it was set into motion the day the plane crashed, but why?

Alicia spoke first, and her remarks were to Kelly. "So," she said, "that chanting is what? Magic or something?"

Kelly, without any emotion, said, "Yeah, pretty much."

"So you're either a wizard or a witch," Alicia said, "like in the Harry Potter novels?"

"One who practices magic doesn't need a title. And as for Harry Potter, I don't know him. What kind of stuff does he do?" Kelly said.

"Well, the wizards in his stories use magic for good," Alicia said. "Well except the evil Lord Voldemort, he is the archenemy of Harry."

"I see. What kind of magic you practice depends on the type of person that you are. I mean there's black magic for those with evil souls, and there's white magic for the rest of us," Kelly said.

Alicia didn't make any reference to Kelly's distinction, but I assumed she was thinking white magic. She went on. "So how does one get to be able to do magic? Don't you need a wand or something?"

Kelly said, "I learned without any devices. If you lose the device or it is damaged, you're kind of limited."

"I see. But how do you get it? I mean are you born with it?"

"Some are. There is magic that you inherit, there's also magic you learn through study." Anticipating Alicia's querulous look, Kelly said, "I got mine through both. The inheritance part is too complicated to explain, and it's not the right time to tell it."

Alicia said, "That thing. We all saw something different. Was that...?"

Kelly grinned. "That's right. Magic. We each saw our worst enemy. Davis saw the bully from school, I saw my father, and you saw some girl from cheerleading."

Now I had a question. "That creature, was it a Chimera? What's the bottom line on that?"

We walked in silence some more before Kelly said, "Davis, it is a Chimera. And I have to tell you; it is going to be a problem. We are in danger. Once a Chimera has your scent, it will never stop hunting you, and that means it'll return. We need to take watch tonight, it will be back."

I said, "But your magic... I'm sure you could fight it, right?"

Kelly interrupted, "No good, at least not in the long run. Not on a Chimera. No. Let's face it, guys, we're going to have to come up with a plan."

Although I, and Alicia too, agreed, I had no idea what to do. I said, "Kelly, do Chimeras have any weakness? You know, like how silver bullets can kill werewolves and vampires and while we are talking about the weird and freaky are vampires and werewolves real as well?

"I'm sure they do have a weakness of some kind or a vulnerability... back home we have libraries with books on all possible creature's weaknesses, in our training camp. But that won't help us at the moment. And yes, them sort of creatures do exist, Davis they are not like your television shows portray them, they are much worse."

Grandpa has a decent gun collection, I'm sure we could get some silver bullets if that sort of thing works."

She chuckled to herself a bit and then she said, "Davis, we are outgunned. There is little chance that we could kill a Chimera by shooting it, trap it maybe... But killing one is nearly impossible."

Alicia said, "Didn't Hercules chop off one's head in a fable?"

I said, "Yeah, but he had the strength of an Olympian God, so I guess we would lack the muscle?"

"I think you, Davis, are that strong, but you don't seem anywhere near ready to embrace what's really inside you..." Kelly said looking at me dreamily.

Alicia and I both looked at Kelly in disbelief. "You are kidding, right? I don't feel like I'm all that strong. Besides, last I checked I was just human."

"There is something special inside of you, Davis, but if you believe you are human, then who am I to tell you otherwise," Kelly said.

This was getting weirder by the minute, and I hated when Kelly spoke in riddles, like was I really as strong as Hercules or not? Could I actually protect us from the Chimera? It was a welcoming thought, but I knew deep down I was only entertaining a daydream. No way could I fight a Chimera and win on strength alone (a rocket launcher, on the other hand, would do the trick, not that I own one).

I looked over at Alicia, her eyes turned sad. I figured she was trying to wrap her mind around everything. I couldn't blame her, I know how hard it is to accept that everything you believed to be true was nothing short of a fairytale. Our eyes had been opened to the real world, and nothing could ever take that back.

I rode up to Alicia and wiped a tear from her cheek and then I said, "Sorry that I got you involved in all of this... I had no intention of pulling you into my mess. I came here for answers and I been getting more than my mind can grasp most days."

I stared at her.

Alicia gripped the reigns of her horse so tight that her knuckles turned white before saying, "Davis, I came here looking for you... It was my choice to come out to the ranch, just the thought of everything Kelly said about were-wolves and vampires and books on killing real monsters is a lot to take in. Like I would think she was crazy if I didn't see the Chimera with my own eyes, I'll be OK."

At the ranch we found Grandma tending an ugly bite wound on my grandfather.

"Grandma, what happened?" I asked.

"Grandpa was out hunting a wolf that had been stalking the chickens," she said. Breathing heavy, she said, "He had caught up with the wolf and got a shot in, but his rifle jammed as the wolf came lunging at him. Fortunate for Grandpa he always carries his pistol. The wolf got in a good size bite on his calf before Grandpa could get the pistol from his holster and shoot it a second time."

Grandpa coughed a spell before forcing out his words in a weak sounding voice, "Think that wolf be rabid, I'm feelin' pretty damn sick or might be the bacteria from the bite. Either way, Davis I need you to go track the blood trail out behind the house and make sure it's dead, if not, finish that critter off quick, nothing worse than a wounded animal."

Grandma and the girls stayed with Grandpa. Me on the other hand, I had a mission. I was about to have a showdown with death and was none the wiser. I took Grandpa's 30-30 lever action rifle out of the gun cabinet and a handful of 150-grain bullets. I fed five rounds into the magazine tube and one into the chamber. Outside on the porch, I held the rifle up, the smooth wooden stock felt at home in my hands as I peered down the iron sight aiming at a buzzard circling the blush pink sky above the corral. It had been awhile since I'd fired a gun, but it was one of those skills you never forgot, like riding a bike.

Out back of the house I spotted the blood trail, it was precisely where grandpa had said and appeared to still be somewhat fresh. Near a puddle of blood, I found a .22 caliber casing. I could only guess that this was where Grandpa was attacked and that the blood belonged to him, the wolf or both.

I followed the blood trail some ways, not knowing what to expect. I lost the trail in dense aquatic foliage, leading into a large pond. So I circled the area looking for any sign of a wounded canine, but outside of spooking myself by kicking up some unexpected frogs, the trail went cold.

I was just about to give up and head back to check on Grandpa and the girls when I spotted the Chimera. It was about a hundred yards out from the pond basking atop a boulder under the hot Arizona sun; it had a distinct red splotch of blood on its neck. I knew at this point that Grandpa was fooled by its magic as well and his biggest fear was a wolf.

Something inside me went off like a bomb, my whole body trembled. I felt a desire for vengeance, a very unfamiliar sensation. I was acutely aware of what Kelly said about bullets being useless, but the immense anger growing inside me was overpowering my common sense and my newfound thirst for revenge was now beyond the point of return.

It sniffed the air as I stared down the iron sight of the rifle. It must have caught my scent because it jumped up on all four paws and started charging straight at me. Puffs of smoke came out of its nostrils like a small locomotive and its goat shaped head reared itself forward, lowering its horns in a ramming gesture as it reached a full sprint.

Taking dead aim, I locked my sights between its broad golden shoulders, squeezed the hair trigger and fired off a round of hot lead. The beast slowed and staggered a bit, before picking up speed. I ejected the round, and let off the next five, connecting each one to its golden flesh, painting its coat red. Just a few feet in front of me it came to a halt, before falling over on its side. There was no doubt that the beast was still alive. Each breath filled its lungs, and its massive chest heaved up and down.

I reached into my pocket and pulled out my last three rounds, I needed these to count. So I loaded them into the rifle and walked up to the beast. Without even the smallest amount of remorse I took aim and discharged each round individually into each of the three heads. It was now motionless, rivulets of blood pooled to the fresh wounds, staining the hide. I tapped the beast a few times with the stock of the rifle, and it didn't move. Then I made the biggest mistake ever, I turned my back on it, and the snake tail lunged at me, biting me on the arm. I tried to pull away, but it refused to let loose. I could feel a burning sensation going down my arm (I assumed it to be venom flowing through my veins) then something came over me. Some of the flashes I saw previously were no longer flashes but a memory. It was training. I saw me doing combat training with Oogle. Once I snapped back into reality, I took my free arm and grabbed the snake's mouth and pried it open.

Its fangs were embedded really deep, with all my strength I pushed; the pain was immense as its long pencil like fangs retracted from my flesh. Free from its grip, I took off running back toward the house. The burning sensation quickly spread, it enveloped my entire body in under a minute. "My training," I said out loud, I instinctively knew I needed nectar, that it would heal me. I changed my direction and headed for the bee boxes -- there was wildflower honey inside.

By the time I arrived, I was staggering, my vision was blurry, and it felt as though I was fading in and out of consciousness. I staggered over to a white bee box nearly falling atop it. I literally slapped the top of the box off, and the bees all swarmed out, like a small black cloud and left; oddly, not even a single bee attacked me. I reached my hand inside and tore a chunk of honeycomb out. I chanted an ancient blessing and then I drizzled the sweet, golden liquid into my mouth swallowing it down as my legs went limp and I crashed onto the ground.

I scrambled back to my feet, walking back to the house had now become a chore, I swayed back and forth fighting the overpowering effects of the venom. The house was not all that far away, but in my current state, it felt an impossible task to reach it.

I knew now that Grandpa was poisoned, I felt it first hand, and it didn't feel so hot. I needed to create a diversion so I could be alone with Kelly. I wanted to keep what had happened a secret from everyone else. After all, for the first time in forever, I felt like I understood what was going on. Most of my memories were now back, from before my adoption.

As soon as I walked into the house, the girls smothered me in a flurry of questions; apparently, they'd all heard the gunshots.

"Did you find the wolf?" Kelly said.

"Was there more than one, Davis, I heard eight or nine shots?" Alicia said.

"Yeah, there were two of them, I suspect the one was the one Grandpa hit, it had some blood on its coat. The blood trail did its job, it led me to what needed to be shot," I said.

By afternoon Grandpa's color was fading. Ordinarily, a healthy, ruddy colored guy he was now ashen. Grandma was talking about calling an ambulance to take him to the hospital.

Kelly caught my attention, whispering to me, "Davis, you sure they were just wolves? Grandpa looks very ill, so I'd be honest if I were you."

My plan was to make a diversion so that I could speak with Kelly alone. So I tried to coax Alicia into having a cup of tea with Grandma in the kitchen.

"Alicia, can you keep Grandma calm, so she can drink some tea and unwind? Kelly and I will keep an eye on Grandpa in the meantime, she thinks she knows what's making him sick," I said.

While steeping Grandma's tea, Alicia said, "I had a feeling she'd know how to help, promise me you will let me know if you find anything out, Ok?"

I promised Alicia that I would let her know if we figured out anything as they disappear into the kitchen.

Kelly started to blubber questions and stopped when I said, "Look, I was working on how to tell you the truth, I didn't want Alicia or Grandma to know what actually happened. Grandpa thought he was dealing with a wolf, but it was the Chimera. I'm poisoned as well, but the nectar is slowing the effects for now at least."

"Oh no," she said. "Its bite is lethal unless you can come up with the right antidote and I don't remember all the ingredients, but I do know a few. It appears your memory is coming back, you remember nectar heals you?"

"Yeah, it's still a bit hazy. But for the most part, I am able to remember some of my training. The antidote that sounds vaguely familiar as well." I said.

Kelly grimly shook her head. "There just isn't enough time, he needs special herbs, and they are really hard to come by."

"Maybe if you name the ones you know it will jolt my memory," I said.

Kelly frowned. "Like I said, I don't know them all, but you need stuff like powdered unicorn horn, a mermaid scale, and things like that."

I struggled to keep my mind in control, the poison was starting to overpower me, I said, "Where the heck would we get stuff like that? Do creatures like that even exist on Earth or anywhere in the universe for that matter."

Kelly said, "I… I'm not sure Davis, honestly. But I can help save some time while we figure it all out."

Feeling puzzled on how that was possible, I said, "How can you do that?"

"It's kind of like science, but using magic… I can freeze time around everyone, but it only buys us three days at best, before I get too weak. At that point, the spell wears off, and we have a few hours before Grandpa dies. So I suggest we do this quickly and then figure it all out," she said.

Deadlines seriously bugged me. First I was told that there were only thirteen days to save the world and now only three days to save Grandpa which dug into the limited time we had available! Like seriously deadlines sucked, and I had no idea how I was going to accomplish keeping grandpa safe let alone the world in just a few days.

We walked over to Grandpa, who was looking a lot worse than before. His skin was still ashen, but he now had a new symptom from the poison, underneath his skin, veins visibly showed through, and they looked pure black. It looked really freaky, to say the least.

"Don't worry, Grandpa, I'm going to fix this," I said, looking at Kelly with approval.

Kelly dropped her arms down limp along her sides and tilted her head back, closing her eyes (my best guess was, that she was entering a state of meditation). She started to chant softly, as her chanting got more audible, her feet lifted from the floor. She was now floating. A blue vortex radiated around her, swirling. I caught Grandpa gasping at the sight, out of my peripherals. Then the blue energy washed throughout the entire house, I could feel it penetrate right through my body, it was so cold that my skin burned and my bones ached. But I appeared to be unaffected for the most part.

Frozen, everyone in the entire house was frozen. Well, except for Kelly and myself.

"Well Davis, if there were ever any doubts that you were actually human, I think we can both safely rule that one out," she said.

Arms crossed, I said, "So, want to shed some light on which species you really think I am?"

Her eyes filled with excitement, her facial expression grew of pure bliss, as she said, "I believe that you're the last Olympian, Davis, isn't that great? Like not all of you were cursed after all, by my ancestors."

"Olympian, so I'm like Greek?" I said.

Biting her bottom lip, she said, "Greek is in your roots, but that's not a bad thing. I find it kind of sexy, in a rebellious teenager sort of way. Daddy would be so upset if he knew I was falling in love with an Olympian, our sworn enemy."

Trying not to blush. I said, "So you admit you're in love with me?"

"Yeah I have been, isn't it pretty obvious? But we need to wake up Alicia unless you want to do this together and just leave her frozen," she said, sporting a mischievous grin.

I thought about it for a while, I played out so many hot scenarios of what Kelly and I would do together, since she confessed her love to me, if we went alone. After snapping out of my hormone-induced high, I captured my common sense and realized we could use all the help we could get. After all, I did promise to keep Alicia in the loop, and I really didn't need to give her any more ammunition to hold over my head.

I said, "Let's wake her up, I guess she is part of this too. I'm not sure how she is going to feel about you freezing her though…"

Kelly brushed her fingers across Alicia's face and mumbled a strange incantation.

Alicia woke, stood up and staggered forward a few steps before regaining her balance. "Why does my head hurt?" she asked.

Kelly explained the entire story, every last boring detail. Alicia looked satisfied and didn't seem mad at all. So I instructed the girls not to follow me, and I took off for the barn. I knew that the only one who could possibly help was

Oogle Doogle. If anyone knew how to save grandpa, it was him.

In the barn, I realized that I didn't know how to get in touch with him (it's not like he left his calling card). I was standing there trying to figure a way to reach him when Alicia and Kelly wandered into the barn. "What are you doing?" Alicia asked.

Feeling really furious (probably from all the stress of the past few weeks all catching up with me at once and not to mention the poison inside me trying to kill me) I said, "One simple request and neither of you listen. Not that it is anyone's business. But I honestly don't know what the hell I'm doing. I'm in a barn calling for a damn creature, that probably can't do squat for me anyhow."

Alicia did a double take. Her facial expression said enough, she was somewhere between being pissed and confused. "You're welcome, Davis," she muttered. Alicia paced for a few seconds and then she said, "If you can't tell, I'm being sarcastic. Like what in the heck is up with you anymore, you seriously need to take a chill pill, and I have to wonder, do you even know what being honest is anymore?"

Her words cut me like tiny daggers, and I knew she was right. She had every right to be pissed at me, but I'd never admit that out loud. I'd been treating her with no respect.

"Look Alicia, I'm sorry for snapping... I've just been under so much stress. You're right, I've been keeping stuff from you. But it's stuff about me... It's just I don't want you to think differently of me. There are some things I found out recently about myself that I even had trouble believing at first," I said.

Alicia said, "It's okay, Davis, I do understand what you're going through. I promise to be mindful. Whenever you feel comfortable enough to tell me, I'll be here, Ok?"

Hearing her say that made me feel better, but I had more important things to do than work out my love life. I was on a deadline to save Grandpa, and we had to find creatures that only existed in fairytales and myths as far as I knew and the poison was now taking its toll on me. So I said, "Ok girls, I need to get in touch with Oogle Doogle, I think he can help."

Kelly said, "I believe you have a telepathic link with him, Davis, so it should be relatively straightforward. Unlike us!"

I looked at the girls forcing a smile, "After we help Grandpa the three of us need to talk. And as far as tele-pathic links go, I'm used to phones; so how do I make calls from inside my head? Seriously, what do I do?" I asked, looking at Kelly for answers.

Kelly frowned, "I didn't talk to him so I don't know, but if I were you, I'd concentrate on him hard. That's the only way I imagine you could reach him."

So we were all quiet while I put myself into a semi-trance by trying to focus all my energy and concentrate on the little elf's name (go figure; I'm making a collect call from inside of my head to God knows where in the universe, trying to contact someone not even human). After a half couple of minutes, I was starting to feel like this sending phone calls from my mind was pointless. The poison was really getting to me—it made my skin burn like a million fire ants were crawling all over me and, if that wasn't already bad enough, my head was now pounding like a jackhammer chipping away at my skull. That's when he popped up right in the middle of us. "Master called?"

"You can't just pop up on me like that, Oogle Doogle, you scared the crap out of me! "

Alicia looked around, trying to discern whom I was speaking to. She said, "Is Oogle here already? I can't seem to see or hear him, Davis."

"Oh yeah, that's right," I said. Looking down at Oogle, I said, "Think you could remove the blinders, so I don't look crazy?"

Oogle gave me a crooked smile, "As you wish, Master, Oogle cure all who are deaf and dumb!" he continued, "Master place amulet on Alicia, then Kelly—Oogle must interface with their consciousness."

I walked over to Alicia and pulled the amulet off from around my neck. Then I draped it over her head, bring it to rest around her neck. "I want you to meet a friend of mine that's not human," I explained. "Don't be afraid he is cute and harmless."

She looked at me wide-eyed like I was losing it.

"Oogle almost done at eighty percent—upload was success," he announced. "Oogle ready say hi."

Alicia spun around frantically, I took it as a sign that she could hear Oogle now. Her jaw went slack when she saw him. "Hi me Oogle, nice meet masters friend."

Alicia took a few steps back, I could tell her mind was having trouble wrapping around what this strange little creature was. "It calls you master Davis?"

"Yeah, it can be a little annoying at times," I admitted.

"Hi Oogle," Alicia kneeled down to meet him at eye level. "Are you digital or physical—like if I touched you would you feel solid?"

Oogle's eyes brightened, "Oogle very much real, you can feel Oogle if like."

Alicia inched toward Oogle and twirled one of his long floppy ears between her fingers. "You're too darn cute," she laughed.

Alicia scooped up Oogle like a teddy bear hugging him if he were a teddy bear stuffing would have burst from his seams. Then she put the little creature back down.

Kelly insisted that she have a chance to wear the amulet, she seemed curious about Oogle, I assumed she wanted to meet her attacker as I'm sure she had some words for him, after the barn incident. So, I lifted the amulet off of Alicia and placed it around Kelly's neck. She spun around with fury in her eyes, waiting for him to appear.

Once Kelly saw Oogle they stared one another down like they were having a showdown in the Old West. I blurted, "Oogle, Kelly, look we don't have time for quarrels. We're in trouble here. Grandpa could die. We have three days before the freezing spell fades!"

Oogle Doogle said, "Oogle no like Master being friends with traitor girl, her family is Masters sworn enemy, we destroy her kind, not trust them for help, no Oogle no like…"

Kelly broke her gaze with me and looked away. If I couldn't get her or Oogle to help me, Grandpa was doomed.

I crouched down on the floor; my head was spinning out of control. The nectar was no longer keeping the poison at bay, my body felt like it was about to combust. I looked up at Alicia her blue eyes were filled with fear. Kelly studied me carefully, "Are you Ok, Davis?"

I couldn't respond I was fighting to hold on. Each breath was harder than the last, my health was deteriorating rapidly.

"Davis, are you OK? Davis, Davis, please don't leave me," Kelly begged.

The last thing that I remember was Oogle placing his hand on my face and an intense white light that sort of reminded me of the plane crash poured into my eyes.

"Bad poison," Oogle said.

I could feel his hand slide down my face and then down the arm that was bitten, his hand stopped at the exact spot the snake tail had bitten me. I could feel the life rushing back to me, and I sat up and watched in awe as the poison dripped out of my arm and onto the floor. The green ooze smoldered and smoked as it absorbed into the dirt.

Alicia's jaw dropped as her bright blue eyes took in the unimaginable; I'm not sure what was harder for her mind to process Oogle or the smoldering yellow poison he drew from me. I could only image how many questions she must have had.

It never occurred to me, how many times I came close to death ever since fate decided it was time for me to be a hero if anything I felt cursed… Like my parents and hundreds of others died, and I was spared… and now my own Grandfather was hanging onto a thread of life, all because I came to his ranch. I felt so selfish and wished more than anything else that I would just die, I resented the fact that Oogle spared me, I was ready to join my parents, to be a family again where ever that might be.

"Master, not one to blame, no blame self for things out of your control," Oogle said.

"My Grandpa… we have to save him Oogle," I snapped.

I hesitated, "Kelly has explained what had happened to my Grandpa and how she borrowed us some time to gather the needed ingredients to make a healing potion."

Oogle Doogle leveled his gaze on me. "Master should not trust anything that comes from her tongue."

"Gee, Oogle Doogle. I don't think this is the time or place to go into some kind of feud. I vouch for her and assure you she will be no issue," I said.

"Well, Oogle tell you. This traitor comes from family that been warring with Gods of Olympus, which master's family. Olympians creator of Oogle; I am a hybrid of imp and advanced nanotechnology. Oogle has been loving, loyal servant for many millennia."

"You need to lighten up Oogle, I appreciate the information about what you are exactly. But far as I can tell from the bits and pieces I picked up, the War seems like ancient history, so in my opinion, the war is in the past. What I do care about is my Grandpa here in the present... the thought of losing him is too much to bear. So are you going to help me or what?" I grumbled.

Oogle was quiet for a moment.

"Oogle Doogle serves Master... so Oogle will help."

"Great! What do we do?" I prompted.

Oogle Doogle said, "First bring your horses over to me."

We went to the stalls and led our horses out to the front of the barn. Oogle Doogle looked at them. "Hmmmm," he murmured. "No way will these mounts be fast enough to solve your problem."

"What is our problem, Oogle?" I said.

"You need to acquire blood from a drake that lives in a volcano, unicorn horn powder and the scale of a mermaid and your freeze spell last only three days," he said.

"Wow!" I said, with a gasp. "What volcano. Where is it?"

"Oh, one more," he said, remembering.

"What's that?" I said.

"You will also need the Hyacinth flower from which to make a brew," he said.

"Sounds easy!" I said sarcastically. "Where do we find all this stuff anyway, does any even really exist?"

He said, "Oogle knows of these creatures, they in several far off places."

My heart dropped. "How are we gonna get there and back in time. What kind of long distances are we talking about? We can't make much more than fifty or so miles a day on horseback. Can we get there in time?" I said.

Oogle Doogle, still surveying the mounts, said, "Not on those horses."

"That's the only horses we have to choose from, Oogle. Would Grandpa's truck be a better option?" I cried, nearing panic.

Oogle put his bony finger under his pointed chin and stroked his wispy beard. "First, Oogle have to supercharge them. Let me do that, no need to use truck, horses just need some extra horsepower."

"Sure. Fine. Go ahead," I said.

Honestly, I could not see how him using magic on the horses would make them faster than a vehicle. Let's face it,

Oogle appeared to not understand how fast trucks could go. Or so I thought at the time.

He did some chanting over the horses and then said to us, "Mount up. Let's try them out."

We got on our horses, and I looked at Oogle. "Is there something we say to make them go fast?"

"No. Just how you would ride them ordinarily," he said.

I said, "Okay" and we moved slowly out of the barn and onto the meadow that was covered with a yellowish green grass, vibrant patches of colorful wildflowers, cactus and red mountains lining the horizon. I didn't notice anything different in my horse. He moved out of the barn area at his usual pace. Clip clop clip clop. Didn't seem to be anything perking him up. The girls followed me. But once onto the grass of the meadow I gave a little kick and we took off like a rocket. Soon we were crossing the vast field at almost supersonic speed. I looked over at the girls. We were all moving like jets, zipping between cacti, and jumping over boulders like our horses were born for this! The girls were smiling and giggling. I had to suppress my own emotions. Even though the pit of my stomach was filled with butterflies like I was on a roller coaster ride, hard as it was I had to keep a serious mindset. After all, Grandpa's life depended on us.

SIXTEEN

A LEAP OF FAITH

The stars looked entirely different but no less enchanting as we roared across the landscape like a thunderbolt. They morphed into a swirling blanket of light that wrapped around all of existence.

We had been riding for hours toward a temple located somewhere in Ecuador. The night air was blistering cold, probably more so racing across the countryside at speeds more than two hundred miles per hour. The wind threatened a possible sandstorm, as each gust bombarded us with sand that stung my skin (as if it wasn't already bad enough being in a dust cloud feeling suffocated). It was crazy to think we were going to be in South America soon; I couldn't wait to get out of the desert.

Oogle confirmed we were almost to our destination, and the best Kelly could figure Grandpa had two and a half days left, so we had to keep focused. In the distance, I could make out a large structure under the light of the full moon. It appeared to be an elliptically shaped building constructed around a large monolith, possibly from one of the early Inca settlements.

"What is this place?" I asked Oogle.

"Sun temple, help buy time to save Grandpa," he said.

"How can a temple help?" I said feeling a bit dumb-founded.

"Time is not constant like master thinks, past, present, future run parallel one another," Oogle explained. "All possibilities already exist, so that means we can take shortcuts to many places. This saves Master time and time is always good to have. Yes?"

"So what you're saying is we can make quantum leaps to different possibilities and then return to prior probabilities, like an event that we already know takes place?" I said, feeling like I needed to brush up on my science studies.

"No—but close to what Oogle try tell master."

I thought about what Oogle was explaining to me, I believe he meant we could reach most destinations through-out the world or possibly the universe by taking advantage of unique locations that allowed this phenomenon to take place. Like I might be able to go back to the past and meet myself or travel to a far off location in the present and save tons of travel time. I guess I would soon find out firsthand what Oogle was talking about.

I dropped back and watched Kelly and Alicia as they rode side by side talking non-stop for what seemed an eternity. Never in a million years would I have guessed they would get along so famously, yet it felt somewhat pleasant seeing them laughing, if not for me they would have been great friends. I just hoped this level of friendship could hold up until I figure out how to defuse things more and sort my own feelings out.

After we had reached the base of the sun temple, we all dismounted and lashed our horses to a large stone structure that Oogle manifested from beneath the soft earth. It erected through the ground, loose dirt mounded near the base as it grew in size, in what felt like a blink there was now a large slab of rock nearly five feet tall greeting us. He was a crafty little imp with immense power. He was tiny, but I'd never want to be on his bad side, that much I knew for certain.

At the foot of the temple, I couldn't help but to feel like an insignificant little ant, it was monumental, to say the least. Kelly was the first one up the stone stairwell, she and Alicia raced to the top (no surprise that she won.)

"So what are we doing here, Oogle?" Kelly said.

"Oogle no speak with you, only Master and Alicia!"

"Then be like that, you selfish little imp. I have half a mind to scramble your circuits!" Kelly grumbled.

I could hear Oogle mumbling underneath his breath in a language that I now remembered. It was Sumerian; I could recall a memory of me as a child speaking it fluently.

It almost sounded like, "If not for Master I'd turn you into straw feed horses."

Once this was all behind us, I intended to get the full story on this feud and see if it could possibly be resolved.

"Master...now we wait!"

"Wait for what?" Alicia said.

"Sunrise, what else?" Oogle said.

I felt a lump growing in my throat. After all, Kelly had stated that we had two and a half days left and we had not yet acquired any of the seemingly impossible to obtain items.

I tried to hold back what I was feeling inside, but a gasket left loose. It felt like a big ball of anger and resentment came rolling off of my tongue as I shouted, "Sunrise? I hope you know what you're talking about... I still can't see how this massive chunk of rock is going to get us anywhere, we need a time machine or something."

Sometimes it is best to ask questions before blowing up, but I suppose I was still under a ton of pressure (like who wouldn't be in my position?). After everything, it felt like I was carrying the weight of the world on my shoulders (You know like the Titan Atlas from Greek mythology, I was starting to understand how he must have felt). Well maybe not quite that bad but you get my point.

Before I could say another word Kelly slapped my face; I definitely didn't see that coming. Then my worst fear came to pass. The bomb exploded.

"Witch or not if you ever lay another finger on my man I'll drop a house on you," said Alicia.

"Your man? You're not even in the same gene pool, girly girl. Compared to Davis you're the equivalent of a monkey wanting to date a brain surgeon. I on the other hand am nearly his equal in all ways that matter," Kelly said.

Alicia grabbed Kelly's hair, and she grabbed hers, they began to scratch and tear at one another's faces like cats using their free hands. The fight escalated down to the floor, they were rolling about screaming and cussing to no end (for a moment Kelly seemed like your everyday jealous human girl having a brawl). But that was short lived.

I grabbed Kelly around the waist, trying my best to separate the two of them, and she backhanded me so hard, that I landed on the ledge of the temple, a considerable distance from where I got slugged. I found myself dangling two hundred feet above the ground (not exactly how I imagined spending my trip).

I screamed so loud that I strained my voice, "Quit it. Stop your damn fighting!"

The girls fell silent; the tension in the air was so palpable you could cut it with a knife. I managed to pull myself up onto the ledge. Alicia and Kelly both calmly inched their way toward me, offering me their hand.

Yeah most people would apologize (after all I did start the whole fight), but I guess I'm a little on the reckless and idiotic side, so I done the only thing that came naturally to me, and threatened to jump off of the ledge if they didn't make up!

"Davis, calm down, you've been through a lot. We can work this out. Please come down off of the ledge," Alicia pleaded.

"I'm sorry I slapped you, Davis, but you seemed like you were losing it, and that is what I've been trained to do under those circumstances," Kelly implored.

Before I had a chance to even step down willingly, Oogle suspended me off the ground kind of like a Jedi knight using The Force. I lost all control of my body. To be honest, I was really scared, I barely knew Oogle, and thought he might actually toss me over the edge and move on with life like I never even existed, looking for the next savior in line for the job. But lucky for me I was wrong, or Oogle had no other heroes in mind.

"Oogle need Master to be calm. Oogle put you down now. No more be foolish or Oogle no help save Grandpa. After all, there much less selfish things Davis need be doing, like save world!"

Once my feet touched back down on the stone floor of the temple I had a whole new respect for solid ground. I felt like I was looking death in the face, but apparently, I'm just as bad at reading imps as I am with girls.

I hated how I felt helpless at the mercy of a small imp, which was no doubt one of the worst feelings you could ever have. But there was no doubt that when Oogle manhandled me, I was just that. Thank God I didn't soil my pants. I'm sure the girls would have never let me live it down!

The three of us hugged like a dysfunctional family apologizing to one another as a pink dawn lit up the world and the valley below emerged, truly breathtaking. Earth colored stone walls stretched out like a maze, and the rocks that comprised them looked super heavy. I was amazed at how an ancient culture could pull off an architectural feat of this magnitude. With further observation, the sun temple was really impressive; the cut boulders fit tightly together, there was no way even a razor would fit between the cut stone it was stacked with such precision.

There were frames for windows and doors inside the temple, but they were filled in with cut stone so you could neither look out of them nor enter. I did not see the purpose they served, they almost seemed pointless. The morning light also revealed how scuffed up Alicia and Kelly were. They did a number on one another's faces. Alicia had a bloody nose, and swollen lips and Kelly had some pretty significant scratches from her left eye down to the base of her nose.

As the sun gained altitude, Oogle instructed, "Reflect the light out of amulet onto floor."

Even though I cherished the amulet, it still draped forgotten around my neck. I had done as instructed. Like magic, the stones rippled, and where there was once stone was now a black liquid suspended in its space. Kelly walked through like it was nothing, and Alicia and I both exchanged a look of disbelief. There was little doubt that we both felt like we knew nothing about the world all over again. Like the life we were living was the dream, and we were now just scratching the surface of reality for the first time.

I followed behind Oogle. I watched him get sucked into the black looking ooze. Before entering myself, I reached a hand out and touched the entrance. It felt almost like freezing cold oil but didn't stick to my fingers.

Then I took a deep breath trying to get my courage up, silently counted backward from ten and walked through. After all, I had little choice, Alicia was behind me, and I didn't want to look too pathetic. Once we all crossed it was crazy, to say the least. A black abyss surrounded us in an arch that was filled with specs of white light that looked like stars.

"What is this place?" I said.

"The fabric of space and time," Kelly said without a second thought.

"Don't touch that!" Kelly shouted.

Alicia pulled back her hand and looked really startled. Kelly quickly explained that the fabric of space was sensitive and we had to not mess with anything, even a single touch in the wrong spot could cause a ripple effect throughout the entire universe and that we were just passing as observers.

The farther we went down the tunnel, the brighter it got, and the wider the arch became until there was no longer an arch at all. Instead, we were standing on an entirely different planet. It was easy to distinguish this because the sky looked off, the sun was considerably smaller, and the moon looked about one-fourth the size of what I was used too, the crater patterns on its surface were more like an ink smudge. Looming in the distance was a familiar blue glow. At first glance, it looked like a second planet, the color of pale blue ocean water, but after staring long enough I could distinguish the bodies, it was no doubt the Earth and its Moon. The Earth was comparable in size to a pea and the Moon appeared as a tiny white heavenly body occupying its lower left hemisphere, it seemed no larger than what you expect the planet Saturn to look like from Earth's surface. This was like something you'd expect to see on an episode of Star Trek (or possibly a dream, but not in person). Taking my focus from the sky, I noticed the sun temple was still intact and oddly appeared to be much the same.

"So this is like another planet. Right?" I said.

"Oogle brings you to Mars, as of now we have exactly two days left. But most important this is where we can find the Drake blood."

I took several deep breaths; I was astonished that I was able to breathe the air. I said, "How is this Mars? It doesn't look red at all; it's lush and green, with a blue sky? Mars is the red planet, it's freezing cold and has an atmosphere that's toxic to humans, right?"

The thought of using temples and pyramids back on Earth as stargates to travel throughout the universe was exciting, to say the least. Someday I planned on having Oogle or Kelly take me on a long vacation to explore the rest of our galaxy, and maybe the home planet where my kind supposedly originated from.

Kelly, now acting as our guide said, "Drake is a tad misleading, I think you call them Dragons on Earth. As far as Mars goes, it's more or less Earth's twin, Davis, it's nothing like the fictional planet in your history books, built purely on speculation. We are currently in the city of Cydonia, it was made in honor of the God of War, known as Ares and Mars on Earth."

Listening to all of this, Alicia's face was becoming increasingly tense. "I'm starting to regret coming along, Davis, I do love you but… being hunted by Chimeras, traveling through space and time with an imp and some wizard chick to other planets and killing dragons was not quite how I pictured my first serious relationship," she said.

"I'm sorry, I never planned for any of this… Honest…" I stammered.

"Don't apologize to a human, Davis, you are above her, she should be trembling at your feet, begging to be in your presence, if she only knew who you truly were," Kelly suggested.

"Look, I didn't even know who I was until recently, so I don't expect anything from her other than treating me the way she always has. It seems to have worked so far, so why fix something that's not broken?"

Once we were back down below our horses were still waiting, lashed to the boulder. But something was different about them; they had horns on their heads. Oddly they didn't travel with us, yet they were somehow here. I figured it must have had something to do with the boulder Oogle conjured. Apparently, when enchanted horses get warped through space and time, they become unicorns. Go figure. We all saddled up, our new destination was Olympus Mons (I remember learning about how it's like the largest volcano in the solar system). And talk about fast, maybe it's because Mars has less gravity, well at least that's what they taught us in science class or the horn is like an Energizer battery, because we moved at speeds that would make even the Flash envious.

Our plan involved heading to Olympus Mons, a volcano in this region that had a dragon nesting inside the lava tunnels or possibly the volcano itself. And we needed to somehow survive the heat just long enough to find the dragon and get its blood. I had a feeling that the dragon would not just hand us over its blood willingly, and this quest was going to get very dangerous!

I looked over at Kelly, "So do we have to kill the dragon for its blood?" I shouted.

Kelly glanced over at me sitting deep down in her saddle, "No clue," she pulled the left reign up to her hip gesturing her horse to slow down. "I've never seen a dragon before they are super rare. But I hear they are immune to magic, only a handful of wizards been able to control a dragon—force might be our only option unless that imp of yours has a better plan."

SEVENTEEN

A GIFT FROM ARES

As we roared over the landscape, I realized Mars was not how I pictured it from all the hype about the "Red Planet" back home. The fine soil was the color of a copper penny, and the landscape was hilly and even mountainous. Plant life seemed abundant, and the sky was dark blue with large billowing cumulus clouds lazing about. The air was crisp and smelled of morning dew; there was little doubt that this truly was Earth's twin.

A metallic object caught my eye in the distance, the sun was reflecting off it.

"What's that contraption," I asked, pointing out into the northern prairie.

"That's one of those NASA rovers they sent here. Most Martians respect exploration of our planet and even dust off their solar panels to help keep them running," Kelly explained.

"This is so freaking cool, they have to know there is life here. Makes me wonder what else they don't tell us," I said.

We galloped east of the temple, looking for leads on any dragon sightings from the locals. I was still adjusting to riding a unicorn (the horn was a bit unnerving, it looked razor sharp) let alone having to mingle with aliens. After a short journey, we reached a small village, where Oogle introduced us to the local aliens. They were little people with large ovular-heads, light olive skin, and dark black saucer shaped eyes. They didn't have much in the way of architectural advancement; they lived rather simply in mud huts like some of the most primitive tribes back home. After we had been acquainted, Kelly asked the locals about dragons. Most didn't know anything, but one couple said a dragon living in a nearby volcano had been eating their griffons.

Griffons, like my adventure was not already weird enough. I said, "Are the griffons here half eagle and half lion, like in Greek mythology?"

"I'm not very familiar with animal names on Earth, so how about you look for yourself?" the male alien said.

As we followed the two aliens, Kelly explained how griffon eggs and meat are prized on Mars, like chickens back on Earth. There were dozens of griffons out in the pasture. They were huge, with impressive wingspans. Eagle heads look cool on birds, but on these they looked damn scary. A few were lashed to fence posts.

"I see nothing is keeping them from flying away? Also, why are those six tied and not free roaming like the rest?" I said.

"We clip their wings, they can still lift off the ground and glide a bit. But we never had one escape; the fences are tall enough to keep them grounded. And those six are trained flying mounts, so they need to stay tied until we are finished up with them, so they don't fly off," said the female alien, her eyes filled with excitement.

Oogle arranged for our unicorns to stay at their stable and rest and for each of us to borrow a griffon for the remainder of the journey; they lent us three of them. Mine was named Moonspirit. They all looked pretty much the same, and it was hard to tell them apart with their indistinguishable features. If not for their numbered collars they wore around their necks, I doubt anyone would be the wiser to which one was theirs.

So we ate and drank the local fare, but I was having trouble keeping my food down, as the air smelled like rotten eggs. Kelly said it was due to Olympus Mons, this giant volcano, in fact, the biggest in our solar system. From what I understood it's like Mount Everest on steroids.

I have to admit I was really impressed with the local culture and how everyone we bumped into was bilingual. They spoke both English and a language that I was unfamiliar with quite fluently, which made me wonder how many other intelligent life forms existed throughout the universe.

After eating, we walked to the blacksmith (it was kind of nice moving slow, I could take in the scenery) and told him what we intended to do. He hooked us up with some sort of flame retardant armor, and a bow with arrows tipped with a rare metal (supposedly it was hard enough to penetrate through the dragon's thick scales), and a single shield which I claimed. He sorted through swords and daggers trying to find a match for each of us. He picked out two black and green daggers and handed them to Kelly, who spun them like a ninja, so I guess he was good at matching blades to their wielders. Alicia was given twin red colored sai's with black leather handle wraps. They were a pretty impressive sight in her hands; she no doubt looked lethal holding the short, trident type swords.

"You there, what be your name?" said the blacksmith.

"Are you talking to me?" I said.

"Yes, you look like a child of the gods, you have the face of Zeus and the eyes of Poseidon," he said.

"I'm an Olympian, I'm not completely sure who my parents are," I blurted.

"I knew it, praise the gods! There may still be hope for us all. Look, long ago Lord Ares brought some materials to my shop. He asked us to fashion him a sword that contained the energy of Zeus's Thunderbolt... I suppose it is only right to give it to his next of kin, after all, it's been around here since my granddad's, granddad owned this shop," he said.

He opened up a large iron safe and pulled out a long object wrapped in a black satin cloth and handed it to me. Anxious like Christmas morning, I unraveled the fabric, and the most beautiful sword I ever saw was unveiled in my hands. It was no doubt crafted for a god.

"Try it out," coaxed the little blacksmith.

The satin floated to the floor as my hand gripped the hilt, and slid the sword out of the silver gem encrusted scabbard. It was now even more breathtaking, the sword glowed with energy and small lightning bolts danced around the blade in harmony. The sword felt light like I was holding a large feather.

"It's true, you are an Olympian... The sword only works for your race. Without the bloodline, it is just a sword, no special powers. The celestial metal was forged, in the forge of Hephaestus on Mount Etna and holds great power!" he explained.

I sheathed the sword and strapped it to my side. I'd be lying if I said I didn't feel pretty badass. The sword made me feel proud of my heritage -- how many guys ever get to wield a sword made for a god?

I strapped light plate mail armor onto my mount, to protect it from the dragon's attacks. After the last piece was secured, we all suited up and mounted our Griffons. Oogle announced that he would meet us at our destination and vanished into nothingness as expected. I honestly had no idea how to fly a griffon. But after riding enchanted horses and unicorns, I figured it couldn't be too difficult; boy, was I wrong! With a whoosh, we took flight, I was holding on for dear life as I soared higher into the Martian sky. I had no clue how to steer this thing (like how do I make it go up and down, horses don't have that capability).

Holding onto my Griffon was the easy part, flying it was not so easy. Flying brought back memories of the plane crash and was equally horrifying! Like I went into a dive, and it felt just like when the plane was falling out of control, and I hated every second of it. The distance between me and a low mountain peak was closing in quickly, and I had absolutely no idea how to steer this stupid oversized chicken before I knew it I was kicking snow off of the peak, but fortunately for me, I was still hanging onto my ride.

Kelly giggled a bit before saying, "Lean into it, guys, find your balance."

I was having so much trouble until now I completely forgot all about Alicia, I glanced over and saw Alicia struggling to stay on her griffon as well. It looked like she was about to fall off. So I did what Kelly said and leaned into the griffon, and it made a world of difference. I nudged the reigns, coaxing it over to Alicia. Once I got beside her, I said, "You have to lean into the animal, look at me. Your body will automatically find its balance."

After we had got all the kinks out and Kelly gave us a few minute cramming session on how to fly a griffon, I calmed down enough to enjoy the view.

From this altitude the alien world below was serene, the streams and valleys looked breathtaking as we darted in and out of low-lying clouds. A herd of some sort of mammals that resembled elephants back on Earth foraged about in the fields of tall grass below. We soon flew over a tunnel system constructed of some type of crystal or glass tubes, ribbed with large metallic rings that covered as far as the eye could see in all directions.

From my vantage point, I saw cigar shaped craft whooshing through the transparent tunnel system by the dozens. I'd never before seen anything quite like this.

"Kelly, what are these tunnels for?" I asked.

"That is Mars' transportation system, it's much more advanced than how roads work back on Earth; we never have to deal with major wrecks or traffic congestion."

"That sounds too cool, I guess we could learn much from this planet!" I admitted.

We could see our destination in the distance; it was a towering mountain spewing smoke. The size was impressive, and there was nothing I could compare it to, it was just that huge! Kelly devised a way to keep the heat of the volcano off of us. She explained that Oogle would channel his energy to deflect the heat around us.

"But this will only last for a while, we will have to work quickly or face the Fates," Kelly advised.

The best I could gather, Oogle would be projecting a massive bubble around us, like an invisible force field.

"Who are the Fates?" Alicia asked.

"The Moirae, you know the goddesses of fate. Clotho spins the thread of life, Lachesis measures the thread of life and Atropos cuts the thread of life. Or in other words, they choose your fate, like when you will be born and when you will die," Kelly said.

The Fates sounded interesting, but I'd rather not meet them. Flying on the back of a griffon was bad enough, but flying up to the largest active volcano in the solar system that was spewing smoke from the top, was even worse!

We circled around the volcano until we found a suitable ledge to land on, we were nearly vertical. The Griffons effortlessly scaled the rough rocky surface with their razor sharp talons digging in. We headed toward a tunnel on the west side of Olympus Mons as the aliens had instructed. They had told us if any dragon's still existed, our best odds would be searching the volcano's lower levels.

At the tunnel entrance, Oogle appeared as promised and took charge. Kelly didn't even need to speak (I sometimes wonder if he isn't always with us, just in the invisible, watching and listening). Oogle chanted for a moment, and then a chilly blast of air washed over us, I figured it was the magical force field Kelly had mentioned. I nudged my griffon to follow Oogle, I found myself seriously having a hard time trying not to laugh at how silly he looked running down the tunnel with his potbelly and long pointed tail, he kind of reminded me of a pet monkey, Alicia and

Kelly guarded our rear. The tunnel was pitch-black, but it appeared that the griffons had keen eyesight and could still navigate very well. I drew my sword, and it illuminated a ten-foot radius. Soon we had made our way deep into the tunnel system, as the Griffons swiftly zigzagged through the passages, I could see some stalactites on the ceiling casting a faint orange glow like they were molten. The light they emitted was just bright enough to see the tunnels formation. My sword still provided much-needed light, and I also found it comforting just in case we got ambushed. The heat so far was bearable, but Oogle warned, "No hot now, but soon. Must find dragon quickly."

As we got deeper into the volcano, the walls began to widen as if we were approaching a larger chamber, and more glowing stalactites and stalagmites cut through the darkness, you could faintly make out reflections on the glassy volcanic rock walls which reminded me of obsidian. Soon we came to the end of the tunnel and the room widened into a large chamber, there floor and ceiling looked like glowing hot coals. My mount was the first to spot the creature it reared up on its hind legs, squawking an ear piercing sound. The other two joined in, and they screeched in unison! The dragon staggered a bit, before overcoming the sound waves and five car-sized heads stared us down, all ten of its yellow wolf-like eyes closed simultaneously, as it rose up on its hind quarters, and belched bolts of blue flame our way. Our Griffons scurried up the side of the tunnel evading the deadly assault, their talons gripped into the volcanic rock like climbing axes. I was now looking upside down at a creature as large as a blue whale, with green armored scales the size of my shield.

Kelly darted through the air at the first roar. She began loosing off one after the other of the special alloy tipped arrows, hitting the giant beast in each of its oversized heads trying to blind it. It turned on her. "Oh no!" she cried. "It's a Hydra."

I rocketed toward Kelly, holding on tight with my legs. I watched her completely astonished, as she peppered its heavily armored body. Each arrow sunk in deep, all the way to this monster's flesh, which reminded me of porcupine quills. I held my sword and shield taut and once in striking distance I brought down the razor-sharp blade across one of the necks, I felt like a sword-wielding lunatic as I lopped off one of its heads. It was surreal how lightning shot off in multiple directions shocking each of the dragons' heads and making it stagger. But I was in for a surprise, the head grew back, and a new one sprouted alongside it. It was now a six-headed beast!

"What the heck, why did it grow two heads back?" I shouted.

Oogle spoke up. "Has many heads. Cut one off. Two grow back."

"You got it!" Kelly mumbled, drawing her sword.

The Hydra waddled forward shooting bolts of flame ahead of it illuminating the walls, the chamber was massive and in the distance was a large chasm, I was defiantly steering clear of that area. I poured on the speed dodging the incoming flames that whooshed past my me, taking the lead raising my shield in front of me trying my best to protect myself from the dragon's fiery breath. Once in striking distance, I could hear arrows whizzing by my ears.

"Watch your arrows, Kelly!" I shouted.

"Don't worry about me, focus on yourself!"

I saw my chance and seized it, you see I had this stupid idea, it was either going to work or get me killed, but I'm not one to weigh my options, I'm way too impulsive for that. My plan was to conjure up lightning again, I knew how powerful it was and let's face it we needed all the help we could get... so I willed all my energy to shoot lightning like I done previously back at the storage unit when Kelly and I were back on the road. At first, it didn't seem to be working, I could feel my rage roaring in my ears as I failed, but Lucky for me I was not a one-time wonder because I started to feel the static electricity building in the air around me. My sword seemed to conduct and amplify the lightning's effect like a Tesla coil as huge white and blue arches of lightning exploded from its tip, lashing out and striking the dragon over and over as I parried each of its massive heads as they lunged at me.

Looking over my should I caught a glimpse of Alicia's jaw going slack; I could only imagine what she must have thought.

I flew about fifty yards out and circled back around, I advanced slowly, lowering the tip of my sword, aligning myself. Once in position, I poured on the speed flying between the beasts' legs, which seriously looked like over-sized tree trunks. I started slashing with deadly precision at anything I could connect with, slicing off chunks of flesh left and right making it roar out in frustration. But it appeared that I was not doing any serious damage. The cuts were not deep enough, and the lightning only stunned the creature momentarily. So, we pulled together to devise a new plan flying out of the Hydra's reach.

"We need to trap it, we seem to be out-muscled," Kelly shouted.

"Does anyone have a plan?" I asked.

As I waited for someone to take charge, I noticed a gigantic stalactite hanging just a few yards away from the hydra, if it didn't flat out kill the beast it defiantly immobilizes it. But the problem was how could I break the stalactite free, it looked way too thick to cut it loose. I knew what needed to be done, I had to conjure lightning once more, but my mind still didn't fully understand how my power worked. Like the first couple of times it just happened, but the one thing I was for certain of, it seemed easier for me to access when I was angry or upset. I also didn't like that everyone expected me to solve all of their problems. I liked it better when Kelly did all the serious thinking, it was a lot less pressure on me that way.

"Guys I have a plan, I need you to both create a diversion and lead the hydra just below that stalactite," I said pointing straight at it.

"Go," I said. "Get the Hydra into position and distract it long enough for me to figure out how to get the stalactite down and planted in its backside."

Oogle ran right in front of the Hydra, but he was so tiny it didn't seem to care.

"Over here, big dummy!" shouted Oogle, as he launched a rock the size of his fist at its massive heaving chest.

Oogle managed to get its attention, and two of its six heads snapped down with such force that it cracked the ground, sending the beast lumbering forward toward my mark. When its heads lifted back off of the ground Oogle was nowhere in sight, he'd done his vanishing act once again. I was starting to think it must be an imp thing.

Kelly and Alicia raced toward the Hydra, Kelly shot off a few more arrows peppering its scales, and Alicia circled behind the beast and pierced one of her sais into its leathery flesh. I was stunned at how amazing Alicia was and even more so at how she took to being part of my world and she barely questioned anything. I'm confident ninety-nine percent of girls would have ran for the hills, but not her, she ran right into the center of it all and proved her love for me a million times over.

The girls were surprisingly working very well together at getting the Hydra into the drop zone. It was now just a few steps away, and that was my cue, so I leaned into my griffon, giving it a nudge and we whooshed into the air closing in on the humongous stalactite. I kept my hand on my sword ready to strike as the distance between me and the stalactite closed.

"Batter up," I shouted, as I slashed my sword into the stalactite, lightning arched up and down the rock, as I flew past it, my sword vibrated in my hand to the point that I almost dropped it. I only chipped a tiny flake of rock away and knew beyond a doubt that I had to stick to the plan.

I hesitated. As I came back for round two, it should be simple enough by now I used my lightning powers multiple times, but it still felt unnatural and complicated. I focused on every bad thing that lead up to now from my parents' death to Grandpa being on his death bed and then I snapped. I could feel the blood roaring in my ears, the air rapidly changed around me, and I could feel every hair on my body stand up. Then lightning poured out the tip of my sword with such force that it knocked me clean off of my mount; I went pummeling toward the ground. I glanced up and saw the stalactite falling toward the hydra. I crashed into the floor hard; my ears were ringing and even worse when I tried to get back on my feet I noticed a stalagmite sticking up through my stomach, it punctured clean through my armor.

I flashed back to the plane crash, the engine's scream, that gut wrenching plunge toward eternity and everyone screaming, most praying, but I felt no fear like I was watching it from afar and was immune. I just refused to accept this as my fate. Somewhere in the darkest, deepest corner of my psyche, I knew I was meant for something else. Not death now.

I glanced up and saw that my plan had worked, Kelly and Alicia were working frantically trying to kill the now pinned down Hydra. When one of its heads snatched up Alicia and started chomping down on her like a chew toy, she groaned in agony as each bite clamped down on her armor. I couldn't just lay here and let her get eaten, so I gritted my teeth and pulled myself up, sliding the jagged rock through the entrance wound as I made my way to my feet, the stalagmite was roaring hot. I held one hand over the wound on my stomach, and the other gripped my sword as I staggered toward the Hydra, with one final thrust I shoved the blade into its chest. The sword began to vibrate, a blue light escaped from the wound, and the Hydra's scales began to ripple like moving water. The creature's heads arched and it made the loudest groan I'd ever heard, one of wrenching agony. And a hole as round as a bowling ball exploded into its chest; my sword clanked as it landed on the floor.

It looked like a bloodbath. We were painted from head to toe in disgusting green dragon goo, worst of all it smelled like rotten eggs. As gross as it was, the only thing I cared about was checking on Alicia. Thank the gods, for the most part, she was only shaken up, her armor did its job keeping her from taking too much damage. I'm positive she would be bruised up in the morning, but she was still alive, and that was all that mattered.

I noticed Oogle was back, I saw him put a small glass vial into his leather pouch and secure it around his waist.

My face was burning, "Oogle where were you, we could have been killed...what kind of guardian are you anyway?" I muttered.

He shrugged. "Just little test for master... see if ready."

He said it with a smirk and gleam in his beady little eyes, which really bothered me. Like who was he to decide on testing me when my friend's lives were in danger. Like if he wanted to test me one on one that is acceptable. But not at the price of potentially getting my loved ones killed.

I balled my fist. "Look, if you want me to be part of your mission...you need to respect my friends and do everything in your power to protect them. Otherwise, you're on your own!"

Oogle stared at me like I was an idiot, but he never voiced his opinion.

Kelly removed my chest armor to inspect my wound. I could see the intensity in her eyes as she prepared to plunge her hand into the bloody wound. I grimaced, my muscles clenched and prepared for the pain. But there was none. Only a warm feeling and then it was no longer there, it was clear that whatever changes were taking place, they seemed to be accelerating. To test my theory, I slid my blade down my arm watching my blood pool back inside of me and the skin mended over top of it almost instantaneously.

There was a moment of awed silence.

I guess Oogle was keeping us safe after all, even when I thought he left us completely on our own. I was reminded of how hot it really was down here when Alicia accidently dropped one of her Sai's I could see it glowing bright orange on the ground almost instantaneously. It made me realize that heat was half the battle.

Our mission on Mars was now done. We landed the griffons back at the stable and Kelly gathered the unicorn horn powder from her mount. It was kind of nice being back on solid ground. I missed my horse. The ride back to the pyramid in Cydonia was refreshing. Oogle revealed how all pyramids intersect and can open gateways and send you throughout space and time, to different planets, dimensions and even into the past, present or future. Using this to our advantage we could travel an enormous distance in just minutes, a journey that would take even the most advanced spacecraft at least several months. As we walked through the suspended, dark liquid portal back to Earth, our mounts waited on us on the other side just as before. They mysteriously morphed back into their original equine form like it was natural for them.

Interplanetary journeys no longer seemed all that odd, I was growing accustomed to this new way of life, it felt somewhat fulfilling as if my broken pieces had been mended and I had a greater purpose. We arrived back at the meadow just outside the ranch a few hours before sunrise. The Saguaro cactus silhouettes were just beginning to appear under the pink blush of dawn. "One day left before Grandpa dies," I muttered. The thought was bittersweet, we now had half the stuff to brew the potion, and there were just two ingredients left to go, the mermaids scale and the rare herb Pharmakon.

EIGHTEEN

ALLURING BEAUTIES

After an unplanned meeting in the kitchen, Kelly told us her plan. Reluctantly, I listened to her as she went over the task of obtaining the remaining ingredients for Grandpa's antidote. Even in suspended animation, he didn't look well, and I realized we needed to hurry (I felt kind of bad, having Grandma and Grandpa in a state of cryostasis, but it was for their own wellbeing). Kelly, Alicia and I voted on getting the mermaid's scale and left Oogle with finding the Pharmakon.

Kelly was waiting for us out in the barn already mounted up. Under different circumstances, I would have been excited to go horseback riding, but we were on the hunt for a Navajo shaman who might know where to find the mermaids. I remembered Grandpa telling me about the shaman and warning me as a child to never follow the dry creek-bed too far because it leads to the Indian's wikiup.

After a short ride, I heard Alicia shout, "Look there is his home."

As we neared I saw the old man, he was knelt down on a red cloth in the center of a circle of rocks that resembled a bullseye pattern of red and white stone. The wrinkled Indian elder had on a woven ceremonial robe, with tribal patterns that reminded me of serpents.

I dismounted and walked over to the Shaman, stopping a few feet outside his circle of rocks and blurted, "Sir, I have a question for you... I can pay for your time."

I fished a handful of crinkled up dollar bills out of my pocket, he stood up from his trance like state and walked over to me, then glanced down at the money and pushed my hand away.

"Yaateeh, wampum not good for everything. One must do what the Spirit tells him. What you seek is living in the Verde River just beyond the low-lying hills bordering the desert."

"But... I never said what I seek."

"I was expecting you; I had vision of Whiteman riding a horse and his female warriors, helping with his quest."

"What quest?"

"You already know, trust your instincts and let the Spirit guide you."

"Thank you," I said and grasped the old man's hand in friendship. "Thank you."

Again we set off, this time east across the desert.

Our horses were just average today, Oogle was not along to enchant them, and I'm not sure if Kelly knew how, or even had the energy to offer if she did since she was keeping my grandparents frozen. Yelling over the hoof beats, I asked Kelly, "What part of the river do we look for the mermaid?"

"The deepest part," Kelly said.

When we arrived at the river it appeared swift but not too deep, the roaring white water rapids looked a bit intimidating but compared to some of the things I'd faced in the past few days, it seemed like it should be a breeze! We eased the horses into the river at a dark place, indicating deep water. I asked Kelly, "Anything, in particular, I need to know about mermaids?"

"There are two kinds. One is benign compared to the other."

"What's the other?"

"She's a man-eater."

Not really knowing what else to do, we just started searching. It was beginning to seem hopeless when suddenly we heard singing. We stopped and listened. It was what I can only describe as a heavenly sound. It did not take long for us to realize that we were in mermaid country. I became enchanted -- literally -- by the singing and began to be drawn towards it urging my mount deeper into the river. Then I spotted them. There was a school of about a dozen splashing about. One was sitting on a rock, her long blonde hair flowing over her breasts and belly. Her beautiful face looked serene, a stunning creature. Their angelic singing seemed to be drawing me closer. I pushed off into the river spurring my horse on.

I could still faintly make out what the girls were saying. "They're getting to him. It's the siren song," said Kelly.

"What does that mean?" Alicia replied.

"Means he can't resist them. We better do something. No doubt they are man-eaters and are luring him in for a snack."

Glancing back, I saw Alicia, and she looked really confused. She tried to yell something, but I was out of range, all I could hear was the sound of running water.

I approached the school of mermaids. The first one slipped up on a rock in mid-river, the current flowing around her. She began to comb her hair. I asked, "What's your name?"

"Melinda. What's yours?" Her speaking voice was as mesmerizing as her singing.

"Davis," I said feeling a bit dazed and disoriented. I'm pretty sure I was drooling; I hung onto her every word being played like a fiddle.

Melinda spoke to me. "Why do you seek us?"

"Well," I said, my eyes glued to her beauty. "I need a mermaid scale as an antidote to save my dying grandpa."

"Oh, how terrible. I will be happy to give you one. Come closer to me," she said.

My heart pounded as I urged my horse forward, now almost in touching distance of her…I noticed her bearing her fangs. There was no longer any doubt about how dangerous she was, yet every fiber of my being was being pulled closer, like a magnet to metal. The closer I got to her, the happier I felt, stirrings of ecstasy danced through my mind's eye.

I used all my mental power to break her spell, but I failed. Miserably.

Kelly and Alicia started riding up onto the opposite bank and sneaking around behind some cactus and rocks, it looked like they were surveying my situation, but my brain was too scrambled to comprehend the severity.

My horse was startled, the mermaids were beginning to surround us, and it looked like they were about to start a feeding frenzy. Kelly spurred her horse hard, riding out to me, I honestly felt a bit relieved to see an ally amongst all the hungry ladies. She approached the mermaids. "Girls," she boldly proclaimed, "I have a deal for you."

Melinda, her face now less sweet asked, "What can you offer us?"

"Well you're going to have a tough time with him if you plan to eat him, my friend over there on the bank," Kelly said, pointing to Alicia, "you see, she and I are very skilled fighters and won't let him go easily."

Melinda with a dirty look said, "What do you propose?"

"We just need a scale from you. Then you can have him."

Melinda said, "Uh ok. You have a deal. We want him tied to that tree near the edge of the water."

I participated in the plan, but honestly had a bad feeling about it. It felt very weird being hogtied to a tree and having my life depend on a plan from a girl who I only knew a short period of time. But I did trust Kelly with my life; after all, she'd proved her loyalty to me many times over in the short time we knew one another.

As Melinda approached the shore to make the exchange, I couldn't help but wish Oogle were here, I'm sure he would have come up with a better plan than offering me as fish food. I hate to admit it, but I closed my eyes for a moment and said a silent prayer. I thought for sure that Melinda was going to have me for dinner. But Alicia and Kelly sprang into action blocking Melinda with their daggers and Si's.

"We had a deal, now move aside before you make me mad!" Melinda said.

Kelly countered her offer with a dagger thrust and Alicia followed her lead, both pressing their blades deep into the mermaid's torso, unleashing rivers of blood. Her color went from blush to a pale gray in seconds, and she let out a bloodcurdling cry that both pierced my eardrums and sounded like a dolphin echo, as her body went limp. Then all hell broke loose, as the rest of the school of mermaids attacked us. Alicia cut me free, and I dashed over to my horse and got my sword and shield. Their singing willed me to turn on Kelly and Alicia, but I managed to fight it this time. Melinda must have been stronger than the rest, like the alpha or something because I had been unable to break free of her spell.

The girls and I fought the mermaids on their turf, sticking to the shallows to give us an advantage. They circled us, and we pulled tight together back to back to defend. The mermaids slapped their tails and spat powerful streams of water at us, testing what we could handle.

I saw an opening and bashed one of them on the head, she fell motionless, and the water turned red as she sank. The other ten or eleven mermaids started dive-bombing us, fangs bared. I retaliated with a sword strike, unleashing bolts of lightning that pulsated through their bodies. The girls followed my lead jabbing and hacking away carelessly. We worked together like a futuristic lawn mower that spat lightning bolts to keep them at bay. Finally, we won, as the mermaids realized they were no match for us and retreated with minimum casualties. We, on the other hand, managed to get away with only a few scrapes and bruises; we had been lucky once more, but I knew sooner or later our run of luck would end.

I slashed a scale off of Melinda and dragged her deeper out into the river. A red amulet that was draped around her neck caught my attention, and I took it as a spoil of battle. The remaining school was watching us from a distance; I could sense they wanted their leader's body back, maybe for a proper burial if they even did such a thing.

All saddled up, the three of us took off. Kelly yelled, "You're a pushover for a pretty face, babe. Lucky you're not sushi by now."

I let her remark roll off my shoulders. I had a deadline to meet, I could feel the sands of time weighing heavy on me. "Let's ride hard," I said. "Grandpa's time is almost up."

Once back at the ranch, I looked over at Grandma; I hated seeing her this way, like a piece of forgotten furniture collecting dust. In the kitchen, Oogle appeared out of nowhere with the lotus flower and then we cooked together the ingredients that we had gathered into a stew. I crossed my fingers, hoping with every fiber of my being that this would work. After all, so many unbelievable things had happened. Lately, it was getting easy to believe just about anything. Nonetheless, it was probably going to be tough getting Grandpa to swallow it as it didn't smell right. OK, putrid! Kelly placed her palm on Grandpa's forehead, spreading her fingers wide saying, "Warmth" and he awoke. He was not very stable, Alicia helped keep him up as I poured the brew into his mouth. Finally, I got him to swallow down the concoction, and then we waited, watching him in anticipation. After a couple of hours, I could see his color returning, a sure sign the potion was working its magic. Without a doubt, he was looking better.

So much better that he was sitting up in bed and smiling while at his request, Alicia fetched him something he did like, a nice hot cup of coffee. We knew he was definitely going to make it when he asked for his pipe.

Kelly brought Grandma back from her frozen slumber, and once the magical side effects wore off, we told her that Grandpa was feeling much better. Grandma hurried into the den, she looked like she was bursting with joy when she saw him sitting up and puffing on his pipe. Grandma ran over and kissed him. "I was so worried," she blurted.

Grandpa was now much better so we could again be lighthearted. Everything seemed pretty much normal so Alicia, Kelly and I walked out onto the front porch to relax, it felt good just sitting and talking after living a life that seemed straight out of a movie the past few weeks. The girls appeared to be getting along better than ever. Unfortunately, I knew it was too good to last very long, with their history together.

Alicia and Kelly rode me unmercifully about the mermaids. Alicia chided me with, "Boy, you're a pushover. All the mermaid had to do was sing and bat her eyes and you were enthralled."

Kelly got into the fun saying, "Yeah, I hope we don't have to knock off every chick who sets her sights on you."

They were both bursting out their sides with laughter; I just took it nodding my head refusing to give into their jeering (they wouldn't think it to be so funny if the siren song worked on them).

Later that morning, Grandpa was up and around and looking great but still a little weak in the knees. In a kind of celebration, Grandma cooked a great ranch breakfast with all the trimmings. We all sat down to eat, except Alicia. Exhausted, she turned in for a morning nap.

When we were done Grandpa said, "I got a lot of haying to do in the barn, kids, can I get some help?"

Kelly and I immediately volunteered. I said, "I have to work off this breakfast anyway."

We pitched hay all morning, and by ten o'clock we were all sweaty and achy, farm work was not easy. We both lay back on one of the hay bales and sipped some water Grandma had brought us.

We were no longer kidding around, and we were both quiet and lost in our thoughts. I sensed something on her mind that needed to come out, but she was still tentative about it. So I said, "Kelly, at some point in our adventures you admitted that you and I had come through some hard-ships together and that should count for something."

"Yeah, I did," she said.

"So?"

She leaned up on an elbow, a straw in her mouth. "What?"

"Don't you think it's time you told me what you're all about? Let's face it you're no ordinary Earth teenage girl."

She smiled. "Which do you prefer, earth-girls or us other worldly witchy types?"

"Maybe, I don't know yet. One of the reasons I want you to level with me."

She chewed the straw and thought for a while. "Okay. But some things you're going to have to take on faith. At least for now."

"Okay. Now," I said gazing at her.

She cocked her head. "If you laugh at any of this I won't go any further."

"Of course I won't laugh," I promised. "Unless you have something funny to say."

"Well first off, I am a Princess." She locked eyes with me for a reaction.

Trying not to look stunned, I replied, "Yes…"

"On Mars. I had run away from home, and my father has been looking for me."

I interrupted, saying, "So the Chimera… do you think your dad sent it?"

"Bingo. I had a couple of reasons for running away. One was to find that necklace you are now wearing."

"That was the only way you could do it?" I asked.

"Well, yeah—I want my dad to give me the same respect he gives my two younger brothers."

She paused looking at me. I figured she was making sure that I seemed intent and interested.

She continued, "Back on Mars my family overthrew the Olympians after they took us in as family and shared all their knowledge. The twelve leaders of the Anunnaki were my ancient ancestors." She gazed at me to see if I was following her. Satisfied I was, she went on. "You see we originated from a dying planet named Nibiru. The inhabitants made settlements on Earth and Mars. They disagreed with how Olympians ruled and felt they had more right to the Earth since their planet orbited it."

She again locked eyes with me. "Now this part concerns you. Your kind comes from the constellation Libra, from a planet roughly three times the size of Earth."

A light bulb went off over my head. "Wait a minute. I remember reading something about this constellation in a magazine. It has planets that are thought most habitable by earthlings. One called Gliese, something or other. And oh yeah I remember now. It has a red sun. Right?"

"That's right. Of course, there is a lot of mythology regarding justice and equality about Libra in some cultures, mostly Middle Eastern, but what you just said is the latest scientific info."

"So I'm not an earthling by birth. Is that what you mean?"

"Yes," she said.

A strange stirring of emotions washed over me, something I couldn't describe but I knew it made me feel closer to her. She leaned forward and kissed my lips. While it's true

I did linger too long, and I didn't break away as I should have, that became irrelevant as Alicia strolled into the barn.

I looked up, feeling my cheeks turn red with guilt. I was too shocked to notice Alicia's reaction.

"Wait...I..." She stormed off.

Climbing to my feet I chased after her, but by the time I caught up with her she was mounted on her pony and I was eating his dust.

Over her shoulder she spat, "Save it, Davis. It's getting old. I think it's time for us to split."

My heart fluttered as I mounted my horse and with my knees I goaded him to go faster: we were in hot pursuit. Nearing twilight, second thoughts washed over me. She had a pretty good lead, and I didn't have Oogle around to snap my horse into hyper mode.

Part of me wanted to keep chasing after her. But I knew it wouldn't make sense. If and when she wanted to talk to me again, she would let me know. I pulled on the reins and turned my horse around, galloping back across the shadowed landscape.

When I got back to the barn, Grandpa and Grandma were there taking a stroll. Waffles was frisking around at their heels, and they were enjoying her company. Kelly had gone, and the old folks kept on their stroll around the ranch.

With my recent women problems, I figured I could use a male around... so I called on Oogle. He was prompt as usual. I told him what Kelly had said about my heritage.

Oogle scratched his chin. "Perhaps Oogle tells Master of his heritage."

Oogle told me in great detail about Mount Olympus, it was more or less a souped-up version of Noah's ark that was capable of interstellar travel through the cosmos and appeared divine by meeting the rigorous criteria for heaven if you were ever lucky enough to visit the city surrounding the throne room. He also touched on my role in things that he had been alluding to.

He said, "Oogle know what Master think. You think you are only a teenager on Earth and have much confusion about identity. Master shows Oogle he is great already, but Oogle no think Master see his own accomplishments. You have big destiny."

My eyes fixated on his big bulgy twinkling eyes as he continued. "Yes, it is true. You and you alone must make choice that has no good outcome but will change much. Master needs training; a rogue planet with an elongated orbit is whirring through space. It is heading directly for Earth, much bad come with its arrival in just ten days' time."

My gulp must have been audible, as Oogle cocked his head honing his ears. "When...when will it hit?" I asked.

"No... Not hit Earth, during the crossing is the only time the curse can be lifted from the Olympians... much bad for mankind, if no save."

I shook my head, sat down on a bale of hay and lapsed deep into thought. How weird. But then again how normal was slaying dragons and mermaids and gathering horn dust?

Oogle had more to say. "Time is short, master must speak with the dolphins and whales to find out the location of Olympus, tomorrow master must accept his role as our savior or all is lost. These are the elder Olympians, and they have been cursed to be creatures of the sea. Poseidon was forced to use his powers to transform himself and all of the Olympians into sea dwellers."

I remembered what Kelly said, regarding the prophecy inscribed on my necklace. This had to be part of that I thought.

I took a deep breath and then poured my heart out to Oogle, "I do accept my destiny, I'm not sure I want it. But it seems I have little say in the matter, no matter how hard I seem to resist it, there is no stopping what is to come. That is what I accept, I know things are in motion that are currently beyond my understanding and that the Gods need me to rescue them from their curse. But how can I accomplish this in under ten days, I don't even know where to start or what is required of me," I explained.

All the pent up emotions were now surfacing, I felt so powerless and so many feelings both good and evil washed over me. I felt so scared and alone, I just wished everything was back to normal and that I was back home in Pennsylvania with my parents in our old house, in my old life. But I knew that was not in my cards, and I accepted that they were indeed gone forever.

Tears poured down my cheeks, and my body trembled uncontrollably. I could feel the sensation of my powers, and it felt like lightning was going to erupt from my hands at any moment, I screamed, "TELL ME WHAT I NEED TO DO. TELL ME!"

Oogle pressed his pointer finger to my forehead, and I had another vision. It was of Alicia, Kelly, and me beckoning the Goddess Artemis. We were performing a strange ritual, and chanting her name."

After I had snapped out of my trance, I looked Oogle deep in his twinkling eyes.

"Master call to her; she and Hades last of your kin in realm. Convince goddess to help, master need shown way to Oracle of Delphi, there master find what need for destiny. Once master has mark of Apollo, then find Rod of Knowing. Only special being can use rod. Must have mark of Apollo or rod is just stick. Master is destined to bear mark of Apollo and have gift of prophecy."

Before I could ask another question, in a "poof" Oogle was gone; he was not one to stick around and chitchat, always right to the point and gone.

This was a lot to digest. One day I'm a run of the mill high school kid. My biggest problem is trying to be popular and finding a date for prom. Now I'm supposed to be some sort of savior and bear the mark of Apollo, what the heck ever that was! Not too much to digest.

NINETEEN

I SACRIFICE MY GIRLFRIEND

What in my past life would have been a supreme thrill for me, two beautiful girls fighting over me, was now just a big problem. I couldn't tell Alicia that I will let her know my true feelings for her and Kelly when we have accomplished our mission. Or could I? At this point, I truly didn't know that answer myself.

I saddled up and rode out to a spot that Alicia and I had found during an exploration of the ranch. It was perfect, a bubbling creek and some mesquite trees for shade. Sure enough, I found her there. She was sitting by the creek, looking solemn and peaceful. When I popped up, she was of course, surprised and I hoped more pliable. "How did you know where to find me?"

"Just an educated guess."

That communion of minds, I know somehow moved her romantic spirit. She loved that I remembered. I too was glad I had remembered the spot.

We were quiet for a while, but it was me who had a lot to say, so I started. "Look, Alicia," I said. "I'm in the biggest spot not only of my life but …." It sounded silly to say, but I did, "but the future of the whole world depends on me. I know we may have a problem right now, but can't we put it on the back burner until we find out if we are even going to have a world to live in?"

She looked at me, some understanding in her lovely eyes. "I…. I… guess this is all too much for me Davis. Don't get me wrong, I'd do anything for you, but this has all been like some crazy dream… one day I'm a cheerleader and the next I'm helping my boyfriend battle monsters in order to save the world."

"I promise when this is over we will be together."

She looked at me, wistful now, and very thoughtful. I felt a little guilty about what amounted to a promise I wasn't a hundred percent sure of. She blew a long strand of her blonde hair out of her eyes, as I leaned in and kissed her soft lips and she melted into my arms.

By the time the sun was sinking behind the sawtooth mountains silhouetting the cactus and sage I said, "Let's get back. We have a lot of thinking and some more planning to do, tomorrow is a big day."

Back at the ranch, we all had dinner together. Grandma, in a celebratory mood cooked up my favorite dish. Baby backed ribs, beans and cornbread. I hoped the girls liked it too. Grandpa sure did and was smacking his lips when we finished.

After dinner, the old folks went to bed and the girls and I gathered up some firewood, walked out into the now cold desert and started a campfire. Everyone knew that we had something to discuss.

I said, "Oogle shared with me the best way for us to get into the Underworld, he also insisted that I need to track down some stick called the Rod of Knowing. Oogle shared a vision with me, on how to do this but I'm not sure I can remember it all."

Alicia said, "Why not just ask him?"

I shook my head. "Oogle is as elusive as Sasquatch, especially when you really need him. I think he likes to test me and see if I can do things on my own. I believe that we'll have a wait till he shows up again."

Kelly said, "What did he tell you?"

"That there are only a few gods left that haven't been cursed to the sea."

"Like who?" Alicia asked.

"Well... Hades is one, and according to Oogle Artemis may still be around. She might be able to help us if she is so inclined."

Kelly said, "And what would make her so inclined?"

I gulped. "What do you know about Artemis?" I asked her.

"She's the chick that looks out for young women. Isn't she? And she hunts. She's the one with the bow and arrow. Right?"

"Well yeah, but she's a lot more than that. She's the daughter of Zeus and one of the most revered goddesses." I wasn't about to tell them everything about Artemis. Like the stuff about virgin bait that I recalled from my vision.

Alicia said, "What did Oogle say we would have to do to get to her. To find her."

"He said very little, he more or less showed me a vision of how we need to summon her. In the vision we offered... I mean showed her a young woman in distress. To do that we'd need a white candle, some white altar cloth, and some white robes. And a symbol of the moon, and animals. There may be more."

Kelly said, "Well, you guys sit here and think about it while I go back for some bed sheets. Will that do?"

I said, "I hope so."

While she was gone Alicia and I gazed into the fire. It was cold at the edges of the campfire. We huddled together and it was nice. We said little, but when the stars came out, I pointed to the night sky. "See that shiny star over by the mountains. That's Venus, the closest planet to the sun. They named a crater on Venus after her. The Artemis Chasma."

"Did Oogle tell you this?"

"No," I said, "I guess I just always been a huge fan of Greek mythology and astrology like I always felt I didn't belong."

Before I could think about it anymore, Kelly came back carrying the sheets and the candles. I asked, "Uh did you think about the symbol for the moon?"

She pulled out a yellow cardboard crescent. "Made it myself," she said.

I found a nice flat rock for an altar and laid the cloth over it. "Let me see, "I wondered aloud. "What's next? Oh yeah. Carve Artemis's name into the candle. Then set them up in four directions." We all did that. Next, I poured water from my canteen on our hands and we washed them, drying them at the fire. The girls looked expectantly at me.

I suggested the next thing we should do is fashion robes out of the sheets and use one sheet for the altar.

"Okay," I said, "we sit around the altar and think about Artemis and what she might mean to us."

Alicia's smile washed off of her face, she now seemed confused.

Kelly said, "I can think of times and a particular time when I needed Artemis's protection."

"Concentrate on her," I said. "Her virtues."

Alicia then added, "Me too."

I knew why I needed Artemis. After we had taken part in a group mindfest, we tried to visualize her, get her scent. "Okay," I said, "now it's time for the chant. Just follow me."

Young maidens we are for thee to claim

By sacred candle and blessed flame

We beseech thee goddess and call thy name

We invoke thee

We invoke thee

We invoke thee

Hail Goddess Artemis

We all looked at each other expectantly. While the clouds did scud across the moon, there was no poof, no burst of smoke or anything much out of the ordinary. We repeated the chant dozens of times expecting a revelation… or something…but nothing happened. I was sure I had done everything right or was I doing something wrong. My mind went into overdrive trying to come up with a logical answer. I didn't want to fail and look like an idiot in front of my friends… after all, I was destined to be the savior, at least that's what Oogle lead me to believe.

Out of nowhere a lone dove landed by the fire, it flapped its wings and then tucked them in and settled down. Everyone was spooked. The dove cocked its head looking at us all and then flew off into the night sky making whistling noises.

"Oh my gods, like I think she heard us Davis," Kelly cried.

"Do you smell that?" Alicia said.

"I think she heard our call, but I don't remember seeing a dove in my vision."

The sweet fragrance of jasmine became overwhelming I averted my eyes from the fire so I could see better in the darkness and that's when I saw her emerge from the desert beyond the fire. I knew it was her when she stood before the fire looking at us. She was every inch the Goddess. She wore a short, white knee length dress, Greek lace up sandals, her hair was light blonde and draped over her shoulder in French braids, and topped with a silver laurel wreath headband. The traditional silver bow was slung across her back with a quiver of silver arrows. She had a regal bearing and like I said, there was no doubt she was a Goddess.

I started stammering. "I uh... thank you so much for coming, Goddess. We need your help."

She looked from Alicia to Kelly. "Which of these young maidens hath called upon me?"

I was stuck. She watched as my eyes ratcheted from one to the other. Then she said, "Thee doth realizeth th're may beest a sacrifice involv'd."

I shook my head. "No, I didn't." I knew it wasn't a good idea to lie to a Goddess but the truth was I didn't know how it worked.

I blurted, "It's me, Goddess. I have the problem. Would you please listen?"

Though her gaze was serene, I didn't know whether to expect an arrow in my gut at any minute or what. Finally, she nodded, and I began my story, trying hard not to leave anything out, I told her how I lost my parents, rescued my grandfather, and found out that it was my destiny to save the Olympian gods.

When I was done she said, "Thee doth forsooth has't a gentle causeth and one most wondrous'r than any maiden in distress, esc'rt thee to thine campeth Davis, alloweth us break with this matt'r furth'r."

She pursed her lips and let out an ear-piercing whistle, and in a blink of an eye, a chariot that looked like it came straight out of a Roman coliseum rolled into our camp. It was pulled by two large stags, like picture a typical deer, but white and make it ten times bigger, and then make it glow like moonlight…now you get the picture. The Stags pulled the chariot so fast that it stirred up a small dust storm. Artemis reached her hand out and beckoned that we come to her, she sprinkled orange looking embers over the stags and chariot, it reminded me of pixie dust from Neverland and then she asked us to hop on, and we did. My heart was beating fast as I was excited to have divine guidance. I didn't feel so alone in all of this anymore and I think the girls felt the same way judging by how eagerly they complied.

TWENTY

I VISIT THE ORACLE
OF DELPHI

Nothing starts off the perfect morning like a long enchanted chariot ride, with a beautiful divine female. The morning sky was a blush of dark purple and pink; we rode in silence, the fragrance of jasmine was intense, and I wondered if Artemis always smelled like that or if her scent changed with her mood or location.

The arid desert melted away into a lush oasis, as we neared a camp filled with dozens of huge tipi style tents, I noticed Kelly's shoulders tensing up. I wasn't sure what was bothering her, but after all the time together on the road, I could tell when something was.

As I made my way through the camp, I said hi to a few of the huntresses, but none of them acknowledged me like I was invisible or something. The tipis lined the parameter in a square formation and then there was an enormous circus-size tent in the center which I assumed belonged to Artemis.

We made our way to the center of the camp, following the goddess.

Two young ladies came out of the large central tipi, both holding spears and wearing full heavy leather armor; they looked both sexy and intimidating

. They had on bracers, gauntlets, pauldrons, and breast-plates that all looked handcrafted and decorated with brass accents and etched with vine patterns.

"Welcometh to mine own campeth, these art mine own two most trusted huntresses Lieutenant Chloe Andreas and Second Lieutenant Leah Maras. Those shall assisteth me with tracking the oracle.

As we were about to enter the tipi, Kelly pulled me aside. "Davis this seems too easy, nothing is ever this simple for us, I think it's a trap."

"Let's just assume it is and be ready for anything," I said.

Kelly nodded.

Once inside Chloe, Leah, Alicia, and Artemis gathered in the center. The goddess and huntresses were working together feverishly, mixing a bunch of strange looking ingredients into a clay bowl. Once finished Artemis invited me over.

"Drinketh this, Davis, if 't be true thou art w'rthy of seeking the Oracle of Delphi h'r scent shall beest known to us, only then can we track h'r."

"Is it safe?" I said warily.

"If 't be true thee cannot trusteth me, whom can thee trusteth young one?"

I glanced at Alicia's face and her smile was reassuring, then I glanced over at Kelly, and her face screamed don't do it! I figured my odds were fifty, fifty at this point that if it was a trap we were probably toast and if I refused we were way outnumbered, so I chugged it down... man was it gross, the concoction had the consistency of slime and tasted like a mud and earwax flavored jellybean smoothie. I had to fight myself not to barf it back up.

After a few minutes, a faint, moon-like glow enveloped me and started to spread in a trail over the ground.

"Thou art w'rthy, Davis, alloweth us maketh haste while the trail is still green," Artemis bellowed.

Chloe and Leah both mounted single stag, and the rest of us climbed aboard Artemis's chariot, with little thought we embarked on a hunt for the Oracle of Delphi, and before I knew it, we were off on the search. Silver Stags pulled Artemis' chariot at a steady pace, and her lieutenants took point tracking the Oracle's scent.

We found ourselves in a new place. There were lots of red rock structures, but one stood out, in particular, it radiated with immense power, and I felt drawn in its direction. It was this large arched stone structure that I later found out was called "Lake Powell's Rainbow Bridge" apparently it was sacred to the Navajos in the area.

Chloe and Leah stopped in their tracks directly under the red stone archway.

"The Oracle must be cloaked by a powerful magic goddess, the trail has gone cold, and I completely lost the scent," Chloe said.

"This charm is nay doubteth the doing of mine own broth'r Apollo."

Artemis walked the distance of the monolith, studying it with great concentration.

"V'ry clev'r... only one can wend beyond. The cloaking spelleth is much m're than meets the eye, our Oracle is enshielf hence in the past, and only a w'rthy vessel may passeth between the timelines." Artemis said, clasping her hands together.

"Davis, thou art the chosen vessel... only thee can passeth between the rifts in the timelines. Nay one else shall beest able to passeth with thee, doth thee und'rstand the task at handeth?"

"Yes, I understand...but why me?"

Artemis cocked her head to the side, brushing a long strand of her hair behind her ear. "Th're is much thee has't f'rgotten."

"Forgotten?" I said.

Artemis gave me a cold stare and looked away.

I walked over to Alicia and wrapped my arms around her, I didn't say anything we held each other for what felt an eternity and when I pulled away. She said, "Promise me you'll be careful sirenboy."

"Sirenboy?" I stammered. "What's up with that?"

"I'm just kidding chill," Alicia said grimly.

"Oh—don't worry about me I'll be all right," I promised. "Like what's the worst that can happen?"

Alicia nodded. "I hope you're right Davis. Come back to me in one-piece OK?"

Kelly walked over between Alicia and I and leaned her head on my shoulder. I could see the tension on Alicia's face, but she refrained from commenting. "You always had Alicia or me looking after you, this time is different, so keep your wits about you, and remember everything I taught you back on the streets, it will keep you alive."

The fact that both girls thought I was a screw up made me doubt myself. But I shrugged it off. After all, it didn't really seem I had much of choice, and part of me wanted to prove them wrong!

"Well see yas," I told the girls.

Before stepping through the archway, I stopped. I didn't notice anything strange about it, but apparently it was going to take me to a place in time meant only for me to enter. My heart fluttered as I turned back to take one last look at my friends my gaze lingering on the girl's faces. Deep down I knew there was a chance that this would be the last time we ever saw one another, so I took a moment to memorize everyone just as they were, in case I got lost in time or worse.

When I walked through the archway, I could feel a slight drop in temperature and noticed a small tent on the other side that previously was not there, other than that nothing extraordinary happened. It was almost an instant shift, it felt nothing like the portal we encountered at the Temple of the Sun in Ecuador. I turned around and could see everyone standing on the other side, I waved and called for both Alicia and Kelly but it become apparent that no one could see or hear me, I was alone on this journey.

After fifty feet, I gripped the hilt of my sword as I neared the entrance of the small tent, ready for anything.

A young woman with long auburn hair draped over her left shoulder, in braids, wearing a white gown, and white sandals stood before me, everything about her seemed perfectly reasonable and harmless until I meet her gaze... her eyes were milky white and glowed brightly like L.E.D.S., there was no pupil or iris. Her snake like voice hissed into my skull sending my stomach into a somersault.

"3,600 years I've waited... Apollo said the boy I meet shall be very special." The woman said.

"Do you mean me any harm?"

"Excuse me?" The woman exclaimed. "I have never hurt anyone in all of my existence, and I don't intend any ill will toward you Davis."

"I never mentioned my name," I stammered. "And I don't mean you any harm either."

"I know much," she brightened. "I've been expecting you."

She was putting off a creepy vibe like she seemed harmless enough, but her milk white eyes made me look away. "Umm, like what happened to your eyes?" I asked.

"They were not always this way. I was once a normal girl, at first, I was so normal I would have never guessed my fate. In fact, there was never any indication of my gift as a child. I was promised by Apollo that they next boy I met would take his mark from me and then I would be granted eternal life in the fields of Elysian for my service."

"Davis will you take my burden and grant me eternal peace, so that I may be with my loved ones, after all of these years... I am home sick. The mark of Apollo is only for those of pure heart and I prophesized that I would meet you one day, and here you are."

"Let's slow down a moment, like I don't even know your name or anything about you..."

I waited for her to say something, anything really as the silence thickened between us. I secretly hoped maybe she could shed some light on some of the major questions that haunted me, like my childhood and the prophecy.

Her shoulders tensed as she rose to her feet, "This way," she motioned for me to follow her.

She led me over to a small tent, it looked like something ancient. It was a burlap material held up by a few wooden poles, and hemp rope. The inside was cramped, I pictured her being a genie trapped inside a lamp for millennia.

"Sit down," she insisted, patting her hand on the bed.

There were stacks of parchment paper stacked in sloppy piles filling both sides of the tent leaving a narrow path to her bed. Above her bed was a Dreamweaver and to the right was a tiny stool and vanity mirror that looked as though it belonged to a child's playset. I cautiously navigated what appeared to be the home of a hoarder and sat down on her bed. It was stiff very stiff, and felt like it was made of bamboo, I could not imagine how horrible it would make my back feel sleeping on it for a night, let alone a lifetime.

After carefully observing her living quarters I took note of all the feminine trinkets, they were very few in number, she owned a small wooden hair brush, a turquoise necklace, and a creepy looking porcelain doll propped against the mirrors frame.

She sat down on the bed beside me, I felt slightly uncomfortable since there was no room to scoot over.

"It's been a very long time since I had company, and saying my birth name feels foreign to me anymore… I've been called the Oracle of Delphi for many, many years. But my actual name is Lorelei Petros, and I was born in Hania one of the larger towns in Crete."

I noticed her eyes dimming, her shoulders slouch, and lips pursing.

"What's wrong?"

"I just miss my home, I've spent so much time out here in the desert that my memories of the sea are all but faded, I have trouble anymore recalling the sound of waves lapping at the surf or the briny smell of the seashore."

I thought about how lonely it must be to be immortal, it made me feel horrible for her. Like how can anyone be isolated to their own conversations for thousands of years, it must have been hellish.

"Now that I have introduced myself, may we proceed with why you are really here?"

"My guardian Oogle put me on this path, he said I needed your mark to complete my quest."

"It's not my mark, it belongs to Lord Apollo… but it is my burden and mine to give to a worthy vessel. I deem you a worthy vessel if you accept Davis?"

"Will it hurt?"

"No, but the temperature shift around you will feel frigid and it will drain my life force since it's the only thing keeping me alive… but you would be doing me an honor to pass my gift, as I am tired and wish to be amongst my family in my promised blessed life in the Fields of Elysium."

"So… you really want to die???"

"My life has been long and I accept this fate, it's only the divine energy inside this vessel keeping me alive. I don't like to think of it as death Davis, it's more like a caterpillar leaving its cocoon as a butterfly to experience a new phase of existence, in that sense I embrace the afterlife."

"I can't take your life… it doesn't feel right."

"Look under my pillow, I know the questions you seek answers to, I am a prophet after all."

I glanced down at her pillow and flipped it over. Underneath was another old looking parchment paper, stained yellow. It was another prophecy; the writing was in ancient Greek. The letters danced around the page until they read as English to me. The first half I recognized, it was the same nonsense Kelly read to me that's inscribed on my amulet.

A child conceived of blood and foam

Shall walk this path by choice alone

His weakness is a friend that's foe

I continued reading the second half.

In the land of death, a choice to make that's his alone

Gods betrayed by the eldest son to undo what once be done

Olympus or Earth the price be weighed

At the end of the prophecy it said, "Sorry Davis, I knew you would never be able to harm me… So, I've taken the liberty of taking my own life. If you wish to bear the mark of Apollo, just kiss me on the lips or don't, the choice is yours."

I heard a loud thud and looked up, the Oracle was on the floor belly up with a dagger buried deep in her chest. Blood pooled on her dress. The last words I read resonated over and over in my skull… I knew I had to make a choice before it was too late, but ultimately I knew this was my fate. So, I did the unthinkable, I leaned in and kissed her soft trembling lips. She instantly gasped as if her breath was being stolen by me, her brightly glowing eyes dimmed to a flicker and then extinguished altogether, a white smoke poured into my mouth choking me and then it was over.

She was gone.

I folded up the prophecy and tucked it into my pocket. I glanced into the mirror, and the color of my eyes swirled from green to blue as if they were trying to find their balance. They did not glow like the Oracle's thank the gods! I walked over to the Oracle and wiped my hand over her now brown eyes that were staring to the heavens, she had a perpetual smile plastered on her face. I guess she actually did embrace her own death. Instead of getting answers to my questions I was left with even more, like this new half of the prophecy what did it mean? And me bearing the mark of Apollo did it make me immortal as well? How did it work? These were some of the questions I had swimming around in my head, driving me crazy.

I left the tent and walked toward my timeline where I initially entered, I could see a campfire burning on the other side and Artemis's chariot parked, it appeared dark there…

but it was sunny and appeared high noon here, which I found very peculiar. When I glanced back to say goodbye the tent was no longer there, so I whispered a silent prayer that she made it to her destination and was with family as I stepped through the timeline anxious to be back with my friends.

***

The following morning, Artemis and her huntress returned to camp, we joined them as their honored guests. Apparently, the Oracle of Delphi was lost to them for a very long time and now that energy flowed through me.　Like there was defiantly something different about me …but I couldn't quite pinpoint what changed. I just knew something about me felt off like I was more connected to the world around me, and my emotional senses seemed heightened. But other than that I was unsure.

When the sun sank beneath the horizon and nights shadow gripped the land, blanketing it in darkness. Artemis had us all gather by a blazing hearth in the center of camp. Dozens of Huntress gathered shoulder to shoulder, making a sea of living flesh.

I glanced at both Alicia and Kelly and their expressions were audible. If we were ever in grave danger, the time was now.

Alicia, Kelly, and I all pushed together back to back, my hand rested on Kerauno ready to fight if necessary. A familiar voice boomed into my head, it was Oogle.

"Davis honored guest, goddess mean no harm."

My shoulders slackened, hearing Oogle relieved my fears. I stepped forward losing my grip on my swords hilt. Alicia and Kelly followed my lead and we joined into the festivities. It seemed that I was being honored and Artemis, she was bestowing a gift upon me. After a huge feast of fresh fruits, raw vegetables, freshly roasted meats, and cheese. Artemis beckoned for me to join her by the hearth.

I glanced around, searching the sea of bodies for Oogle, but as usual my advanced A.I. was nowhere to be seen…like he was the worse protector and advisor in history!

Artemis revealed a black velvet pouch the length of a bottle. It was tied shut by a black lace. I untied the lace. Inside was a strange knotted sick with odd symbols. The symbols appeared to be an incantation. When the stick touched my fingers I felt a strange sensation and the most peculiar thing happened, the stick glowed, emitting a faint blue light.

"As I suspect'd thou art the chosen se'r Davis, thee highlone shalt writeth the st'ry of the god's," Artemis said.

"And if I refuse?"

"Davis, thee has't been chosen by the gods to beareth the gift of sight. T is thy sacr'd duty to shareth thy gift with those whom art w'rthy of seeing past 'r future events." Artemis looked deep into Davis' eyes, her liquid moon-like eyes piercing his own. "One cannot simply refuseth thy fate. Davis, thou art the charm yond weaves ev'rything togeth'r—you've been known by many names in the past. doth thee accepteth this hon'r and gage thy allegiance to Olympus?"

What she said sounded like lunacy on the surface, but deep down in the pit of my stomach I knew truth resonated in her words. It was hard to believe. I learned that much first hand with all the creatures I've encountered, and all the strange things that I witnessed.

"I accept…I will do as you wish," I said.

"Yond wouldst beest wise as timeth is not on our side. In eight days the crossing shall beest completeth and mine own broth'rs and sist'rs shalt f'rev'r remaineth in the accurs'd domain of mine own broth'r Poseidon."

"The Crossing?" I said.

"It's at which hour Nibiru passes near earth. Ev'ry three-thousand-six-hundr'd years."

"Why does Nibiru affect the God's?"

"T don't directly, but the curse Hades putteth on his broth'rs is did tie to the planets crossing. Nibiru is the home planet of the Anunnaki, humans known those folk through-out the ages as angels."

Hearing what Artemis said, made complete sense, for the first time I fully understand what Kelly was. Like I could completely wrap my mind around her now, she no longer seemed so mysterious. The thought of Kelly being an angel was really exciting, and everything just made so much sense, like how she could heal animals and stun people. I couldn't help but wonder if she could go full-on angel mode and grow wings.

"Thee wilt doth thy sacr'd duty Davis, anon closeth thy eyes holding the Rod of Knowing firmly in thy hands and focus thy thoughts on the god, Poseidon," Artemis instructed.

I did as she said. After a few moments of thinking about Poseidon, I swore that I could smell the sea. In an instant, a beach came into view, "I see white sand, jagged rocky islands, and bright blue water." My back tensed as words echoed inside my mind, "Rocky Point, The Sea of Cortez."

"I knoweth of this lodging. I've hath spent much timeth with mine own broth'r th're. At first lighteth, we rideth to the The Sea of Cortez," Artemis said, lifting her fist skyward.

TWENTY-ONE

WE GO TO THE SEA
OF CORTEZ

It was now September twenty-fifth, only seven days left to complete our mission. The sun had been up for a while, but it was not real hot yet. The desert was still, but a few horses in the corral would whinny restlessly. I was sitting by the hearth trying to sort out the complications of my life, as impossible as it felt, the word impossible seemed to have less meaning than it once did. After traveling through portals, riding enchanted beasts, battling mythical creatures, and facing uncertain death anything seemed possible these days.

I was thankful that we were all still alive. My mind was still trying to wrap around how I was able to regenerate or channel lightning like I got that my parents were Zeus and Poseidon. They were two of the most powerful Olympian Gods and all, but I still had no idea how two guys make a baby—I guess I was in no position to question how Gods make babies...it could be worse like Aphrodite was the product of her father being castrated by Cronus if I remember correctly. But first the plane crash and then Olympus Mons where I became a shish-kabob and somehow still walked away. My powers were defiantly growing stronger by the day, but I felt no less vulnerable than I did before the plane wreck. Unfortunately for me, the fate of the world was resting on my shoulders, and time was not on my side. I could not wrap my mind around one thing, if the curse was set nearly three-thousand-six-hundred years ago, then where was I all this time, if that is when I was created? What did Artemis mean by me being known by many names in the past? Trying to wrap my mind around this was nothing short of a massive migraine.

Even though most of it made little sense, I knew in my heart that this was my destiny to save the Greek Gods. After all, the two most powerful Olympian Gods created me of their blood, and I was carried on the sea foam in the domain of Poseidon until my birth.

I now thought of this as my new life as Oogle and Kelly had revealed that so much was expected of me. I just wasn't certain of all the details, even with most of my earlier memories restored, it was hard to think of myself as anything but normal. To say I was feeling overwhelmed would be a massive understatement. Hopefully, there would be some more guidance from Oogle or Artemis. I defiantly needed it.

I was in deep thought when I noticed Kelly's shadow and looked up at her. She sat down beside me and we were both quiet until she broke the ice. "I really don't want to complicate your life. I know Alicia was here before me and I don't want to get into a fight with her over you."

I nodded.

My feelings were so mixed about Kelly and Alicia like I didn't want to pick either of them, in fear of losing my friendship with the other, I cared deeply for them both.

She went on. "To tell you the truth if you are happy then so be it. I'll be happy too."

I firmly grasped her shoulders, and she lifted her head up locking eyes with me. I swear for a moment I could see a flicker of guilt in her eyes, but I put it aside thinking I had imagined things. Like seriously what would she have to feel guilty about? Like she saved my butt more times than I'd ever admit.

I could hear the huntress stirring about in their tents, and soon Artemis came out and greeted us by the fire.

"Davis aft'r we consume, lets gath'r supplies and taketh one day's rest to ready ourselves f'r the journey ahead," Artemis announced. "At twilight, we shalt maketh a sh'rt journey south of h're to the Sea of Cortez, is saf'r f'r us to traveleth und'r the camouflage of moonlight, so yond we art eyeless to any whom mean us harmeth."

She continued, "Th're I shalt require thy guidance in locating mine own brethren and freeing those folk of their wretch'd curse."

"I'm here to serve, but what about my Grandparent's. What should I tell them?" I asked.

"Those gents art having breakfast with thee as we speaketh."

"How is that possible?"

"I've enchant'd the ranch…they won't even knoweth thy missing."

"Wait," I said, "So…they have no idea that we are even gone? But what if someone would visit like Aunt Lisa?"

Artemis pursed her lips. "Mine own charm is v'ry stout, Davis. Thou art very much th're because I madeth shades yond art thy exact replicas, with access to thy mem'ries. But their mission is spending timeth with thy family and thy mission is saving Olympus."

I wisecracked, "I could have used a shade for Mill Creek that would have made school a lot less complicated."

Artemis gave me a bewildered look disregarding my comment and whistled for her stags.

So far our journey was not met with any delay or complications. Things had been progressing smoothly and I had no idea what to expect once we arrived at the Sea of Cortez. Like I knew my job was to save the other Olympian Gods from some ancient curse, but I also had no idea what dangers lay ahead. Nothing this far was easy, every turn was met with obstacles. The only real question was…what mythological creature would stand in our way next, and would we be able to overcome the threat or would we find ourselves on a one-way trip to meet my uncle, Hades in the Underworld.

Artemis was no doubt immortal, or she secretly had a death wish. Either way, I was not complaining like I didn't have my driver's license or even a learners permit yet (however I was really looking forward to both in the near future) but she still allowed me to drive her silver chariot. Like I'm no stranger to riding fast animals such as the supercharged horses from Grandpas ranch or the griffons on Mars, but there was no comparison to Artemis's stags.

We blazed across landscapes zipping through congested highways, red lights, up the sides of buildings, through forest and even over the top of lakes and rivers. I can only image what people saw if they caught a glimpse of us, I guess we were probably moving so fast that even if someone did see us, it would be just a blur and they would probably shrug it off as nothing. That is human nature if it doesn't make sense just shrug it off, or take some pills to help you forget what you saw until it feels like a bad dream. Or maybe we were invisible as Artemis did mention earlier about the moon camouflaging us.

We reached the coast about twenty-five minutes into our journey, we stood at the edge of a steep cliff. The scenery was breathtaking, the full silver moon pierced the veil of the clouded sky. Below us, moonlight and fog meshed together forming a coastline. Beyond that squid ink waves moved in rhythmic patterns.

"Let's maketh campeth h're f'r tonight. The climb down wouldst beest dang'rous without prop'r visibility." Artemis said.

Chloe nodded in agreement.

"The sea is dangerous enough without Poseidon's protection," Leah said.

I found us a large, flat area a fair distance from the drop-off. Leah and Chloe went to work setting up two tents. This seemed so natural for them like they didn't need to pause to read instructions or even verbally communicate to snap them together, it was evident why Artemis picked them as her lieutenants. I took notice to Kelly and Alicia gawking at them as they meticulously pieced the tents together by muscle memory. The tents were not your typical modern variety. They looked old and inspired by nature, they were made of tanned animal hides. If I had to guess what type of animal the furs came from, I would put my money on Buffalo.

Kelly, Alicia and I shared a tent together, and Artemis and her huntress slept in the other tent. The inside of the tent was not very spacious, it fit one queen mattress inside. The bottom was made up of a pile of large animal furs, it appeared to be a mixture of animals the huntress slain over the centuries. I was fairly sure some was wolf and rabbit, but the others I had no clue about or even if all the animals were of the standard breed and not mythical. I claimed the middle of the tent, Alicia was to my left and Kelly to my right.

I'm not going to lie, my heart was racing, I never slept in a tent with a beautiful girl before, and now I was going to be sleeping between two of them.

We sat and talked for a while, Kelly and Alicia prodded my memory for any clues regarding the Sea of Cortez. I honestly had no additional information to share. As the vision was kind of hard to fully absorb, it came at me in waves, and the arrangement of images was defiantly out of order. So it made it a bit confusing on my end to piece them back together into a meaningful order. We discussed a vague plan of action for in the morning about not risking our lives too much and then we all laid down, both girls were on neutral terms for the time being with each. They both rested their heads on my chest, using me as their pillow. Kelly was the first one to pass out, leaving just Alicia and me alone to talk.

Alicia whispered softly in my ear, "Davis do you ever just wish things could go back to the way they were…like before you got expelled from Mill Creek?"

I tilted my head toward her. "I guess. Like ever since the plane crash my life has been crazy. I don't know if my life could ever go back to normal. Like my parents are gods, and I'm supposedly their prophesized savior." I looked up at the roof of the tent and took a deep breath, "I think this is the new normal for me, I'm pretty sure after what we been through there is no going back."

I didn't really feel like staying on the subject so I told Alicia, "I'm drained, so I'm like going to crash. See you in the morning."

Alicia leaned in and kissed me, dragging her teeth softly over my bottom lip, which sent chills down my spine. "Sweet dreams," she said.

I lay there silent, naughty thoughts swam in my mind. Kelly was snuggled into me, and Alicia was teasing me, driving me wild. She would randomly caress my side by reaching her hand up under my shirt, just to drive me crazy. She traced her finger across each individual muscle on my stomach. I couldn't take it anymore and lost my willpower. I left my hand wander a few times testing my boundaries. I slid my hand up her shirt, letting my fingers glide gently over her tummy hovering near her bellybutton and waistline, and then I walked my fingers further north and squeezed her firm breast through her bra for a brief moment, I could feel her body growing tense with each touch. But that was my limit, I didn't feel like we were ready to do anything more. At least not now, the timing didn't feel right, and I was also confused over Kelly. Like I had an attraction to her that went beyond just physical appearance, and I didn't want to get caught messing around with Alicia and screw up a good thing.

TWENTY-TWO

I RIDE A KRAKEN

At first light, Leah woke us all up. The girls and I grabbed our belongings and crawled out of the tent. The tent was surprisingly comfortable, I felt well rested and ready to start the day. I rubbed the sleep from my eyes as I watched the sun rise above the horizon, casting its reflection onto the Sea of Cortez. There was a thin fog covering the coast. The main thing that caught my eye was the jagged rock islands about one-hundred yards out from the sandy shore below. They jutted out of the water like daggers. It looked primitive, I could imagine what explorers must have thought long ago when they discovered this place in their long wooden ships. I'm sure it made them weary.

The Huntress worked together very synchronized as they dismantled each tent and packed them away.

Kelly patted her belly. "I'm starving."

Alicia nodded in agreement. "Me too."

I rummaged around in my backpack, our food was nearly all. All I could rummage up was some beef jerky and a pouch of peanuts. Lucky for us Artemis and her huntress were prepared and offered us a nice spread. We sat down on the ground legs crossed, around a red sheet. On top of the sheet lay a mixture of fruits, bread, and cheese. We picked at the food until we were all satisfied. I ate a combination of berries, a yellow delicious apple, and fist size chunk of bread.

After breakfast, Artemis called me over. I could tell she had something important on her mind how she was pacing back and forth.

"Davis, I has't aid'd thee longeth enow. Gods doth not square battles, as this is our children's right, to defend our hon'r." She paced around for a moment and then heaved her chest, "I am going to alloweth Chloe and Leah h're with thee, they shall keepeth thee safe, and taketh thee the rest of the way."

Artemis leaned in and gave me a hug, her face was pressed against mine, I could feel the moister from her tears.

"I've nev'r been valorous at declaring o, farewell," She said sobbing.

Artemis called to her huntress. "I turneth Davis and his companions ov'r to thy careth, keepeth those folk safe as thee wouldst me."

Chloe and Leah slammed their fists against their armored chests and said in unison, "yes goddess."

Artemis climbed onto her silver chariot and took the reins in her hands. "Davis, one lasteth thing bef're i wend. I bethink thee shall findeth these useful on thy quest."

She tossed two small, golden discs into the air. I had caught them before they hit the ground.

"What are they?" I asked Artemis.

"Golden Drachmas," she said. "It's the currency of the gods."

Before I could say another word she zipped away in a blur! I seriously needed some enchanted stags they were awesome!

Since Artemis left, Chloe took the lead. She had us follow her down the cliff, she found an incline narrow enough for us to climb down. I never climbed down a rock wall before and it was harder than it looked on T.V. every few steps down I found myself struggling to get my grip. Alicia was having the same issue, in fact, she was severely struggling. She lost her grip about forty feet above the shore and went into a dive. My heart was pumping hard in my chest. I had no clue what to do, so I decided to jump after her and somehow get her to land on top of me. Kelly launched herself off the face of the cliff without any warning. Her body began to glow and shimmer with intensity and then the strangest thing happened, huge ten-foot wings sprouted out of her back on both sides. With laser precision she swooped down, scooped up Alicia about fifteen feet above the ground and then glided down to the beach, making a soft landing.

We all caught up with Kelly and Alicia. She seemed a bit in shock, just sitting on the beach.

"Did you know Kelly was an angel Davis?" Alicia stammered.

"Umm...I suspected she might be able to fly, but this was the first I ever saw her do it."

Chloe huffed like she was unimpressed. "The Anunnaki and the twin brothers Zetes and Calais always been renowned as angels by mankind, because of their wings and human-like appearance."

"Zetes?" Alicia said turning the word into two syllables.

"He was the son of Boreas, God of the north winds," Leah said.

"I kind of miss them two, they were always so much fun. Shame Hercules had to kill them." Chloe said.

We walked the length of the beach looking for any possible sign of the Olympian's. Before noon we finally spotted a dolphin offshore. As it closed the distance between us I recognized them same green eyes, they were the same eyes the dolphin from the plane crash had.

I looked at my friends.

Without a second thought I jumped into the water and swam towards it, Kelly, Alicia, and the huntress all followed my lead. I was first to speak. "Who are you?"

He stopped swimming and floated on the ocean swells. We did the same.

His permanent smile seemed to be mocking us, that is until he spoke! "Yes, you are on the right track. I am Poseidon."

I tread water, thinking a mile a minute. "Did you all hear what the dolphin just said?"

"It just made eeekkk noises," Alicia said.

Chloe swam up to the dolphin and gave it a hug. "We will save you from this curse, Poseidon."

"So you understood what he said Chloe?"

"Not a clue," She said. "But I know a god's essence when I see it."

Then I remembered that I was the temporary new Oracle and in possession of the rod, somehow it was allowing me to understand the high pitched sounds of the mammal. Finally, I said, "You mean the Poseidon of Greek Mythology? The Son of Cronus and of Rhea and brother of Zeus."

"Yes. That be me."

"But I always saw Poseidon as a muscular bearded man carrying a trident. You...you are..."

"A fish?" He said.

"Well, yeah."

"I am a god. I can turn into any being I wish. Right now I want to be a dolphin."

I believed him, yet this was almost too incredible to conceive. "But don't you derive your power from your tri-dent?"

"My Trident is not the source of my power; it does carry a small amount of my divine energy and is a means of protection when I need it."

"How old are you?" I asked.

"Older than the ages," he replied.

Suddenly, a rumbling distracted our conversation. The water began rippling all around us. But before I could fully absorb what was going on, a massive sinkhole the size of shopping mall opened up, twisting the water, rapidly rotating in a swirling vortex-like whirlpool just a mile out, revealing Polybotes, the same giant that I battled in the boy's room at Mill Creek. But this time, he was much larger, like T-rex big and headed in our direction.

I looked over at Kelly, and again she had a guilty look plastered on her face, but I now had a sense of when people were not being honest with me being in possession of the Rod of Knowing. I said, "What is this, Kelly? I know you are hiding something from us."

"I'm sorry, Davis, I really am! I never intended to have feelings for you. I was just trying to stop this silly prophecy from happening and make my father proud of me, honest," she said, lips trembling.

Before she could breathe another word Chloe and Leah had the tips of their spears pressed to her throat.

Chloe pushed just hard enough to draw blood. "I was waiting for you to slip up Anunnaki scum."

I pushed Chloe's blade from Kelly's neck. "Let me be the judge if she is a traitor, am I not the new seer?"

The surf swelled as Polybotes got closer, I had to hurry. I needed to know if Kelly meant me harm if anything we had was real. I pulled the rod out of its pouch and held it. Looking deeper into Kelly's big doe eyes, I knew she was sincere, and I inaudibly asked the Rod to show me the truth. In a flash, I was watching Kelly being tormented by Hades in her dreams (I never met him, but trust me it was obvious who it was). I saw their first meeting, by a large lake surrounded by a thick forest. She looked so scared and he told her if she ever wanted to be loved by her father all she had to do was stop a little prophecy from happening. She hesitated, but eventually Hades won her over with his charm and instructed her on my location and insisted that she had to obtain both amulet pieces before I did. I saw Kelly following me when I ran away from Aunt Lisa's, she was my shadow, and I was none the wiser.

The last vision showed Hades and Kelly meeting in Grandpa's barn, she called him and said the deal was off, that things had changed. But he refused to let her off the hook and threatened to take her soul if she backed out. In one fell swoop, a ghostly visage was reaped from her chest. Crippled in agony she fell to the ground, and then he exploded into black smoke, sending her soul slingshotting back into her body and leaving Kelly to her thoughts.

As fast as the vision came, it was gone. The vision could not have ended any sooner like the earth was literally shaking around us that was how close Polybotes was.

"Chloe she was forced by Hades to do this," I said. "Let her go."

Chloe lowered her blade. "We will continue this conversation later."

Oogle manifested on my shoulders and whispered, "Master need armor forged by Hephaestus."

"That be awesome…but seriously Oogle we need a strategy or we are toast."

"Master have Zeus's body armor, it is amulet. Just press finger on both crescents at same time."

I tugged open the collar of my shirt and revealed the amulet, my eyes fixated on the location Oogle mentioned. I wasn't sure what to expect, but I touched my finger between the two crescents'. "Please work!" I thought to myself.

The amulet started vibrating, its intensity grew until it morphed into black goo, the goo spread over my entire body, it was cold to the touch like thick oil. Then it began to harden and turned into a blinding white light, brighter than the sun that enveloped my entire body, leaving me blinded. The feeling of power flowed through me. It was a new and strange feeling, unlike anything I ever experienced. As my eyes readjusted coming back into focus, I could make out the light solidifying around my body. As the armor finished materializing around me, I could feel the strength it gave me, I felt invincible. The pale morning light reflected off my armor inching across the cold sand. I looked at myself over admiring the new look, it was super reflective metal which felt weightless. All my clothes were under the new armor, the only thing that remained was my sword still strapped to my side.

"Now master has much power, Oogle protects master from harm. I use to be called Troy Body Armor long ago."

I glanced around looking for Oogle, "Where did you go?" I muttered.

"Oogle is armor," he explained.

The thought of the imp being some liquid Nanotechnology that could morph into body armor was mind boggling in the least. But Zeus's body armor, the God of all gods... this was just crazy!"

"How is that possible?"

"Oogle is advanced guardian or living armor, but never both. Oogle can only be one at any time."

"What do you mean by only one?"

"Oogle imp or armor never both. Can only be changed back on Olympus."

"Then how do I still hear your voice and does Kelly and Alicia?"

"Oogle shares same consciousness as master and girls, but only master hear me when in armor form."

Kelly and Alicia looked astounded by my new look, and Chloe and Leah looked at me like I was insane for talking to myself. Only Kelly and Alicia knew about Oogle.

The advancing Polybotes was now near and threatening.

"So I guess it's time to settle an old score, this guy is going down once and for all," I said.

"Wait Davis… let me reason with him, I think he will listen to me." Kelly insisted.

Before I could protest, she lifted into the air like an eagle and went soaring toward the giant. Kelly circled Polybotes head several times. I strained my ears trying to figure out what they were saying to each other. On her fourth time around he swatted her like a common house fly, sending her hurtling through the air out of control and she slammed into the ground hard.

I felt anger wash over me, this creature from my past was haunting me yet again. But this time, it was more personal… he hurt someone I cared about.

I'm not sure what came over me, I've never felt so much bottled up anger inside me ever. It's like everything bad that ever happened to me hit me all at once. I couldn't save my parents, but I was no longer that powerless boy anymore, I had the power of two powerful gods coursing through my veins and I was going to smite this beast back to Tartarus! I charged at him. The distanced narrowed between us, and he noticed me charging him and started hefting up boulders out of the ground and launching them in my direction.

I dove, rolled, and ran over the top of them. Oogle was in full combat mode, calculating every move I should make and commanding me to do as he instructed.

When I was almost in striking distance, I heard Kelly wail, "Davis no."

But I disregarded her warning. "So how do I kill this beast Oogle?"

"Master roll between his legs fast, then you must scale his back with much speed before he tosses you off, then when at his neck draw sword, stab deep and then hang on to grip tight while sliding down his back and cutting him all the way down."

As I neared the giant, I felt dwarfed but continued my pursuit. Like the hydra inside Olympus Mons seemed like a walk in the park compared to this guy. When I faced him at Mill Creek he was formidable, now in his true form, he was just plain scary.

It almost felt like I was not controlling my own body, as it was near effortless to carry out these instructions. I rolled under his legs, and he pounded the ground with his fist making car size dents on the beach. I launched myself off the ground and landed on the back of his knee, I held on with all my strength, then I shot myself forward pushing off his leg with my feet, and landed on his waist, I gripped onto his shirt as he thrashed about trying to send me flying. He swatted at me a few times, but I stayed near the center of his back. I started to lose my grip, so I focused all my energy,

Oogle explained what I needed to do again, and I followed his every instruction. With lightning fast precision, I scaled the remainder of his back and landed right on the mark, pulled my blade from its scabbard, thrust it into his neck up to the hilt. I could see his skin ripple beneath the surface from the arcs of lightning boiling his blood, his skin was starting to burn giving off an awful stench. Then I grabbed the hilt of my sword with both hands and dropped off his back as dead weight. The sword tore away his flesh, opening him up wide. Pools of golden ichor poured onto the sandy shore, splitting his back and shirt in two.

He reeled in pain, screaming out curses at me. He was no longer focused on me, so I took the opportunity to check on Kelly.

Kelly groaned, blood spilled from her mouth, her wings folded back which was kind of weird. I still had trouble wrapping my mind around the whole wing thing she had going on.

"You have to go." She said under the gurgle of blood.

"I won't leave you."

I heard Alicia scream and looked back. Polybotes had her clutched in his fist. His back was nearly healed my plan had failed. Chloe and Leah were peppering him with arrows, but they just seemed to annoy him, making him angrier.

"Kelly, get up," I crooned lifting her to her feet.

She made it to her feet but was a bit wobbly.

"Davis look away, I am taking my real form."

I looked away, and a bright flash washed over the ground and then faded away. When I looked back, Kelly was now ten feet tall and had glowing blue eyes. An aura of light faintly glowed around her entire body. She hurtled herself into the sky darting toward Polybotes.

I pulled Kerauno from my side and ran back to the battle to join my friends, once in earshot I screamed, "Drop Alicia you overgrown buffoon."

Kelly pulled her bow and notched an arrow of light, loosing it on Polybotes hand. Her light arrows seemed to get his attention, as she loosed one after the other with hawk-like precision turning his hand into a dartboard. He groaned in frustration until he finally dropped Alicia. Chloe and Leah were slicing and dicing his legs with their spears. Alicia wasted no time and pulled out her Sai's going work on the back side of his legs. The girls down below did not appear to be a threat as he swatted at Kelly like an insect missing her over and over again.

With Alicia free of his grip, Kelly now focused her shots on his neck and face which really agitated him. I ran up beside Alicia and started chopping at the backside of his other leg. After a good twenty minutes of us slashing him to pieces I realized this was pointless. "Oogle how do I stop him?"

"Master use your lightening, it is powerful."

"Who do you keep talking to?" Chloe hissed.

"Nobody."

"Everyone get back," I bellowed.

The girls all looked at me like I had a death wish, but they didn't argue with me. Once they were out of the way, I closed my eyes and focused my mind on channeling lightning.

I could feel every hair on my body stand as I focused my mind. A tingling sensation started at the base of my spine and flowed to my fingertips. When I opened my eyes lightening flowed out of me like a river, bolts of chain lightning struck Polybotes one after another forcing him back toward the sea. Polybotes pushed through the pain and power of the lightning and gained ground, I focused so hard that blood started to drip from my nose. Then my powers backfired making a sonic boom sending me flying through the air. But lucky for me Kelly swooped in and caught me.

"You're not getting out of this fight that easy sirenboy."

"I didn't plan on it," I muttered.

"Enough of these games," Polybotes rumbled.

He raked his humongous hand over the white sand beach making five long trenches. Next, he reached into a pouch that hung forgotten around his waist and revealed a handful of oversized bones like they were so big that they could have belonged to an elephant.

Polybotes tossed the bones into the trenches, then he clamped his teeth down on his own hand making it drip blood. He dripped the blood overtop of the bones and then covered them with the loose sand. The sand that covered the bones began to vibrate and then hands started to sprout up from beneath, like rows of cornstalks. Dozens of animated corpses that looked gruesome emerged from under the sand, they staggered with uncoordinated steps in our direction.

Chloe shouted, "Let's send these abominations back where they belong."

She and Leah charged them with their spears, piercing and slashing at them feverishly. But more kept crawling out from the trenches, like an endless army of hungry ants. Like don't get me wrong I did find this kind of cool, like who didn't at one-time wonder what it is like to fight a horde of zombies. But at the same time, I feared for Alicia like I knew Kelly and the Huntress could hold their own. But Alicia never signed up for this, and I felt horrible that she was here with me. Like if we survived this I doubt she would ever want to spend time with me again because it was way too unpredictable and often dangerous.

Kelly swooped in and started loosing arrows on them when one of her arrows pierced their skull they would turn to ash. Alicia and I charged in, Alicia if I didn't know any better was made for killing monsters. Like she did flips over the top of them plunging her Sai's into their heads incinerating them. Her acrobatics actually came in handy for slaying zombies, she was seriously making me look bad, and I was the one with the powers and Troy body armor.

After a while the zombies began to overwhelm us, surrounding us so much that we backed ourselves into the surf.

I was jarred by a familiar voice. "You are my son too, you have my regeneration and can command the waves," Poseidon said.

"How? I never done it before."

"Since discovering who you are, have you been to the ocean?" He said.

"Not until now."

"Let your body be free, as free as water. Feel the waves wash over your feet, become that wave. The waves move as freely as you breathe air."

I relaxed the best I could and done as he instructed. When I breathed in the waves came to me, when I exhaled they went back out to sea. Now that I could feel their rhythm I tried to make them larger, after a few attempts, I could seriously feel myself controlling them like I had no doubt it was me. I raised my hand over my head, focusing on the waves.

"What is this?" Polybotes roared with anger.

A giant wave stood still, taking the shape of my arm and hand rising out of the water twenty feet high. When I bent a finger, the wave mirrored my every move. So I reached forward and grabbed a handful of the undead soldiers and pulled them out to sea when I slammed my hand down the sea ate them up. I sent my hand wave back into shore, this time, I balled my fist and slammed it down like a hammer about ten feet in front of my friends. A dozen or so zombies turned to ash. But more kept crawling out of the trenches so I knew what I had to do, destroy the source of their power, the bones. I lifted my hands as far as they would stretch over my head, the mirrored version was now forty feet tall.

"Get out of the way," I screamed.

My friends all fled behind me, and I crashed down the enormous tidal wave on top of all of the zombies and Polybotes. Then I dug my hand into the sand and squeezed its contents, then I jerked my arm back pulling a large handful of sand and zombies out to sea and submerged them into the endless abyss.

Since my friends were safe behind me, I slammed a wall of water onto the remaining zombies, washing them out to sea. This time, I focused my mirrored hand on grabbing Polybotes, I hammered it down on top of him hard, then I grabbed him squeezing so hard my knuckles turned white. But he pushed through the water not even phased.

"Davis he is too strong for us, we must retreat," Chloe said. "I'll hold him off, everyone else run. That is an order."

Everyone retreated but me, I was done running. If I had to die this day so be it. Just as I drawn my sword, I heard Poseidon. "I can help you save your friends."

"Please," I gasped. "I'm desperate."

Poseidon told me to remove my armor. I had no clue how to do that so I asked Oogle. "Master just press center of your chest where amulet normally is. I touched the center, and my armor flashed once more, a lot less intense as the first round and turned back into my amulet.

"Swim with me," Poseidon commanded.

I swam behind him out into the sea for a good ten minutes, the shore was now a good distance off.

"How is this saving my friends?"

Before I knew what had happened, I felt a sharp pain on my thumb, Poseidon bit me.

"Ouch," I cried out. My blood made a small murky circle in the water like I just dipped a paintbrush. Then the water bubbled all around me, and looking down I could see a huge black creature rushing up to the surface.

"What's happening?"

"You've released the Kraken, young one. He is my protector, guardian of the sea king. My blood is your blood, and any child of mine is protected in my domain.

"The son of Poseidon," I said, allowing the words to roll off my tongue. "I'm the son of the sea king... I doubt I'll ever get used to saying that.".

"You should feel pride in your gut, you were born of hope for Olympus and mankind," he said. "As a son of the two eldest gods you have been blessed with traits from each of us, you have great power stirring inside of you."

My heart thudded as I watched in horror. It felt like we were about to be devoured by a Megalodon shark as it erected from beneath the water, lifting me onto its head. Water poured down its sides like Niagara Falls as it stood upright. I was looking down from a thousand-foot tall creature, with tentacle-like arms longer than skyscrapers.

Kelly flew over carrying Alicia and landed on top of the Kraken.

"What are you two thinking, this thing seems dangerous."

"Put us down!" I wailed.

"K—raken... Waiting order from the son of sea king," it replied, in a loud clickety sound that only I understood.

Polybotes now had living reinforcements, a few dozen Anunnaki soared towards us bearing spears, swords, and bows that had a heavenly glow.

Pointing at the army of angels closing in I shouted, "Strike them down!" and the Kraken went into motion. It felt like I was riding atop of a living Empire State Building with eight skyscraper-sized tentacles.

With one mighty thrash, the sea swallowed up over a dozen angels. The wake of the immense impact made a fifty-foot swell that shadowed the incoming army, before unleashing havoc and crashing down on top of the front line, sending even more to their deaths.

"Davis stop," Kelly said. "Let me talk to them, I am the princess of the Anunnaki, they won't dare harm me."

I took a moment to collect my thoughts, I looked over at Kelly and said, "I know about Hades and your deal, how our meeting was no coincidence, my only real question is where do your loyalties lie?"

"Well," she replied, "I don't want to lose my soul, but I don't want to betray you either. I do love you, Davis, this is far from easy on me."

"Do what's in your heart, Kelly," I replied, her eyes fixated on me in deep thought.

Before she could say anything, two muscular male Anunnaki swooped in from behind and snatched Kelly up. Her bow and quiver fell from the sky, landing beside me. Quickly I picked them up, loaded a light arrow, took aim and let loose. The arrow spiraled through the air at a high velocity and penetrated the leg of one of the men. He screamed in pain but held his grip, they were now too far away for a second shot, and I was not a skilled enough archer to risk a long shot. Also, I didn't want to risk knocking them out of the sky with the Kraken, it was way too risky. I watched as they landed back on the beach beside Polybotes.

Even though I was still a little upset about Kelly's betrayal, she didn't deserve this. My biggest issue was trusting her again entirely. Like what else has she been keeping from me? Everything I thought I knew about her was staged, just one big act and I was none the wiser. Was anything true? Like did she ever really have feelings for me, or was that part of the scheme?

Alicia looked upset; she didn't need to say anything. I knew she too had mixed feelings. She did really like Kelly, minus the fact that she and I shared feelings for one another.

"We need to save her, babe, I don't trust Polybotes or Hades. I saw what he did to her in a vision, he tore her soul out, and she collapsed on the floor," I said.

She locked her intense blue eyes with mine, and for a moment it was as if our souls touched. "Fine, let's risk our lives for the little back-stabber! Hurry before I change my mind, Davis," she hissed.

I urged the Kraken ashore; the Anunnaki army charged it, tossing grappling hooks at its tentacles (not sure how much good that would do them, if it fell over it would kill their entire army!). The Kraken kept a slow, steady pace, crushing any soldiers stupid enough or just too slow to clear its path. I recognized the guy beside her it was Hades, he was so much larger than her. He pointed his finger at her furiously; my best guess was that he was displeased in her shift of loyalties. She never even once tried to apprehend me, and she had more than adequate time and opportunities.

We closed in on Hades; I commanded the Kraken to thrash all eight tentacles down at key points. Like a giant nutcracker, it was on, the creatures limbs smashed down so hard, it felt like a five point nine earthquake on the Richter scale. Angelic or not, they looked scared, when those gigantic tentacles pulverized them. Far below, the freshly cracked earth swallowed up heaping piles of bodies and debris.

I gave Alicia the bow and she went right to work pelting Angels. This hero stuff must have been swelling my head because I told the Kraken to firmly plant an arm to the ground.

"I'm going to get Kelly, cover me," I said.

"Promise me you will be careful? Don't do anything foolish, Davis," Alicia said, choking back tears.

"I'll be all right... after all, you got my back, right?" I said, sliding down what could most likely pass as the world's longest slippery slide. Nearing the bottom, I pressed my amulet, and in a flash of light I was armored, I pulled my sword from its scabbard and slashed wildly at several angels that were now circling me, the arcs of lightning kept them at bay as my ride came to an end.

I raced toward Lord Hades, slashing and bashing through angels left and right. Caught off guard, a giant hellhound pummeled me to the ground. I pushed back hard with my sword against all three heads. They snapped and snarled as they tore at my blade, my gauntlets held up well against their teeth, dog saliva pooled around my blade and dripped over my face. All of a sudden it went silent and they stopped attacking. Lowering my sword, I saw that all three heads had been shish-kabobbed with light arrows.

Looking back (well I suppose it was more like up) at Alicia, I shouted at the top of my lungs, "Thanks, excellent shooting by the way."

I ran the last hundred feet and then stopped dead in my tracks. Hades looked downright scary. He had black hair, draping out from beneath a black plate helmet covered in black spikes. Shadows of lost souls flickered and danced around his robe and helm. His skin was albino pale, I guess there was no sunlight in the Underworld. I had no plan, heck I didn't even know how to fight a god. But I didn't let him know that. I looked fearlessly into his gray eyes, images of people burning alive flashed in my mind. Kelly was shackled to his flaming chariot, parked a few feet behind him. There was little doubt that things were about to go south as dozens of Hades' soldiers surrounded us.

"Hello nephew, glad to see you could make it. Guess Apollo's silly little prophecy turned out to be true and here I was starting to think he'd lost his touch," Hades said.

"Let Kelly go, or there will be trouble," I shouted.

Hades laughed, and his laugh was no ordinary one. It made my mind swim with an overwhelming desire to kneel. But after having my mind twisted by a siren, I had enough practice to resist.

"How rude, too good to respect your elders? Hades asked. "Now hand over your amulet like a good little boy, so we can put an end to this, I would hate to harm that lovely girlfriend of yours—."

I felt my blood boiling. Done talking, I let Hades meet my sword. I pointed it at his chest, it arched bolts of lightning up and down the length of the blade.

"It's been awhile since I had a blade like that drawn on me, a worthy sword for the occasion."

A skeletal warrior broke the circle, coming right at me, then dissolved into ash as an arrow passed through the top of its head and left foot coming to rest on the ground (it was good to know Alicia really did have my back). I instinctively knew what the name meant. It was Greek. I said, "Kerauno, or thunderbolt?"

"Precisely, nephew. Now about that amulet."

Kelly interrupted, "Don't do it, Davis, I recognized one of my friends, and he flew away to warn my father. His army will handle Hades. He should be here any time now… they are tracking me I turned on my rescue beacon. Besides, if my ancestors overthrew the twelve Olympians, one God should be easy enough with all of our advancements."

I took a moment to process what Kelly had just said. Maybe she was right, maybe this really was not my fight, and I could just stall Hades until backup arrived.

Hades faded in and out of existence as he paced about, he sometimes was solid and other times transparent like a ghost. "Listen to me, girl, I don't know what you have been told," he said, with a smirk. "Truth is your ancestors were not nearly bright enough to pull off the plan, they were loyal to the Olympians like good little puppies, trying to please their masters… Well, until I tempted them that is."

Kelly thrashed against her restraints, clanging the chains and then shouted, "What do you mean?" She stammered. "More like forced them! If you shared the same kindness with them as you did me."

"No use my dear, those chains are enchanted adamantine, it's virtually indestructible. What I mean is, I'm the mastermind behind everything from the Olympians being cursed, Davis' parents dying to give him a kick toward his destiny, and even you blinding Davis with foolish love, leading him right into my trap."

I slashed at him hard. My blood was boiling, I finally had someone to unleash all that pent up anger. I now had a face to match to my parents' killer, and now Hades was marked for death by me. I was dead set on sending him on a one-way trip back to the Underworld wearing a toe tag. He disappeared into a black smoke, but I knew he was behind me, so I spun around slashing. Every move he made I was there, he could not outmaneuver me. The Rod like gave me a sixth sense for what he was about to do next. Hades used his helm of darkness to go invisible, and I met his battle-axe with the clank of my sword. Clank after clank we fought, sparks of lightning and flickers of shadow surrounding the connecting blades. I jumped over his battle-axe, rolled out of the way of his flame attacks and even dodged his smoky green bolts of what I assumed to be poison.

Hades erupted into flames shouting, "I'm done fooling around, child, now it's time to be punished."

Large flicks of flame lashed out at me, there was no way I could fight him now, he proved his power was far beyond mine. So I ran dodging and rolling across the ground until

I reached Kelly. One swipe with Kerauno and her shackles were severed, freeing her of the chariot. I guess my blade was an exception to the unbreakable rule.

Hades again went invisible, and this time, I didn't have a chance to react, I saw what was going to happen, but I was too late. He grabbed Kelly by the throat.

"I call a truce, uncle, the amulet for the girl, we can settle our differences at a later date."

This must have pleased him because for a moment it appeared as if he started to smile. "You had your chance to barter, and I don't take kindly to liars such as this one," he said. "Leave the Olympians cursed to the sea, don't aide them or you will reap the souls of all you love."

I guess he smiled just to insult me. "I'd rather die than help you!"

"And so you may, but for now let's make a trade, send away the Kraken in exchange for your other friend's life." He said and waved his hand making Alicia appear at his side. "Love is a great thing, makes a man weak on the battlefield, great for leverage."

I heard Oogle speaking in my mind. "Hades tricky one, call goddess Iris see if cursed, make oath if goddess not, swear on Styx."

I recited word for word what Oogle spoke in my mind; Hades' face turned a lighter shade of pale if that were even possible. In a flash, a strong gust of wind swept over us and rainbow colored light enveloped our area. As the light dimmed, a beautiful winged maiden appeared holding in her hands a wooden staff. The staff was elegant; I recognized it as the same type of caduceus used by Hermes the messenger god (used for divine purposes such as healing). It had a central staff entwined by silver twin serpents.

"IRIS," Hades hissed. "Thought you were cursed to the sea with the rest of my siblings."

"Thanks for coming, Iris, I wanted to make a binding oath with Hades, on the river Styx," I said.

"Very well," she said, her caduceus shrunk down to the size of a pen and she pulled out a parchment and wrote up a contract. Then a golden vase materialized in her hands. Inside was water. "Both of you place a hand on the vase, and make an oath."

I put my hand on the jug. "I swear on the River Styx, that I will send away the Kraken, in exchange for Alicia Thomas (I made sure to say her full name just to be on the safe side)."

Hades placed a hand on the jug as well and said, "I Hades, ruler of the Underworld, hereby make a solemn oath, to not take nor harm a hair on Miss Alicia's head, in exchange for the Kraken being removed."

We were both in agreement. So, Iris placed the contract on the ground and had us pour the water from the river Styx over it binding us to our agreement. The letters glowed gold and floated off of the page slightly like a 3-D movie. Iris was gone as quickly as she had arrived leaving behind rainbow sparkles popping momentarily around us. I placed my hand on the Kraken's tentacle and ordered it away, and Hades gave both Kelly and Alicia a nudge closer to me. He seemed satisfied that I held my end of the deal and turned into black smoke. I walked up to Kelly and Alicia followed me. The army of angels flew away and the few skeletal guards that protected Hades sunk back into the earth. The huntress ran over to us.

"Why did you send the Kraken away that is the only thing stronger than Hades." Chloe hissed.

I shrugged, "Hades gave me no choice he was going to kill Alicia," I said. "Anyway how I see it, we had a triple win… both girls are safe, and we won the battle."

We all glanced around the beach and then at each other. Everyone smiled. We won this fight, now I just had to restore the Olympians. I touched my hand to my chest removing my armor.

Kelly leaned her head on my shoulder and Alicia followed her lead and rested her head on my other shoulder too. I wrapped my arms around them both. I was happy this battle was over and that we were safe for the time being. Before I realized what was happening Hades reappeared behind the girls and ripped their unwilling souls from them. They both went limp in my arms.

"Nooo! You swore on the Styx not to harm Alicia," I shouted.

"Yes I did—I swore to not take nor harm a hair on her head," he mused. "As you can see I held my end of our deal—I never once mention her soul."

As he vanished into smoke clutching their screaming apparitions, that looked much like the real Kelly and Alicia, a spear penetrated the smoke, right where his head just was. Good job Chloe, but it's too late.

I dropped to the ground by their motionless corpses, and then I noticed they were still breathing. Hades did not kill them after all. I could hear Oogle say, "Body is still active, no last long without soul, separated from soul long body dies, only three days can wander."

I hung my head in silence. First my parents, then Grandpa and now this, it seemed like everyone I loved was in danger around me.

"I'm sorry Davis. They knew the risk, and they died honorably," Chloe said. "We must remember the bigger picture time is running out to save Olympus."

"They are not dead. It's my fault they are laying here fading away," I said. "I refuse to let them completely die, I'll save them we have three days."

"We need help, maybe Poseidon can help?" Leah said.

I had almost forgotten all about Poseidon and the prophecy. My heart ached. I was under no delusion. I betrayed Alicia during my trip with Kelly, and now she might die over loving me too much. And Kelly I know she had done me wrong. But at the same time, she never once really did anything all that bad, she tried to turn her back on Hades and look where that got her. If anyone should have died, it should have been me. I was the villain, the one playing with both of their emotions, because I was selfish and not wanting to choose one over the other, out of fear of losing the other or worse both of them.

TWENTY-THREE

I FETCH MY FATHERS TRIDENT

Down by the water, I saw Poseidon. There were nine other dolphins with him and two killer whales (I figured the Orcas were most likely Zeus and Ares). I could still make out Poseidon this round, I'm positive the Rod must have done more than its fair share with breaking the language barriers.

"I need you to shapeshift into a creature of the sea for me," he said.

I didn't feel like being the errand boy for the gods, I already did plenty. Now I need them to help me for a change.

"Look I know you need my help... but I also need yours," I said. "So I hope your open to negotiations."

Poseidon dove under the water and shot up into the air splashing down hard enough to get me soaked. I took it as a sign of him not negotiating very well. So, I turned and started walking away. I figured the heck with it, I'll figure out how to save the girls myself.

Chloe and Leah ran to my side. "What was that Davis?" Leah said. "No one refuses a god, especially Poseidon."

I shrugged my shoulders. "Well I just did," I said. "I asked for his help in exchange for mine, and he went all Flipper on me."

"Wait here, let me talk to him," Chloe said.

Chloe came back a few minutes later grinning ear to ear. "He agreed to help, but you're not going to like it very much."

"So spill, bad news first," I insisted.

"Poisoned is willing to support your mission but…" Chloe lowered her head. "He is assigning you two huntresses for your journey."

"Why is that bad news?"

"The huntress he chose—were Leah and me," she said swallowing hard. "The living doesn't regularly return from Hades realm."

"Sorry you got picked," I said. "but if I had to go to the Underworld, I'd rather do it with Leah and yourself than anyone else."

"Thanks, I think!" Chloe said flipping a long strand of hair behind her ear. "If we plan to survive we will have to use our wit more than brute force."

"I'm open to your suggestions… I need to get to the Underworld the girls are counting on me."

"Don't worry Davis," Chloe's shoulders heaved as she took a deep breath. "If anyone can save them—you can."

I shrugged. Like I was willing to risk it all to save the girls…but would it be possible, after all, Chloe made it clear that no one returns from the Underworld, so I had doubts that I'd be the exception. But I had to try, this much I was certain of.

Chloe and Leah walked back to the shoreline, and I followed them, this time Poseidon seemed in better spirits.

I locked eyes with Poseidon. "So, how do I shape shift… I never did it before."

"You can't!" Poseidon said. "Well, not naturally I mean. But since we are cursed any demigod, god, or goddess that steps into my domain and stays in the vicinity of me falls victim to this dreadful curse. But you are different, you were born to be stronger than this wretched curse. You will be able to reclaim your form of your own free will once you're a safe distance from me."

I walked into the surf waste deep beside Poseidon and placed my hand on his back. I knew beyond a doubt that he saved me at this point. His skin felt exactly like what I remembered after the crash.

"Thanks for saving me after the plane crash," I said. "I never got to thank you."

Poseidon nodded his head from side to side. "I'd never let a son of mine drown in my domain!" He said. "Besides your more useful if you're not trapped in the Underworld, though my brother Hades would have loved that."

"Thanks, I think!" I said straight-faced. "Will it be much longer before I transform?"

I could hear Oogle whispering in my mind, trying to guide me through the process of speeding up the transformation. I finally started to morph into a dolphin. I could hear the bones in my body snapping and moving into position, it felt painfully uncomfortable. The worst part was my head; it was seriously like the worse migraine headache you could ever imagine times a thousand. My skull literally pulled apart and reassembled itself, I could see my nose elongate right before my eyes... sort of like how Pinocchio's nose grew when he told a lie.

"Follow me, quickly," Poseidon said. "We must hurry."

I looked back at Chloe and Leah, they didn't join us. So I slapped my tailfin up and down a few times saying goodbye and then I dived in a fancy porpoise kind of arcing dive, and followed Poseidon and the other Olympians out to the sea.

It was a strange world under the sea, glimpsing it from the eyes of a sea mammal was surreal. The vibrant coral reefs and schools of fish were breathtaking. Not to mention the rays of beaming sunlight cutting deep into the dark abyss far below me. A memory washed over me of my mom telling me as a child, about how the sun's rays protruding though the clouds were really escalators to heaven.

Swimming forward, there was little time to adjust, lucky for me maneuvering my new body and holding my breath extended periods of time felt pretty natural. The Olympians surfaced for some air, and I followed, expelling air from my blowhole upon breaking the surface (it kind of felt like sneezing, minus it coming out the top of my head).

Poseidon locked eyes with me, his permanent smile turned somewhat serious as he said, "I don't have my usual powers, this curse forced us, gods, to surrender our power. Without my abilities, the human's are doomed as is all of Olympus along with me."

"How can I help?"

"You must locate the pantheon inside of Olympus, go to Zeus's throne and activate his Thunderbolt, then place it in the central hearth to get the ship fully functional," he grinned in deep thought. "Once the ship is live it will handle the rest."

"How will I know when it's live?"

"Trust me you will know!" Poseidon said. "We are almost to the resting spot, of Mount Olympus. You have one thing I don't, the power to take back your original form. You need to pass a hand scan to access Olympus, and well I only have flippers--!"

"How would my hand pass the scan I never been to Olympus?"

"The scanning part is not all that important my boy. Your blood is the key. You see it takes only a droplet of your blood to test, but it requires a hand to trigger the screening process, and if you pass as Olympian you're granted access," Poseidon said.

"Sounds simple enough, but what if you don't pass?"

"You're incinerated, it's quick and painless." He explained. "Nothing to concern yourself with, child."

Easy for him to say, it's not like he was the one going out on a limb to risk his life for strangers. They disappeared back into the sea, and I took in a few deep breaths before submerging back beneath the surface. Oogle's voice filled my mind, this was oddly starting to feel normal the longer we were connected, but I kind of missed seeing him. "master doing good, Oogle knew you would set things right."

There was little doubt Oogle could read my mind, so I refrained from responding. We came to a halt. "Over there," said one of the Orcas.

Poseidon shifted directions, and my eyes were drawn to Mount Olympus for the first time. The feeling of astonishment was immense, there was no mountain at all. Instead, I was facing what appeared to be an enormous metallic structure; before I had time to think for myself, Oogle chimed in, "Not Mountain, this mother ship, and home on Earth for Olympians like you." It was huge, even bigger than the Kraken, so it made sense why they called it Mount Olympus.

Down at the sea floor, in front of the massive craft, an opening appeared, and I followed Poseidon inside. He showed me the hand scan panel, now I just had to figure out how to go human again. After Poseidon and the other Olympians had gotten a safe distance away, I started concentrating on how I remembered myself in a mirror. After several minutes I felt the familiar bone breaking sensation overtake me once more. I was reeling in pain as my body shifted back to its natural form., leaving my lungs begging for oxygen. The sensation of being air deprived made me instinctively want to rush toward the surface, but it was out of reach (being incinerated and drowning both seemed like horrible fates). As the first set of honeycomb doors bubbled shut, I saw Poseidon on the other side, and he appeared to be wallowing in a dolphin sort of way. I held out my hand, every fiber of my body willed me to gasp for air, but I resisted. He took notice instantly like I was feeding him a fish. He did not swim to my rescue as I had hoped, so I willed my mind to calm down, I swam over to the next set of doors and pressed my hand on the scanner. It glowed a dull red and then I felt a slight prick on the palm of my hand. The red light became green, and the doorway bubbled and started to open, the sound reminded me of gears grinding together. Soon as there was enough room to squeeze in, I swam inside. The doors slammed shut behind me, and the water began to drain rapidly. There was a suction sound, almost like the sound that a bathtub makes when you pull the plug. In just seconds the water level dropped below my mouth. It couldn't have happened at a better time I was really feeling lightheaded from the lack of oxygen. I took in a deep breath filling my lungs. It felt amazing being able to breathe again. I'd never even give any thought to breathing air, but this I appreciated.

A strange sensation washed over my entire body, it almost felt like my soul was being torn out. Crouching down to my knees I braced my hands on the floor holding myself up. Then the weird sensation passed.

"Ouch, what was that," I said.

"Davis body went into temporary shock from changing so rapidly."

"That was a bit weird for my liking!" I said. "Now how the heck do I find this Thunderbolt, there must be dozens if not hundreds of rooms in this massive ship."

Glancing around the entrance I noticed a sliding honeycomb doorway up ahead, I pressed my hand into the scanner, and this time it didn't prick me. Maybe my fingerprints were now saved in the ship's memory bank. The doorway ground open, inside was a massive circular room, with many consecutive levels. It reminded me almost like giant metal donuts stacked thousands of feet tall. When I walked to the center and looked down, the levels went down like an endless pit. The bottom was pitch black, and I realized that what I saw outside was only half the ship; the rest was burrowed deep into the sea floor. After a bit of exploring the endless dimly lit corridors, I found myself alone in a maze of constructed metal and out of nowhere memories of the plane wreck hit me like a ton of bricks and then another flash washed over me of Kelly and Alicia's souls being reaped. After I had snapped out of the blanket of bad memories, I felt horrible. Part of me blamed myself for all of this. I know it was not really my fault… but it just felt like I was bad luck to be around and if I never existed, none of this would have ever happened.

My negative mindset had a firm grip on me. Maybe I was doomed before I ever had a chance. I pushed aside my feelings and focused on finishing this task. I had to see it through, I knew in my heart that the girls were counting on me to save them. Because I know for a fact if I were in their position, I'd be expecting them to rescue me.

"There has to be an easier way to navigate in here," I said. "Even a god would get lost in this labyrinth of metal."

"Oogle can boot up ships main power system and jack into mainframe computer and get coordinates of Poseidon's chambers."

"Why didn't you suggest that earlier?" I said. "Don't you think that be useful information for me to know?"

"Sorry master," Oogle said. "Sometimes Oogle forget that you don't understand all my functions."

"Well, it's not like you came with an owner's manual," I snapped.

Oogle barked out directions. "Go straight one-hundred feet, then make sharp left to stairwell." Oogle made several odd clicking sounds. "At end of stairway open fourth door on left."

The corridors felt endless, as I made twists and turns in different directions. I was starting to get played out, there was little doubt in my mind that you could easily get lost inside of Olympus, it was a cold, dark and endless maze.

Could be worse be worse, I told myself. I could be being hunted by some ancient monster.

After an hour or so Oogle said, "Destination in fifty yards."

"I hope they have a refreshment stand I'm thirsty!"

"Oogle no see food stands on map."

"Never mind Oogle," I said. "I hope the inner chamber is a bit more inviting than this."

The inside of Olympus did not resemble a spacecraft; it looked nothing like the endless corridor's I just left. It was like everything good in the world, condensed into a single area, like what Heaven must look like. The architecture was superior to even the best-constructed buildings on Earth. There were giant golden and marble statues, large gold and copper-trimmed skyscrapers. Breathe taking gardens, sporting flowers and fruits with sweet smelling aromas that I can't even begin to describe. My favorite was the pools with fountains, they had one every twenty or so feet, and there was literally water everywhere. But the strangest part of all was the blue skies above and the eerily familiar looking sun. They must have been artificial, yet they seemed so real.

Creatures that I thought only to be myth ran shops and played musical instruments, such as satyrs and centaurs. The pools teemed with fluorescent colored fish that changed color as they swam, making the water look like a living rainbow.

Oogle guided me to the pantheon of the Gods, on the way a small centaur ran out onto the street in front of me, it was just a kid chasing his ball. He glanced up at me than done a one-eighty running back toward his parents. Bleating out nonsense that I could not understand. I walked for a good fifteen minutes down the path from where we entered, as I got closer to the pantheon I had to stop for a moment to take in all of the detail. Like the size of this thing, it looked like a white marble coliseum, etched with history, showing events that occurred over the eons. Such as ancient battles, and moments of architectural triumph such as the construction of the Great Pyramid of Giza. All of mankind's greatest accomplishments were engraved for the gods to observe on these walls.

Once inside the Pantheon I saw twelve giant thrones, each sat about ten feet off of the ground. They had Greek symbols etched into their tops which I assumed were unique to each god. But the design of each throne was very unique like they were customized for their owner. Like I recognized Poseidon's throne right away, the back had fishnets etched into it, and seashells embodied the arms, the biggest giveaway was his bronze colored three-pronged trident, with barbs leaning against it. I was only supposed to locate Zeus's Thunderbolt and place it inside the central hearth, but seriously who could resist picking up Poseidon's trident. He was supposedly my birth father, so I figured why not.

As soon as it touched my hand, I could feel its power pulsing throughout my body. A bright green hue appeared around the top of the spear.

"Master have trident of sea god, you have some of his power, what is your plan?"

"No plan Oogle," I thrust the spear forward. "I just couldn't resist picking this bad boy up… like how cool is this."

"Oogle not understand definition of 'cool' temperature is a steady 86 degrees."

"Never mind!" I placed the trident back down in its resting spot. "So Zeus's chamber must have his Thunderbolt… but which one is it."

I walked around the room, one throne had wild animals and moon phase symbols, the one beside it had images of the sun and a chariot. Then I stopped in my tracks when I saw a throne with a lightning bolt on the armrest. I walked up to it, studying the detail, I had no doubt this belonged to Zeus. But where was the Thunderbolt, it was not here. I searched all around it, but there was nothing. Not thinking I rested my hand on the armrest and it began to glow. When I looked up at my hand lightening was weaving between my fingers. Quickly I pulled myself up on to the throne, and before my eyes was Zeus's legendary Thunderbolt. I picked it up, and I could feel its immense power surge through my body. Unlike Poseidon's trident this thing made me nervous, like I was scared I'd blow myself to pieces or blast a hole into the side of the ship, and the ocean would burst in on us.

I jumped down onto the floor and walked over to the hearth clumsily. I felt like I had two left feet. I saw an empty cylindrical spot in the center of the hearth that looked like it was bored out perfectly to fit Zeus's bolt. So I lined them up and slowly pushed the Thunderbolt into the slot. It was snug at first, I pushed down with all my weight, and it wouldn't budge. Then all of a sudden it slammed down like a super magnet took hold of it. The whole ship began to vibrate, whirring sounds echoed throughout the pantheon. Then the ship rumbled, and it felt like it was pushing me toward the floor, the sheer force was intense, I struggled against it. Then it stopped.

"I guess that's what Poseidon meant by I'll know if it works."

The hearth came alive, and blue flames grew, flickering and licking at the air around the hearth. One by one the Olympian gods emerged, walking out of the fire. As they walked from the flames, they were shimmers of bright light shimmering in and out of existence until the final process of their metamorphosis. They were left in the nude and like an illusionist, clothes magically materialized, covering their flesh. Hundreds walked through the portal, I suppose it was a mixture of gods, goddesses, and demigods, each of them took in deep breaths and stretched a bunch before leaving the pantheon. After a while only twelve remained, I recognized a few of them such as Zeus and Artemis.

Poseidon was the last one through the flames. At first, he shimmered in and out of existence like the others, then he reclaimed his resplendent godly form, he was at least eight feet tall and beefy in a muscular sort of way. He reached out his hand in a thankful gesture, and I took his hand. In a flash of blinding light, the twelve major gods and I, we were back on the beach.

I looked over at the gods, I'd be lying if I said I didn't feel anything. There was a great sense of accomplishment. I felt like I was bursting with joy as I observed the gods and goddesses enjoying the simple pleasure of having their curse lifted.

"See, master bring peace and make all right," Oogle said. "This is dawn of new age, Davis heroic actions will be shared through the years, as the savior of the gods."

The Olympians had been restored. They were back to their former selves. Everyone was wiggling their fingers and toes, mucking up sand on their feet. They all looked so joyful, I suppose being a creature of the sea for that long would make anyone miss his or her limbs.

"You did a good kiddo," Poseidon patted me on the back. His flowing black hair was held back by a golden circlet, he had a long black beard, and when I looked into his eyes, they shifted from green to blue, like how a mood ring shifts colors when your mood changes. He was ripped; I bet he weighed like five hundred pounds from all his muscle. His skin was a bronze tan like he spent all of his time out in the sun.

"Thanks," I said.

Poseidon brightened. "Come with me, kiddo, let me introduce you to Zeus."

Zeus seemed less than gracious to see me, he looked just as I expected, a large beefy man that must have worn an XXXL T-shirt, he would have made an NFL lineman look scrawny. However he did look rather young in appearance, minus the long snow-white beard and hair.

Zeus announced, "Nice job saving my brother here and the rest of us," He chuckled. "After all, you do share my blood—so victory is to be expected."

"Thanks, I guess," I stammered.

Zeus had some advice for me. "You have some ways to go before I consider you a son of mine. That title is earned by giving tribute through your actions, in my name. A good starting point would be delivering this message for me."

"What message," I asked. "Who do I give it to?"

"If you survive the Underworld and see my brother, tell him that his King has informed you that a storm is blowing his way and a debt payable only in blood is due from his followers the Anunnaki, in just thirty days' time!" Zeus said his eyes flickering with electricity. "Tell him to ready a sacrifice of a single member for each family, as tribute for the sins of their ancestors! And let it be known throughout the lands, that Olympus has been restored to all of its glory."

I agreed to deliver the message but had no intentions of letting a bunch of Kelly's people die in the name of Zeus. This monstrosity had to be stopped. But I had bigger fish to fry; Hades was going to meet the tip of my sword very soon. I was dead set on fighting my way through the Underworld to bring Kelly and Alicia back, no matter the cost.

Before I could set out to rescue the girls, Poseidon insisted on introducing me to another being, whom I instantly knew must be Aphrodite. She was as beautiful as legend says, with long locks of blond hair and intense blue eyes. She wore a golden, laurel tiara, and her hair draped over her shoulders, revealing dangling emerald earrings. She wore a white dress made of fine silk that covered her long slender frame, down to just above her knees, like a short dress and in her right hand she held a gorgeous jeweled staff, worthy of a goddess.

A bit awed I ask, "Are you, Aphrodite?"

"Yes I am, your love for Alicia and Kelly really touched me. I've not sensed love this strong in many ages." She blushed. "you and Kelly have a connection unlike anything I've ever sensed, I'm jealous of the way you feel for her."

"Jealous?" I asked. "But we just met!"

"I'm not jealous of thee, in that way," she said. "I'm jealous of such affection, I am the goddess of love, and no man nor woman has ever felt this strongly toward me, not even with a little coaxing."

"I'm sorry to hear of your misfortune," I said. "Is there anything I can help you with other than loving you in that manner."

Aphrodite burst out loud, giggling to herself. "I'm amused that you think thy would love thee," She said. "I, however, do owe thee a debt of gratitude and will tell you that Kelly is your soulmate."

"Kelly... my soulmate!"

Aphrodite laced her fingers together, looking more serious. "Love is all I know Davis. What you and her share is what I call star-crossed," she said. "Two souls of the opposite nature drawn to one another like you were molded of the same clay."

"I appreciate your gift... I'll keep that in mind," I said. "But if I don't rescue her soon, I think that will be a deal breaker on the whole star-crossed thing."

I said bye to Poseidon and Aphrodite and headed over to meet up with Chloe and Leah. They were chatting with Artemis about some beast they were hunting before she got cursed, from what I overheard.

Hermes walked over before I interrupted their conversation. He said, "You have something that needs to be delivered, son, a spoil of battle that you possess." He was

just as tall as Poseidon and Zeus, but he was younger looking and clean shaved, he had a winged cap covering most of
his sandy blond hair and was more of an athletic build, not
nearly as beefy. I didn't follow at first, and then I remembered taking the necklace from Melinda.

"Oh, you mean this?" I said, reaching my hand into my
pocket to fetch the necklace.

I dangled the necklace by its silver chain, the pendant
was gold, the back half looked like a scallop shell, and the
front was encrusted with lots of beautiful blue beryls and
aquamarine gems. In the center was a detailed image of
a girl, standing on a mat with bees, sparrows, and a swan.

Hermes' blue eyes twinkled as I handed him the necklace. "This belongs to Athena, and it was a gift from her
father Zeus at her birth. I'm pleased to be able to return
this to her, so glad that I am going to personally lead you to
Lake Acheron, where you can seek out Charon for passage
into the Underworld."

"Let me get the huntress, I'm ready to save the girls."

I saw Poseidon wrapping Alicia and Kelly in a seaweed
colored cloth, so I walked over to him, to see what was up.

"What are you doing?" I asked.

"I'm taking them back to Olympus to watch over
them," he explained. "Be safe in the Underworld, and don't
forget who you truly are."

The thought of Poseidon watching over the girls brought me peace of mind. I thanked him for watching over them, and said goodbye.

I caught up with Chloe and Leah and we joined Artemis, the goddess whistled, and her stags came zipping up the beach. Chloe and Leah prepared the chariot. Artemis turned around and waved her hand motioning for me to join her, so I climbed on.

"T seemeth thou art coming to t'rms with thy h'ritage Davis, I nev'r hadst any doubteth in thee saving Olympus," she said. "Thee remindeth me much of mine own cousins Perseus and Hercules."

I smiled. "Thanks."

Hearing those words made my cheeks warm. But I shrugged it off, after all, I'm sure it takes time to learn how to be a god anyway, that's probably why they are immortal.

In the lead, Hermes lazily zipped through the air using his winged shoes as transportation and Chloe and Leah ran with leaping strides over the rugged terrain effortlessly behind him, like they were part cheetah.

"Thou art a true h'ro Davis," Artemis admitted. "Thy journey thus far hast been fraught with dang'r and many obstacles to ov'rcome."

She continued, "Yet thee ov'rcame those folk challenges. I can't waiteth f'r thee to meeteth Chiron, that gent is a most wondrous teachest'r and hast did turn many of demigods into legends."

"Wasn't Chiron the centaur that trained Achilles?" I asked.

"Thou art c'rrect," she laughed. "I knoweth thy fath'rs beest joyous. Thee hath broken Hade's curse with five days to spareth."

I stood in the middle of the chariot, listening to the hoof-beats of the stags as they galloped full speed ahead. We didn't have a map showing us where the Underworld's entrance lies, but I guess we did have something better— Hermes was like divine GPS, leading us straight to Charon. I suppose it was his business to know the locations of all the gods, being their messenger and all. A strange deja vu like feeling washed over me, it's ice-cold grip coiled me like a serpent before it slithered down my spine. I couldn't shake the feeling that this was a one-way trip to the afterlife and I wasn't going to be lucky enough to cheat death this time.

TWENTY-FOUR

I PLAY SOUL CHESS
WITH MY UNCLE

After a while, we found ourselves deep inside a dark and foreboding forest. Where two of Artemis's Huntress caught up with us, apparently they were tracking an ancient monster, unlike anything they ever saw before.

One of the huntresses remarked, "The big brave man isn't afraid. Is he?"

I looked deep into her smoky gray eyes, she was younger in appearance, my best guess about thirteen, but I knew she was probably hundreds, if not thousands of years old. She had a wary look on her face, a face framed in tribal tattoos and she had long, straight copper brown hair that flowed out beneath a brown hooded cloak. Her bangs hung to just above her eyes.

"I'm heading to the Underworld, to jab my sword into Hades, so I think I can handle a forest monster."

Since she didn't answer me, I figured she was out of comebacks or just plain shocked that I was stupid enough to pick a fight with Hades. When we emerged from the forest to face an impassable mountain range, the other Huntress said, "Oh I hope the big man's strength holds out. Those mountains are so high."

Glimpsing over at her, she smirked. She looked about sixteen years old, with a tattered brown tunic and brown hooded cloak, which covered her slender frame. She had jet black hair and eyes as dark as midnight, there was little doubt about her real age, her eyes seemed to reflect the depths of eternity. I didn't say anything out loud, but I was thinking how those mountains looked like a walk in the park compared to Olympus Mons, back on Mars.

Artemis must have noticed that her huntresses were getting to me and she offered some kind words. "Don't mind mine own Huntress, those girls has't been besting men for ages. It's not arrogance it's parteth of their character by now."

I shrugged.

"I'm just used to Chloe and Leah," I said. "I suppose the other Huntress are not as well mannered."

Artemis glanced at me, "Yond is wherefore I pick'd thy as mine own lieutenants."

The search continued over mountains and forest and plains. Time dragged on. I tried to keep up my strength in order not to be ridiculed by the huntresses. However, Artemis continually encouraged me throughout the search.

Eventually, a few days later we emerged from a glade to find the Acheron River. Hermes swooped in, and I tried my best to hold back my laughter. He just looked so funny, with his winged cap and boots flapping, a very peculiar look for a grown man.

Hermes said, "This is as far as I go. Follow the river southwest, to Lake Acheron. You will find passage to the Underworld there from Charon as promised."

"Thanks for the help," I said.

"It was the least I could do, after all you returned a family heirloom."

Hermes pulled out a foot-long golden cylinder, it dimly glowed, and two golden serpent's inner twinned with one another, locking together to form a full-length staff. At its top two serpent heads came alive, flickering their tongues.

He spoke to them, "Now, now no fighting!" He said. "I know it's been a long time since you saw one another... but remember your promise."

A loud boom of thunder came out of nowhere as we stood below a beautiful blue sky. One of the serpent heads lashed out in confusion nearly biting Hermes.

"Calm yourself, or I swear—," Hermes said. "Well was nice traveling with you all, but the boss man needs me back on Olympus—official business—can't wait!"

"Yes, boss I'm on my way," he said, as he vanished into fragments of colored particles.

I looked over and saw Chloe and Leah talking, as I got closer their conversation became apparent.

"Alicia is such a brave maiden we could ask her spirit to join us before her link fades to her body. With Artemis's blessing she would be saved," Chloe suggested. "I mean she would be young and beautiful forever, surely that would be better than an unjust death."

"That's not going to happen, we are doing this my way!" I said abruptly.

They both seemed startled and then Artemis leaned in and whispered something in Chloe's ear, then walked away. It made me a bit paranoid thinking about Alicia being made a huntress. The thought of losing her to a bunch of man haters made me nauseous. I valued our relationship together and was no way letting her join them, at least not easily.

The walk along the Acheron River was too silent; the entire stretch we walked seemed

desolate. There was no birds, insects, or plant life anywhere, the skeletal remains of large fish littered the river bank. A few times I swore something was following us in the water, but I suppose it was just my imagination.

We soon found ourselves at the Acherusian Lake.

Artemis said, "We has't hath reached our destination, but th're is nay way we can passeth into the Underworld in the same figure like this. We must useth a guise to appeareth as shades."

Artemis waved her hand, and a human skeleton appeared at our feet. I stepped back a bit. I had no idea what she was up to, but dead people creep me out.

"So… what is the plan?" I asked.

"I wilt useth a conjuring spelleth to fake our deaths."

I watch Artemis and her four huntresses go to work etching strange runes into the bones. Then all five of them joined hands and fell into a chant. They were chanting in an ancient Greek dialect which made little sense to me. Something about bone and flesh becoming one, other than that I got nothing. Once the ritual was finished the skeletal remains burst into blue flame, the heat was intense and concentrated where the symbols were etched. The bones smoldered and cracked, from the extreme heat as they became paste white, and turned to ash. Her huntress scooped up the ash and started to rub it over their faces, and then down their necks and arms.

"Davis, you must cover yourself as thy," Chloe said, as she rubbed her legs in ash. "Tis not so bad."

I scooped up a handful of the ash, it had bone fragments littered through it, some were thick chunks. I felt sick rubbing some dead person's ashes over myself, but if this was the cost to save the girls… then so be it. We were all covered in the enchanted ash of the dead John Doe, and no I had no desire to ask who they were, as I didn't need that image haunting me. Artemis laid her hand on my shoulder and said a silent blessing.

"I've did bless thee with the gift of true sight Davis," Artemis said pursing her lips. "Don't freak out at which hour thee turneth 'round, thy now seeth shades, the restless spirits of those who is't hath passed on."

She was not kidding! Like seriously we were surrounded it looked like Woodstock, but with spirits instead of living people. Some of the spirits looked like ordinary everyday people, while others looked from different eras in time, and some... well, let's just say, if you had a weak stomach I'd steer clear of them. They were disfigured like they died violent deaths. This one girl's head was literally dangling over her shoulder, and the inside of her throat was visible... too bad the blessing didn't censor some of the most gruesome spirits.

While I was adjusting to being around all these apparitions, Artemis handed me three more gold coins.

"Addeth these golden drachmas, to the two I gaveth thee," She said. "'Twill payeth f'r our passage with Charon."

"Thanks," I said.

It felt like I was in costume for a Halloween party like I kept accidently smearing my makeup, err I mean bone dust. You know what I'm saying. The one time I rubbed some in my eye, and if that was not bad enough I licked my lips since they felt dry... well, you can guess how that turned out. I was freaking out bad, spitting like a rabid camel. I swear some of the nearby shades didn't know what to think of me, I was seriously disturbing the dead!

Waiting on Charon's Ferry to pick us up felt like an eternity. The water looked black, and Artemis warned that five rivers flow through the Underworld, I knew one was the Styx, I remembered the story of Achilles' mom dipping him in the river by his heel and making him nearly invincible. Looking around at all the restless souls, I spotted one that appeared solid. Walking closer, I noticed it was not a soul at all. He looked very familiar. "Hephaestus?" I blurted.

Hephaestus, a muscular man, sported long black hair and a large bushy beard; he limped forward with the aid of a stick. As he got closer, I could see a body and face with a lacework of scars. You could tell that he did a lot of work with a fiery hot forge.

"Hello, lad, just stopping by to pay my thanks is all. Thought you might find one of my automatons to be of use on your journey," He said reaching around inside his tool belt. "My brother is not all that jolly, probably from a lack of real company. I'm sure being around souls all day would drive anyone crazy, even a god," he chuckled. "So, I'm sure ya will need all the help ya can get."

He handed me a small bronze sphere with a winding key. I never owned an automaton before—so I seriously had no idea what it did.

"Thanks for the gift, I'm sure I will find some use for it," I picked it up studying it carefully. "What does this key do?"

Whatever ya do—don't touch da key!" He insisted. "Well, lad, I won't be holding ya up, if ya find yourself in danger—then ya can touch it. Just wind it three times and toss it at whatever be bugging ya."

I nodded. "Thanks for the automaton!"

"I suppose ya deserve a proper welcome, so welcome to the family lad," he said heaving his shoulders. "We be a dysfunctional bunch, but when push comes to shove, we always got each other's backs."

I looked at the big guy, he looked rough on the exterior, but there was little doubt he had the biggest heart of all of the Olympians. I reached in and gave him a big bear hug.

"Now, now don't be going all emotional on me," he blushed, pushing me away. "I best be heading back to my forge on Mount Aetna."

Then he vanished into a cloud of thick black smoke, I inhaled some of and started to have a coughing fit, it really irritated my throat. It felt like I breathed in the powdered glass that's the best way I can describe what I felt.

I reached into my pocket, to stash away the miniature automaton Hephaestus gave me. I had no idea what it did, but I had to trust that it would help. After all, he said if I found myself in trouble that all I had to do was turn the winding mechanism three times and toss it. It seemed simple enough.

In the distance, I could see a faint flicker of light. After a while, it was visibly Charon on a small wooden skiff. A rusty old oil lamp hung several feet above the boat illuminating the inky waters, as the small skiff pulled to shore. Charon was not what I expected. He was a frail old man, with a crooked nose, milky white eyes and a long bushy white beard. Wearing a tattered brown cloak with a hood and holding a long pole partially submerged in the water. I was both nervous and excited for his arrival after waiting hours. There were thousands of troubled souls wanting passage. I heard a young boy and girl talking, they both sounded really excited, their one-hundred-year wait was up, and they could now enter the Underworld without the required fee. They looked like brother and sister, I heard the little girl no older than five say, "Think we'll make Elysium brother?"

"I'm not sure sis. But we are both just kids, so we should have a good chance," he said.

The flames of the lamp flickered on the shore and reflected in the dark water. I could feel a lump in my stomach; was I nuts? Why was I even doing this? I shook off the doubt, I knew deep in my heart that Kelly would do the same for me. There was no way I was going to be a coward and back away now.

"Those with payment for passage will be boarded first and if there is any room only those who waited one hundred years or longer shall be permitted passage to the Underworld. We work on a first to arrive first to exit basis so no butting in line," Charon explained.

Artemis nudged me. "I have payment for passage, for my friends and myself, sir--."

"Very well, dead-lings, step forward," his eyes lingered on my hands scanning for coins. "Silver and gold are my preference. hat payment did you bring, come on, don't be shy--show me!"

I walked to the shoreline and Chloe, and Leah stayed within touching distance of me. Artemis and her other two Huntress kept to our backs.

"Hmm, let's see…Five of you… Let's say two obolus per head, so ten total in case you forgot how to count," Charon snapped.

"All I got is this," I announced. I reached into my pocket and revealed five golden drachmas. Charon studied them as I dropped them one by one into my hand, clanking the cold metal coins together.

"Gold drachmas, why I haven't seen them in centuries. Where did you get them?" he insisted.

"From me!" boomed Artemis.

"Oh Lady Artemis, I barely recognized you under your guise of a dead one. Rules are rules, my dear; I can only offer passage to souls. Well unless you sweeten the deal, say ten drachmas, and I turn a blind eye?"

"Thee at each moment been a greedy one!" She muttered, fishing five more coins from a pouch. "Thee nev'r did see us."

We boarded the skiff after Artemis paid our dues. Charon looked overly excited. I had no idea what an old man would want so much gold for. His clothing looked worn and ragged, I saw better dressed homeless people in Baltimore when I visited the aquarium in fifth grade. Anyway, that was not my concern, I was seeking Kelly and Alicia's souls and demanding them to be returned to their bodies. I remembered back on the beach, how Poseidon wrapped them in a seaweed colored silk wrap, I knew their bodies were safe in his care. I just needed to get their souls back.

"There will be no passage for anyone else today, I'll be back tomorrow," Charon shouted.

"Wait, there are two souls I want passage for or the deal is off for the ten drachmas!" I said.

"Davis, what are you doing?" Chloe chided.

I whispered to Chloe, "I have this under control. He is greedy but fair if he's anything like the guy in the stories I've read about."

"Very well then, not like I'm going to give these back. Pick quickly because we leave in sixty seconds," he exclaimed.

I pointed to the young boy and girl, and in a flash, they were gone and on the skiff with us.

The ferry ride lasted awhile. Charon made many puns about the undead, mocking them. He seemed shallow and a tad cruel. We were heading inside the mouth of a cave, silhouettes of stalactites adorned its roof. Artemis warned us that Cerberus would be guarding the gates of the Underworld and that we would have to make it past him.

The little boy apparition kept staring at me, his tiny transparent frame fading to the point of being nearly invisible when the skiff would make a turn. Finally, I broke the ice. "Hi, I'm Davis, what's your name?"

"I'm Charles, and this is my sister Isabella. Thanks for helping us get a ride," he brightened. "It used to be really scary for us, being around so many spirits. But after a couple decades, it becomes like home."

The skiff slowed to a halt, Charon reached our destination. His boney hands clung to his submerged pole as he steadied the skiff for us to exit.

"Now be gone with ye," Charon laughed, shuffling the drachmas in his free hand. "This was a one-way trip--no one leaves the Underworld."

Charon chuckled to himself in a shrill voice.

Once ashore we faced a dark stone tunnel, there was just enough dirt floor to hold our party, I looked back at Charon his long, yellow teeth were visible under his lantern, he looked ecstatic he skipped about on his skiff doing a jig.

"Good luck with the hellhound, I'm sure I'll be seeing some of you again real soon," Charon said, still chuckling to himself.

I looked at Chloe, "What did he mean by hellhound?" I asked.

Chloe frowned, "Cerberus guards the entrance to the Underworld, no living may enter."

"Oh," I stammered.

We were literally stuck on a fifteen-foot-long peninsula, as there was an endless river behind us and to either side were rock walls. There was no other direction to go but forward and we came too far to go back now. I was feeling a bit claustrophobic, so I thought to myself, "Oogle you will be with me right?"

"Oogle always with master," he paused. "Master must trust in self—embrace greatness inside. No need Oogle all time."

After that Oogle had gone silent mode, I tried to reach him a few more times but got nothing. I hated when he did this, especially since he was always invisible now.

The whole feeling of this environment oozed with fear and had me on edge. What Chloe told me reminded me of a movie I watched where Hercules battled Cerberus. So, I was aware that his job was to sniff out any living thing that tried to sneak into the Underworld. In the movie, he was not bothered by the shades or souls as they passed by unnoticed, either Cerberus was unable to sense them, or he was just so used to them that they were like background.

After feeling our way through the darkness of the caves entrance, we soon came to a dimly light tunnel which merged into a congested line of spirits. After making our way down a mile or more of twisting stone corridors that smelled of putrid, rotting flesh we got our first glimpse at Cerberus. He was a massive, immovable three-headed dog, with thick black fur and kind of looked like a black wolf minus having a serpent for its tail. He reminded me of a science experiment that went horribly wrong, but I guess a three-headed dog the size of an elephant was not all that strange considering the location. Cerberus blocked our path, we needed to find a way through the giant stone archway just twenty yards ahead, but his body completely filled the entrance, which seemed to be the only way into the Underworld.

Taking the lead, I cautiously approached him, doing my best impersonation of being a spirit. At first, he was uncertain of me, he sniffed several times with each massive head, and drool poured down my face, as I stood motion-less, trying not to breathe. My mind raced—what if his drool washes off the ash. Finally, he decided to move on--his serpent tail coiled back stopping just inches from my face its tongue flickering in front of my eyes. I guess his front half needed a second opinion. Trying my best not to look into the serpent's large slitted, yellow eyes which were hypnotizing, made me flash back to the Chimera at Grandpa's ranch. I snapped out of my trance and saw Cerberus sniffing Chloe, my stomach turned at the thought of his massive heads turning her into a disposable chew toy. I was happy to see her keeping calm, I was expecting her to freak when it licked her forehead, especially when strands of drool started rolling down her face. After Cerberus was satisfied Chloe was dead, he moved on sniffing the rest of our group one by one, then he ran off checking out the other shades as our group passed into the Underworld undetected.

Once through the gate, there was a gray stone path that paved the way, with hundreds of spirits lining it shoulder to shoulder, uniformly moving in one direction, forward. We followed the line of spirits until the path split; the left path led to an ancient looking pavilion.

We took the other path leading right, which led to the Fields of Asphodel, Hades Palace and the Pits of Tartarus. Inside the Fields of Asphodel.

Artemis whispered to us, "Yond is the Pavilion of Judgment wh're the three judges, Alakos, Akos, Monos and Rhadamanthys det'rmine thy lodging in the Underworld. Some shall wend to the Elysian Fields or the Blessed Isles, oth'rs to the Fields of Asphodel and many shalt beest did punish in the Fields of Punishment the po'r choices those gents madeth in life f'r."

The subterranean domain was void of sunlight, and it was cold; patches of mist lingered over a lot of the land.

Everything was ashen gray, even the fields of wheat; the area was lined with groaning, transparent apparitions that blended in with the scenery when looking straight on at them but appeared solid out of your peripherals. Also, dead looking black trees called poplars were spread out in small clumps, I'm not sure what a poplar tree is exactly, but that's what Artemis called them. Cautiously, I walked past the spirits anticipating them to grab me or something, but none of them seemed to be alerted to our presence, and they were completely undisturbed. It looked as though they were left without memory or purpose, I could not help but think how horrible it must be to spend eternity like them.

A tear rolled down my cheek as I thought of the possibility of my parents being amongst them, all I could do was hope that my parents were given a better fate than this. Artemis took the lead with her huntress. After hours of walking through endless rows of souls, we came to a stop.

Artemis whispered, "Behold above, those art the Fates flying toward Hades palace."

Looking up I saw three giant bat-like creatures gliding through the air a hundred feet below the ceiling, which looked black as obsidian and was so high above that it could easily pass for the sky, if not for all the giant stalactites dangling from it. I knew enough about the Fates that I could safely say I'd be perfectly fine never having the pleasure of meeting them in the flesh.

The souls seemed endless, imagine being at a football stadium with hundreds of thousands of people crowded together, now times that by the biggest number that pops into your head and you would still not even be close. After what felt like weeks of walking, my limbs and lungs burned to the point of collapsing, the ashen soil had turned to a sandy obsidian mixture, it felt solid like frozen ground and crunched under your feet. But when you touched it, it had the same feeling as touching fiberglass, an irritated poking sensation. Also, the souls were starting to thin out, until there were no more, just another crossroad with two paths, leaving us with the choice of which path to choose, which I took as a good omen. Since we already passed the Fields of Asphodel, I assumed the roads led to the other two destinations Artemis had mentioned earlier. Looking around I noticed on my left a faint glow; it looked heavenly in all of this darkness.

"Is that Elysium?" I said, pointing in the direction of the light source.

Artemis's lips curled in a faint smile, it was the first real emotion I saw from anyone since we had arrived in the land of the dead. After all it was no walk in the park, the stench of rotten eggs filled the air, which I recognized as sulfur and it burned deep down into my lungs with each breath. I had to literally force myself to inhale, I could see the pain in Leah's face but never once did I hear her complain. The best way I can describe the pain, it reminded me of breathing in powdered shards of glass, I could almost visualize them embedding into my throat and lungs.

Artemis said, "Nay, yond is the Isle of the Blessed, res'rv'd f'r the greatest of h'roes, the ones yond w're b'rn three times and three times madeth t to Elysium. Ev'rything is p'rfect th're, it's a wint'rless blissful w'rld, did fill with music and feasts."

"Do many people make it?" I asked.

"Well, t is not easy to receiveth th're." Artemis said. "But th're art oth'r ways to has't a wond'rful existence Davis, such as earning imm'rtality."

I was intrigued at the thought of being immortal, but I think any human would feel the same. It's like being offered all the positive things of being a vampire without being cursed to kill and drink blood.

"How does someone like me join the immortals club?" I asked.

Artemis stopped and turned her attention to me, "You're already doing a most wondrous job earning the fav'r of us gods," She crossed her arms. "As a demigod you earn favor by accomplishing good deeds, and honoring the elder gods."

I continued walking, like as much as I was enjoying the conversation this was not the best place to chit chat.

Looking around all I could see were ashen colored boulders and wheat that looked trampled by the billions of souls dwelling here. In the far distance, I could faintly make out what appeared to be an impenetrable, black rock wall that ran the length of the entire Underworld as far as the eye could see in any direction. When I mentioned it to Artemis, she said it was the Walls of Erebus (supposedly he was some primordial god, a son of Chaos if I got the gist of it). This place was really huge, but I guess it had to be to hold so many souls. I couldn't help but wonder if the souls in the field of Asphodel were stuck here forever or if they had a chance at reincarnation.

Leah said, "We are nearing Hades palace, it should be visible soon. Be warned, no matter how tempting, never eat any food of this place. Doing so will keep you here forever, it is a rule of the Fates. Whoever eats or drinks of the Underworld shall be doomed to dwell here for all of eternity."

"Eating makes man healthy, he must eat to have strength for his death with Hades," she giggled. "I mean to win fight."

The other Huntress joined in laughing at me until Artemis glared at them and they fell silent. Chloe and Leah just shook their heads at the other huntress like they were immature.

Seriously though who would want to eat anything from this dump, it reeked of death and decay. I tried to picture myself or anyone else for that matter finding any type of food here anything but appalling.

I soon forgot all about the idea of eating food in the Underworld, when the sound of tortured souls became unseeingly audible. Images rushed through my mind of what sort of punishments they must be enduring. Like an idiot, I had to peek, I couldn't just move along and mind my own business.

"I'll be right back, I have to see what's going on. See if I can help, I know if I were being tortured I'd want someone to help me," I pleaded.

"Davis, stand ho, we shall beest spott'd bef're we ev'r maketh t to the castle," Artemis warned.

I've never been one to listen, and I suppose a goddess made no significant difference in this regard. I have always been bullheaded. I ventured off on my own toward the echoed wails. There was a large tunnel up ahead, and souls were being dragged by ghoulish looking creatures that looked like horribly disfigured and partially decayed humans with chunks of flesh missing. There were also a few specters; they looked like scythe-wielding reapers in black hooded robes, with glowing red eyes glaring out of their dark, skeletal eye sockets. It didn't take me long to realize there was little I could do. Like what could I do to stop all the souls from being tormented? The only thing that was clear in my mind is that I'd never want to end up here. I heard one soul scream that he was judged wrong, he didn't belong in the Pits of Tartarus. At that moment I knew exactly what I was looking at, the entrance to the depths of the Underworld, a prison reserved for the most horrible of mortals and immortals.

A voice pierced my skull like nails on a chalkboard the voice boomed in my head. "Turn back, turn back while blood still flows through your veins!"

It took me a moment to register who's voice it was while I shook off the after effects. My ears were still ringing, the shrill voice felt like a drill burrowing into my skull. A horrible, horrible feeling.

"NOOOO!" I screamed. "I'M DONE RUNNING!"

Like it or not this was my life. I didn't want it really. But it seemed like I didn't have much choice in the matter. After all, I wanted to walk away after saving Grandpa but then I got myself in too deep with Artemis and the Oracle of Delphi. Now Alicia and Kelly's souls were on the table, and that pulled me all the way down this rabbit hole. I never openly admitted it, but deep down I knew that I accepted that a normal life was no longer in the cards for me. If I wanted, to be honest with myself, I suppose this way of life was growing on me. It felt more natural and less forced than before the accident. Like no matter how hard I fought it, things greater than me drew me to this point. I'm not saying my old life was horrible or anything like that deep down I still missed my parents and even living with Aunt Lisa. But getting to fight bad guys and feeling like I'm really doing something good, in a saving, the world kind of way just felt right. Also, it has its perks like having beautiful women by my side which always makes things more exciting.

Chloe and Leah caught me off guard. They crept up on me as I was digesting my thoughts and the warning Hades gave me. "Are thee OK?" Chloe huffed out of breath. "When I heard you scream I came fast as I could."

"It's Hades he warned me to turn back," I said. "Well more like threatened my life if I stayed."

"Don't worry Davis I got your back," Leah wiped her hair from her eyes. "You will save your friends."

The other two huntresses and Artemis walked up beside me. The huntress with copper hair said, "Did the man get lost, men always have such poor sense of direction. Come on, follow us, Artemis grows impatient."

The huntress with black hair rolled her eyes at me as she turned to follow her companion. Once back on the path, I noticed how foggy it had gotten, the patches of mist condensed into a cloud as thick as pea soup that blanketed most of the terrain, making for poor visibility up ahead.

I looked at Artemis, feeling a bit stupid for disobeying her and said, "I think Hades just spoke to me, he more or less told me to leave or die."

Artemis paced for a moment and began tapping her fingers on her arm and then said, "Davis, th're art much most wondrous'r f'rces at w'rk. Hades might has't ang'r f'r mine own broth'rs Zeus and Poseidon. But I feeleth something much m're ancient than Hades is pulling the strings," She admitted. "Something hast hath felt off from the beginning, and now yond mine own family is rest'red, I shouldst beest reliev'd but mine own huntresses has't been rep'rting ancient creatures roaming in the wild, creatures yond been did trap in Tartarus f'r millennia art now surfacing."

"Who would want to curse all of Olympus?" I asked.

"I has't mine own suspicions," she readjusted her quiver. "But what I am c'rtain of is yond we art all being mislead, as bigg'r f'rces art at playeth and we art just the distraction."

"That's just great—so, what you're saying is I'm in the middle of a divine peeing contest!" I balled my fists. "Look I get why I'm here and understand why I was needed to break the curse, but I refuse to be anyone's puppet!"

"Davis, we doth not controleth 'r manipulateth thee in any way. Ev'ry action you've done up until this pointeth hast been of thy owneth freewill, thee w're b'rn f'r this, this is thy destiny and thou art m'rely just walking the path yond hast already been pav'd," she said gripping my shoulder. "I am v'ry joyous with thee so far—lets wend saveth thy companions."

After digesting what she'd just said, I realized that she was right; no one had forced me to do anything, every choice I made was of my own choosing. Like even Hades killing my parents had no real power over my decision. Like after their deaths I could have chosen to accept what had happened and moved on with my life, but that was not me. That would have gone against my character, and I knew at this very moment that I lead myself down this path of my own free will.

Not saying another word, I walked blindly into the fog taking the lead. Leah sprinted up beside me and took my hand.

"It's OK to be scared, Davis. We can't control anything, the sooner we understand this--," she said, her voice becoming shaky. "When Artemis first found me and made me swear an oath to her, my life had ended—I had cut thy own wrists, I was done being abused by my stepmother."

"I—I am sorry—, "I said. "I didn't know."

I wrapped my arms around Leah. "I know you didn't have to share that with me—but thanks!"

"It has been a very long time, but them memories still haunt me," she said. "Being a huntress for Artemis allows me to help others like me, and gives me purpose."

Holding her made all of my fears temporarily melt away, just feeling her warmth felt reassuring in such a horrible place. Artemis walked past me taking the lead, a few moments later she stopped.

"I can senseth mine own broth'r his essence grows stout'r," she waved her hand back and forth. "Parteth from this lodging!"

With a final wave of her hand, the fog parted, clearing a path in all directions. At the end of the road was our destination, Hades palace.

The exterior wall of the castle looked like polished black marble with a huge, old bronze gate covered with a green patina. Inside the gate was a courtyard with a beautiful garden, filled with exotic colorful plants, bright, vibrant colored mushrooms and pomegranate trees that filled the air with a sweet mouth-watering aroma. The smell was tantalizing. I found myself mindlessly walking toward it when I caught sight of a young woman out the corner of my eye. She walked around humming a familiar lullaby. Every step she took, different types of flowers sprouted up all around her, like in fast forward going from a tiny sprout to full blossom in just seconds. And then they wilted into silhouettes of their previous selves succumbing to their own weight and becoming piles of ash on the ground.

The courtyard and garden were littered with gold and silver coins as well as diamonds the size my fist.

Artemis motioned to the young woman and said, "Persephone, art thee going to greeteth thy family."

Artemis and Persephone rushed toward one another and embraced in a long hug.

"How is Father?" Persephone asked. "I'm sure his temper is getting the better of him with the curse and all."

"That gent is fine, joyous to beest out of yond dreadful sea," she said giggling. "His temp'r hast not tam'd much ov'r the centuries."

Artemis explained how Persephone's husband had broken an Oath on the river Styx. And assured her that they were here for girl's souls and had no desire to fight.

"Follow me, let us straighten this matter out at once!" Persephone spun around stomping off toward the palace in a fit of rage.

While passing through the garden the sweet aroma from a pomegranate tree caught me off guard, I found myself mindlessly walking toward it again with my hand out reaching for a fruit. Lucky for me Chloe was paying attention and slapped my hand, knocking me out of my daze.

"You must resist Davis," she said. "One bite of that and you will be stuck here for all eternity!"

Persephone led us into Hades' throne room. Almost immediately, some transparent specters swooshed around the room, as if making sure we were not a threat.

Persephone called to her husband. "Dear we have company, come down from your study!"

A moment later Hades entered the room. He glanced around ratcheting his gaze. Then his eyes stopped and lingered on me, before shifting his focus back on Artemis.

Hades said to Artemis, "Ahh—well, hello sister, what brings you all the way here?"

"A broken oath," she said holding her hips. "How dareth thee braketh a promise on the Styx."

Hades tugged at his chin. "Was merely exploiting a gray area to keep things entertaining," he explained. "It has been boring for way too long, I miss toying with demigods."

My blood boiled. "ENTERTAINING!" I screamed. "How is it entertaining to take the two girls who meant the most to me away? Not to mention how you robbed me of my parents!"

Hades paced, with an amused smirk on his face. "It's been nearly four-thousand years since I had the pleasure of a family squabble," he admitted. "I have been very bored as you might imagine, being immortal and all."

"Bored, lonely, whatever," I wailed. "It gives you no right to screw with people's lives like this!"

Hades let out a demented laugh. "Boy, I have every right to toy with souls, living or dead anyway I so desire," He flipped his cloak to one side. "I am the eldest god, the god of wealth, king of the dead. It is I, and I alone who controls Death."

A familiar sensation washed over me. It was the same desire to kneel, like when I first encountered him back on the beach. The urge was nearly irresistible like Melinda's siren-song and I struggled with all my might not throw myself down on the floor and grovel for forgiveness. I figured his domain must have intensified his power, but I somehow resisted his aura.

Chloe stopped in front of Hades. "You may control much, but some fates are beyond your reach," she hissed. "Give back Kelly and Alicia, or I'll order them to become maidens of Artemis."

"How dare you raise your voice and make demands in my home!" Hades boomed. "You are out of your league girl."

Artemis rushed to Chloe's side. "Mine own lieutenant is right these girl's fates hadst already been decided by me!" Artemis said. "As thou knoweth those maidens hath called to me, and I answ'r'd their calleth."

"Did they swear an oath?" Hades asked.

"Nay— but in timeth those maidens wouldst has't," Artemis suggested. "We w're busy stopping the prophecy."

"Then it seems we are at an impasse," Hades smirked. "May I suggest a game of skill, the winner gets both souls, if the player of my choosing loses I keep them—if we have a draw we each get one—sound fair?"

"What game of skill and who is't doth thee dare?" Artemis asked.

Hades laughed and turned to me. "So what do you say nephew care to play your uncle a game of Soul Chess?"

Just then Persephone intervened and spoke up on our behalf. "Husband you are always telling me how important it is on keeping my word, yet you broke an oath on the Styx—please reconsider.

"My mind is set," he boomed. "So—nephew do you accept my challenge?"

I walked up to Hades and looked him deep in his soul-less eyes. "I came here to deliver a message from Zeus!" I balled my fists. "He said there is a debt owned in blood, all Anunnaki must offer they're first born as tribute!"

"His threats are insignificant to me," he said. "While he was cursed I was the ruler of all, not he."

I shrugged. "Anyway back to the game—I'll play your stupid game on one condition—it stays clean, no more tricks!"

"Very well," Hades said. "We have a deal."

"Your word means nothing these days," Leah chided.

Hades rolled his eyes at Leah like she was an insignificant insect.

"Follow me to the game room," Hades started walking. "Hurry and do not wander off as its very dangerous in the next part of the palace."

We followed Hades through several large rooms. Most of them were mostly empty except random torturing devices and skeletal guards standing guard at the doorways. Finally, we came to a room with a single door at the far end, I figured this must be his man cave err I mean game room.

"Please, please come in!" Hades snapped with authority. "Nephew take a seat at the roundtable, everyone else pull up a chair to watch."

I walked over to the roundtable, under closer inspection, I swear its legs were carved out of bone. The chairs were a black wood and felt timeworn, they had a musky smell to them. I took a seat and waited for my host to join me. I thought to myself Oogle I know you said you were letting me do this on my own—but if this game is like real Chess, I could actually use a super computer to help me gain an edge.

"Oogle will help Davis with game."

Hades walked over carrying an eerie looking chess set, it looked like he picked it up from the set of a horror movie. The board was carved out of wood that looked like blood, the usual squares you would expect on a Chess board were nonexistent. In their place were squares that depicted different deaths of humans, such as decapitations and eviscerations they were very detailed and gruesome. Some were so bad that it made me feel sick to my stomach. The chess pieces caught my eye when Hades sat them down. They were miniature souls that appeared alive. They were modern era people, a mixture of all ages and ethnic backgrounds.

Chloe pulled a chair up beside me and gave me a smile like she was saying good luck, you are going to need it! Leah pulled her chair up and sat on the other side of me. Artemis and her other huntress pulled their chairs up beside Hades on his left side, and Persephone sat to his right.

"Are these the souls of dead people," I murmured.

Hades let out a deep laugh. "Now what fun would that be," he said. "These are a random bunch of living people if you lose a piece—Death will collect them for real."

With a wave of his hand, Alicia and Kelly's souls appeared on each side of the table, and all of the little soul-pieces arranged themselves on the Chessboard.

Hades put his thumb on his king, which looked like the real king of Saudi Arabia and rocked it back and forth under the weight of his finger. "The rules are the same as the game Chess," he explained. "But it's more interesting since you control who lives and who dies, makes for a better challenge."

"Let us begin, you move first Davis as your side is the traditional white pieces," he suggested. "A little word of advice—avoid naming your pieces or getting too attached, as it's a pity when they die."

I studied the board making my thoughts audible for Oogle, we don't want to kill any kids or young people, if we are forced to sacrifice a piece, please make sure it's someone very old. If we have to take a piece from Hades also target the eldest pieces first. Seriously though I was not a fan of this game at all, it just didn't settle right in my stomach.

"Davis move far left pawn up two," Oogle instructed.

Without any thought, Hades moved a pawn forward to meet mine.

Oogle guided me through each move, we were six moves in and no pieces were swapped when Hades accused me of cheating. "You are cheating," he flipped the table over outraged sending the pieces rolling across the floor. "I don't know how you are cheating, but no one ever makes it past three moves with me."

Kelly and Alicia were just floating in the air where the table used to be. I stood up, my adrenalin was pumping. "So, you admit that you invited me to a challenge you knew I could not win?" I exclaimed, "Did I not say no more tricks?"

My heart was pounding hard in my chest, I've had all that I could stomach of my uncle. It seemed like there was no escaping a fight, if I intended to take the girls home, so I gripped the hilt of my sword ready for a fight to the death.

"WAIT!" Persephone pleaded. "MY husband intended to cheat by having an unfair advantage, so in the good nature of us all being family. I call the game a draw or a stalemate in this case."

Persephone walked over to Kelly and placed her hands on her cheeks. "I release thee—return to thy vessel."

In a flash, Kelly's soul was gone. I assumed it returned to her body back on Mount Olympus as that is where Poseidon said they would be waiting.

Hades was enraged and stomped over to his wife. "How dare you meddle in my affairs!"

Artemis and all four of her huntress rushed over and circled Persephone, offering their protection. "You cunning snake, speak to your wife in that tone once more in my presence, and I'll cut out your tongue!" Artemis said.

"Are you OK?" Chloe asked.

The goddess nodded.

Hades hesitated. "I offer you a game to play, and you cheat me, in my own realm," he said. "I'll be taking this one to the fields of punishment."

"I told thee she was already claimed by thy!" Artemis boomed.

Hades reached into a leather pouch dangling on his side and revealed a silver crown, when he placed it on his head he vanished into the background, becoming completely invisible.

"Show yourself, coward," Leah wailed.

The huntress pulled their spears, Artemis readied her silver bow, nocking a silver arrow. "I doth not wisheth f'r a square broth'r, but if 't be true this is thy wisheth, then i shalt oblige."

The Fates flew in, cracking flaming whips that lashed out at everyone. They forced us all away from where I suspected Hades was hiding, as they hissed and whipped at us in defense of their infernal king.

Persephone screamed, "Husband stop this where is your sense of chivalry?"

I guess his wife was the only one who was able to reach him and make him consider his actions, even if on a small scale. It seemed to have worked.

Hades voice boomed from in front of me. "I will offer you this nephew, as I'd rather lose to you than Artemis. Your choice Alicia or your mortal parents, choose wisely," he removed his crown becoming visible once more. "You have three minutes; I feel it is fitting given that there are three souls."

The three Fates eyeballed us carefully waiting for any one of us to look at their king wrong, or make a move. Trust me I fought a lot of crazy things in the past month, but I didn't want to mess around with these ladies. They reeked of death, and I didn't want to join them here or be cursed by them. I weighed my options, Hades really liked to hit you where it hurt, like how in the heck was I supposed to make such a life changing choice in only minutes. As badly as I wanted my parents back, I decided dead is dead and Alicia was still alive in every practical sense, minus missing her soul.

So I made my choice. "I'll take Alicia's soul," I said. "My parents would understand I'm sure."

Hades gave me his famous evil grin. "One stipulation, you must exit the Underworld the same way you came in Alicia's soul will follow you," he said. "I'll alert my soldiers and Cerberus of your presence and let them know you have my blessing to leave. If you look back, even a small glance I will keep her soul. Once you've reach the water's edge where Charon dropped you off, only then may you look back.

"Must I do it alone, or can the huntresses and Artemis join me?"

"You must do it alone," Hades said. "Artemis and her huntress shall await you on the other side."

"You have a deal!" I said.

I looked back at Chloe, Leah, Artemis and her huntress they all offered me a smile as encouragement.

Persephone walked up to me, "I just want to tell you that the stories I hear of you make me proud to call you brother, she said. "I'm not sure if you know this, but Zeus is my father as well."

Persephone leaned in and whispered softly into my ear. "You misinterpreted the prophecy," she said. "You were tricked if you waited until after the crossing you could have saved both heaven and earth. Now as we speak Hade's father Coronus stirs in the pits of Tartarus becoming whole again, the curse drained the Olympians energy to heal him."

I stepped back feeling sick. It's like every step forward puts me five steps backward. I looked at Persephone. "Thanks for the words of encouragement," I said with a cough. "I'll pass this task and then I'll make sure I give your father that message about how much you miss him."

I told everyone goodbye and insisted that I would be fine and see them all on the other side. Alicia's apparition was aware of me now. I didn't know it—but spirits could cry as she had what I assumed to be tears of joy as she beamed a smiled at me.

"Don't worry Alicia—I won't fail I promise."

"Take one final look at Alicia Nephew, as it will be your last if you fail."

I looked at Alicia for a long stare and then said, "I'll see you on the other side."

Heading out was not as bad, at least this time I knew what to expect. I retraced my steps and left Hades Palace through the garden, this time, I managed to resist the pomegranate tree. I felt half tempted to load up my pockets with gems and gold coins but I figured with my luck they would be cursed or worse, and I didn't want to entertain what worse could mean, so I just left them. I managed to get back on the path, after several hours of walking I wondered if Alicia was still following me. It seriously was tempting to look back, like was she even with me, was this another one of Hade's traps. I had no idea, but I reassured myself that she was with me.

After I had passed by the Isle of The Blessed, I knew I was on the right path. "So Oogle I guess your back on silent mode," I asked.

He didn't answer me, so I suppose I was back to being tested. Like got that I needed to be more independent on missions, but I seriously wanted some friendly conversation as this place was so dreary, if I were the emotional type, I'd probably curl up in a ball and just lay motionless on the ground. That was the aura this place put off, it was very, very dark.

I walked through the endless wheat fields trying my best not to stray off track when I noticed the Pavilion of Judges in the distance it gave me a warm, happy feeling.

"Alicia not much further now, we will soon be to the tunnel that leads to Cerberus."

She didn't answer, I was not even sure she could. It nagged at me in the back of my mind, was she even following me. Was she with me, was she ever with me was the bigger question. It killed me inside not to look back, but there was no way I'd fail her, not again. I'm sure Hades was loving how much this was torturing me. I'm certain that this was his plan all along, to make me suffer.

Since Oogle and Alicia were both not talking to me, my mind wandered off to what Persephone had told me. Like I knew Coronus was a Titan and was bad, but I didn't grasp the full extent of what him waking meant for the humans, Anunnaki, and Olympians. But how Persephone emphasized on me being tricked made me fear the worse. I thought back to the lines of the prophecy, to see if it was completed.

The child conceived of blood and foam was defiantly me and during my visit in the Underworld I realized I was walking this path of my own accord and that was the second line in the prophecy. A friend that's foe—I figured maybe Kelly since she was initially working for Hades but I've made several friends on this adventure, so I was not sure. The fourth line was defiantly about the Underworld, I was not sure if it was regarding me choosing Alicia over my parents or if it was me choosing not looking back to save her. But I was fairly sure that's what it meant. The fifth line was something about the gods being betrayed by the eldest son, I figured this is what Persephone warned me about, and the word son in the line made me think father, I wasn't sure what was being undone, but I assumed this was regarding Cronus. The final line in the prophecy Olympus or Earth the price be weighed—this I had a feeling did not come to pass. Like I understood Persephone said I was tricked and could have saved both heaven and earth…but my gut told me this last line had nothing to do with that and meant something much worse.

Once I reached the tunnel, I found myself walking against the moving flow of soul traffic. Lucky for me not only were they transparent, but I could easily pass through them. When I walked through one, I could feel the temperature drop around me, like a cold spot. After a while I finally reached the Archway and this time I was staring at Cerberuse's backside, it didn't take long for his snake tail to sense me, its tongue flickered tasting the air around it.

Since Artemis and the Huntress were no longer here to save me. I decided to say a silent prayer to Poseidon and Zeus. "Hey Dad's—like I know we just met. But since I been risking my life for you for like awhile now. I thought maybe I could ask a small favor. I really could use some help, like if for whatever reason Artemis's enchanted bone dust wore off, and Hades didn't give Cerberus the memo not to eat me, I' appreciate your help."

I didn't hear any thunder boom or see any divine signs as a message of them hearing my prayer, heck I didn't even know for sure if they could. I was kind of hoping that they sent Hermes down to fly me out of here. But no such luck, it felt like if I was going to do this, I had no choice but to do it on my own.

I cautiously inched forward until I was inches away from Cerberuse's tail, it didn't take long for it to find me. Its yellow eyes hovered in front of mine, its tongue flickering. Then all of a sudden I heard one of the dogs three heads leave out a blood-curdling howl. It struggled to turn around under the stone archway, dust from above rained down. I couldn't turn back, or I'd lose Alicia forever. So I ran and slid between his legs like I was stealing second base. His heads came slamming down toward me like the buckets on a bulldozer taking up chunks of ground around me. I scurried to my feet just barely keeping out of his massive jaws.

I ran forward strafing left and right in random patterns, zig-zagging all over faster than I ever ran before. Gods I wish I had one of Artemis's Stags, it be a breeze to escape then! I ran so quickly that my upper thighs burned, and my stomach muscles were starting to cramp up. But I pushed on, I had to survive this, I had to make it to Charon's skiff. One of his massive heads latched onto my shoulder I thrust myself forward tearing away cloth and flesh. My shoulder started to throb almost instantly. I couldn't turn around and fight him like I wasn't even sure if I stood a chance if I could—but I knew that was not an option at this point. Think Davis, think I thought outloud. Then I remembered the gift from Hephaestus, I had no idea how or if it worked but I was nearing the end of the tunnel and had no more options, I'd soon be cut off by the river, and if Charon was not there waiting I was going be turned into a living chew toy!

I fished around in my pocket, I could feel the cold metal sphere, but it was not an easy task to get it out while running full speed. Finally, I managed to free it from my pocket, I held onto it tight. Once I got to the water's edge, I planned to spin around and toss it at Cerberus. Just I seriously had no idea what to expect, and if for whatever reason it failed, I had no backup plan. The tunnel was so dark I could barely see anything up ahead, I was plowing through spirits left and right as I pushed myself to stay a few inches ahead of Cerberus's deadly fangs. I could now hear the gurgling of water up ahead, I was closing in on my destination. I went over my plan over and over again in my mind, it had to work, there were no other options at this point. As soon as I crossed the threshold of the tunnel, my body was in full on flight-mode it took me a moment to process what I needed to do—I vaguely recalled the instructions. Oh yeah. Wind it up three turns and toss it at him. In a nanosecond, it pinned Cerberus to the floor covering him in a magically woven net. Cerberus, even with his massive strength and size, could not escape. He struggled futilely, growling and snapping at the net with all three of his heads. He was tightly pinned down, and the net was growing tighter constricting what was left of his movement.

I looked ahead into the darkness. I saw no sign of Alicia, maybe she returned to her body, maybe this was all just another trick. There was no way to be sure until I left the Underworld and spoke with Artemis.

After Cerberus had calmed down, I walked over to the net. Seeing him trapped made me feel sick, but at the same time, I didn't want to be torn to shreds by his heads as they played tug of war with me.

"I'm sorry boy," I said. "Your master was supposed to call you off, but I guess that was another lie."

After being pinned down, Cerberus kind of reminded me of a super-sized Waffles, so I walked over and reached my hand inside the net and scratched its ear, the hellhound responded with some happy panting. I'm sure Cerberus was just misunderstood, probably just needed some attention, someone, to pat him on the back, scratch behind his ears and toss him a ball once in a while.

I saw a faint glow in the distance, Charon was on his way. Knowing that I was soon leaving calmed me down. Now that I was thinking clearly I remembered about my shoulder, I reached up and touched it. Everything felt fine, it had already healed. Like I loved the fact that I had the gift of regeneration, but I also was not under the delusion that I was invincible, I could think of a dozen different things that probably kill me—like my head being cut off, or me being dropped into a vat of acid or a volcano. But I felt my powers were justified with all the danger that I attracted, I'm like some super monster-magnet!

Charon arrived, and I got off the skiff, he looked at my hand for payment.

"I don't have any cash this time, but I think it is wise to get moving—I'm not sure how long that net will hold Cerberus," I said point back at him. "We better be going."

Charon did not argue with my logic. Time felt somehow different like it was moving faster. I guess being in the Underworld has that effect, maybe it's the ashy scenery or the lack of a sun and moon. Either way, it didn't matter—after a while, I could see sunlight peeking through the darkness, the Acherusian Lake was a stone's throw away. I hoped that Kelly and Alicia would be waiting for me on the other side, but part of me was expecting Hades to have pulled a fast one on me.

Charon pulled the skiff ashore and motioned for me to get off. I scanned the endless crowd of spirits, being transparent gave me greater visibility since I could see right through them. But I didn't see Artemis, Chloe or Leah, or anyone else living for that matter. My mind raced with a million possible and horrible scenarios that all had Hades in them. Then I saw Hermes zipping in above the crowd of souls.

As he drew near, I could see a nervous grin plastered over his face.

Hermes landed in front of me. "Davis you are needed back on Olympus," he said. "Artemis sent me to fetch you."

I locked eyes with Hermes, "What's wrong?"

"No time for chit-chat—your mortal friend is grasping to a thread of life."

"Take me to her," I insisted.

Hermes gripped my shoulders, and a beam of light flashed over us. I rubbed my eyes everything looked white with blue spots. Then my vision came back into focus, I was now inside Mount Olympus, inside a large room decorated with dozens of marble statues. They were different mythical creatures such as centaurs, harpies and satyr's

TWENTY-FIVE

THE COUNCIL GOES MEDIEVAL

Hermes motioned for me to follow him. I didn't move more than five steps when Kelly ran over and wrapped her arms around me.

"Hey Davis," she said. "What happen to your shirt?"

"Let's just say I been to hell and back," I patted my shoulder. "But I'm happy to see you're feeling better—where is Alicia."

"She is not doing so hot," Kelly sighed. "Artemis is with her now."

"Take me to her, I have to see her."

Kelly lead me to where Alicia was resting. Artemis, Chloe, and Leah surrounded her. I walked over to see for myself how bad off she was—and she looked on the verge of death.

She was flush like I could see the life draining from cheeks, even the pigment faded from her hair making it white.

I walked over to Artemis. "Did Hades betray me?"

"Nay, mine own broth'r hath kept his promiseth just h'r vessel is too weak t won't holdeth h'r spirit much longeth'r."

Artemis locked eyes with me. "I wait'd f'r thee to arriveth as the lady cannot speaketh an oath in h'r condition, only someone the lady loves can do t f'r h'r," she said. "We needeth to act apace if 't be true we art to saveth h'r."

"Is there any other way?"

Artemis looked at me contently. "Davis I'm s'rry but th're is nay oth'r way, we might not but maketh Alicia swear an oath to me 'r the lady shall beest t'rtur'd by mine own broth'r."

"Do it—I can't bear her to suffer!" I said lowering my head. "I owe her more than that."

Artemis knelt by Alicia's side. "Mine own quite quaint one alloweth mine own w'rds seep into thy mind and Davis speaketh on mine own behalf."

My heart lurched when Alicia gasped, and her eyes rolled back into her head. Only the whites were now visible. I was so scared. Artemis chanted, "Oh virgin goddess of the wild places, cleanse mine own body pure of sineth and alloweth mine own s'rvitude beginneth. By lighteth of moon and silv'r boweth the hunteth is all I wisheth to knoweth.

As thy maiden, I f'rsake all men until battle doth take me 'r did free again."

I recited the words in Alicia's place, I caught my voice lingering on freed again, this line gave me some hope—but nothing seemed to happen.

"I thought you said I could take the oath for her," I snapped. "Why is it not working!"

"H'r flesh is already rejecting h'r spirit th're is nay coming backeth from this," Artemis said. "we might not but cleanse h'r body and protecteth h'r from Hades."

Chloe walked over and placed a hand on my shoulder. "Davis I think I have an idea," she brightened. "If Apollo would give his consent, you could transfer the Spirit of Delphi into Alicia, it save her—I'm sure of it!"

Artemis patted her first lieutenant on the shoulder in approval.

Artemis bellowed, "Apollo, broth'r—come apace!"

Apollo joined us he was about seven feet tall, tan and chiseled. His hair was golden blond shoulder length and wavy. He looked like a supermodel that just came back from a beach photo shoot.

Artemis explained Chloe's suggestion of using the Spirit of Delphi to save Alicia. Apollo tugged at his clean shaved chin, considering the possibility.

"Well if I allowed her vessel to be the next Oracle of Delphi, it is permanent—no take backs," he said. "So she would need to stay in Olympus for a while before she could ever entertain having a semi-normal life. As she would need training and protecting, at least until we are sure this prophecy has ended because in the wrong hands she could be our undoing."

I bit my lip trying to hold back the information I learned from Persephone until Alicia was safe. Then I'd spill—but not a moment sooner.

"So do we have your blessing Lord Apollo," I said. "Alicia has been a great asset on all of our missions."

Apollo beamed a smile at me. "Sure why not, we need a dedicated Oracle anyway," he said. "Besides I don't really think you to be the oracle type Davis, I believe that you would go mad waiting in a cave to give out my prophecies every seven days—like my last male Oracle Trophonius. You are as untamed as the sea like your father, Poseidon."

"You do remember how this part is done, the passing of the spirit," Apollo quipped. "Just lean in and plant one on her, but unlike an ordinary kiss think about a transferring of energy."

I looked at Alicia she looked so weak, I leaned in and softly kissed her lips. I thought about Delphi's spirit transferring to her and tears pooled in the corners of my eyes and streamed down my cheeks. Out of nowhere my back muscles tensed and my back uncontrollably arched as Delphi's spirits expelled from my body and into Alicia's, sparks of blue and white energy poured from my hands. I felt drained afterward, but if it worked it was worth it. I leaned against a nearby marble statue of a satyr holding a goblet and flute. My eyes lingered on Alicia. Please work, I thought to myself, come on wake up!

I knew it was working when the color rushed back into her cheeks, and the white hair was replaced by her natural color. Alicia sprung up on the table, she looked dazed. Her jaw slack, her eyes wide as she gazed all around her and found that she was alive. "Where am I?" she asked meekly.

Alicia received a warm reception from the huntresses. Apollo reached out his hand and laced his fingers with Alicia, helping her stand up. "Welcome back to the world of the living gorgeous my name is Apollo," he announced. "It be such a shame to lose such a marvelous creature."

Alicia's cheeks turned two shades of red. "Thank you Lord Apollo," she stammered. "And thank all of you for rescuing me."

"Umm—Lord Apollo I need an audience with Zeus," I said. "I learned of some dire news while in the Underworld that he needs to hear."

"Zeus don't do audiences without appointments, sorry kid."

"I think he will want to hear what I have to say," I said. "It regards his father."

Apollo stood up straight, saluting me with his full attention the bronze color in his cheeks turned a shade of pale white, "I shall call a meeting in the pantheon at once," he said. "Hurry along now, follow me."

I waited at the doorway. Just inside the Greek Pantheon were the twelve Olympians walking inside and sitting down on their thrones, the room was in the shape of a horseshoe wrapping around and the gods and goddesses sat in this order Zeus, Hera, Poseidon, Demeter, Athena, Apollo, Artemis, Ares, Aphrodite, Hephaestus, Hermes, and Dionysus. In the center of the room, the hearth burned with brilliant bright blue flames. The Gods were in their pure form around fifteen feet tall. Otherwise they would have looked pretty silly sitting on oversized thrones!

The gods began to chit chat amongst one another, it had been a very long time since they enjoyed the simple pleasures they once took for granted, and they all were so happy and overflowing with joy. Chloe gave me permission to enter the pantheon and Zeus stood up from his throne towering over me like a telephone pole. His voice boomed, "Silence let us hear what my son has come to say."

The words "my son" caught me off guard, like this was unexpected and got me choked up.

I walked closer clearing my throat, "I gave your message to Hades but—I don't think he took it seriously," I said. "But that is not what I came here to tell you—Persephone warned me that I miss understood the prophecy."

Zeus nodded taking in my words, "You may continue."

I leaned back to see his face, "Persephone said that Hades cursed you all with a deeper purpose other than getting you out of his way and making you miserable," I took a deep breath. "I guess the best way to describe what he did—he turned you all into batteries to energize your father Cronus, and now he is restoring himself and growing stronger by the minute in the pits of Tartarus."

I continued, "Also during my journey through the Underworld I went over the prophecy and am certain it's not over. Persephone explained to me that if I waited, I could have spared heaven and earth. I have no idea if this is true or not, but I don't think it had anything to do with the last line of the prophecy, 'Olympus or Earth the price be weighed' what do you make of it?"

Zeus stomped his foot outraged, the white marble cracked under the weight of his foot snaking out in a v-line right at me, and spider webbing under my feet. "How dare he awake Father," Zeus boomed. "It will mean the end of all that we know, we must put a stop to this at once!"

He continued, "I do agree that last line is unsettling for me as well, prophecies are never easy to understand, they can be interpreted in many ways."

All the other gods and goddess stood up their eyes ratcheted to Zeus awaiting further instructions.

Hera walked over to her husband, "We must locate our demigod bloodline and start training at once," she said. "Once we have a count we can bring back some of the older demigods like Jason and Perseus—I know we swore to never make clones of them again after what happened—!"

Ares interrupted, "We need a strong army if grandfather wakes we must strike him down before he is at full power," he said slamming his fist down on the arm of Aphrodite's throne, a chunk of white marble fell from it and sprouted wings flying up in the air. Then it circled around and came back down in the form of a white dove landing in the palm of her hand. She gently placed the bird where her throne was broken, and it seamlessly meshed back into the marble until, bird and marble once again became one.

I guess gods needed infinitely durable furniture that could endure their abuse in times like these. Dionysus stood up holding a wine goblet in his hand, a bottle of wine hovered over his cup filling it from time to time as he drank. I wondered if he had an invisible servant or if he purposely enchanted the wine bottle to do that.

After he drank a few big gulps of wine he let out a belch that reminded me of a sonic boom, grabbing everyone's attention, "I say we clone Hercules he was always fun to have around," he took another drink from his cup. "Besides no one could hold their drink quite like him, fun guy."

Hera glowered at Dionysus, my best guess was she was thinking keep your mouth shut you are a drunken idiot.

Dionysus sat back down. "That shall be all—," he said gesturing with his hand to dismiss everyone.

Zeus took center stage. "Hermes locate my old friend Chiron I will be needing his assistance in training our newest arrivals," he commanded. "Athena I need you to check on our training camp for heroes and make sure that it is architecturally sound.

Hermes and Athena both said, "Yes sir." And vanished in sparks of light, I figured they didn't want to make Zeus wait as he seemed like the impatient type.

Then Zeus shifted his attention on me, he tugged at his flowing white beard. "You have done me proud," he said. "I shall grant your friend Kelly immunity to my punishment for the Anunnaki, this is my gift to you."

I looked into Zeus's glowing blue eyes, they looked electrifying. "Must innocent blood be spilled to bring justice father?"

Zeus sighed, "I know my punishment seems harsh," he said. "But—I've learned over the millennia that fear is the only way to rule, trust me I tried doing things the nice way and see where that got my family—at the bottom of the sea!"

I sighed, "Well it seems we have bigger problems then the Anunnaki at present—what can I do to help?"

Zeus took a knee, kneeling down in front of me. "You have done enough, take Kelly with you and just be yourself for a few days," he said. "Let us figure out how to stop Cronus when it's time I'll send Hermes for you, I want you to meet my friend Chiron, I have a feeling you will become good friends."

"What about Alicia," I sighed. "Can she come with us?"

"In time she can," Zeus said. "But it might be years until that is possible, she is a weapon in the wrong hands."

"Can I at least say goodbye to her for now?"

Zeus patted me on the back, "Sure kiddo, but you both will be much closer than you think," he gave me a wink. "I have big plans for you."

"Umm—OK," I said.

Alicia was over with Artemis and Apollo they were explaining her new role as their Oracle. Chloe walked up to me and punched me in the shoulder.

"Ouch—," I rubbed my shoulder. "You have a mean right hook!"

Chloe flipped a strand of hair out of her eyes, "Not bad for a girl huh?" she said giggling. "It has been a long time since I was in the company of a man Davis, I think of thee as a brother now."

I hugged Chloe. "Thanks, I always wondered what it be like to have a sister," I said. "You would be an awesome sister to chill with!"

Chloe shoved me away, "Get going before I cry," she sniffed. "I've never been good with goodbyes."

"I don't think I'll be gone for long—Zeus said he has big plans for me," I chuckled. "Whatever that means."

Her jaw dropped. "That's great news," she said. "May our paths cross often. I'll try my best to convince Artemis to put us on a quest together sometime soon!"

"That be awesome," I said. "I'm holding you to that!"

I was really starting to feel at home amongst the Olympians. I walked over to Alicia, I was excited to talk to her. Like I had so much I wanted to share with her about my journey to the Underworld and what I went through saving her, and how sorry I was for getting her caught up in all of this. That's when it crossed my mind about her Mother, like if she had to stay on Olympus wouldn't her mother need to know?"

"Alicia—," I said wrestling around in my mind for the right words. "I'm sorry."

Alicia turned toward me giving me her full attention. "You have nothing to be sorry about sirenboy," she placed her hands on her hips. "It was my choice to come with you on this adventure, and I would do it again in a heartbeat!"

"But you—almost died," I shuffled my feet nervously. "I felt responsible and would have never forgiven myself if you—."

Alicia interrupted me. "But I didn't Davis," she pleaded. "And now I feel special like I have somewhere that I actually belong. After my father left when I was young, I never felt like I fit—."

I interrupted her. "How is that possible, you had so many friends in school, and you were super popular."

Alicia sighed, "Just because I was popular doesn't mean I felt whole inside, with the spirit of Delphi I feel at peace with myself," she smiled. "It's such an enlightening feeling Davis—I can't even begin to explain it."

I asked Apollo and Artemis to give us a moment alone. Then I wrapped my arms around Alicia and just held her. The world felt like it paused just for us like time was standing still. For now, this moment was ours and ours alone. I placed my hand on the side of her face and leaned in for a kiss, she met me half way, it felt amazing when her soft lips met mine. Then I pulled away, my eyes stung—all the emotions I had felt from her being gone, being near death rushed at me, hitting me full force. I fought to hold back the tears as they stung at my eyes.

I sniffed. "I thought I had lost you," I said. "How would I be able to live with that guilt?"

Alicia smiled. "Davis you're the most amazing man I ever had the pleasure of knowing," she said. "Like seriously I don't know anyone that go to hell and back to keep me safe!"

Her last comment brought a smile to my face, we both giggled at the thought. Just then I remembered the rod, and I reached into my pocket and pulled it out, unwrapping it from the velvet material.

"Here take this—it really helps with the whole prophecy thing," I handed the rod to her and as she grabbed the other end, both of our backs arched in unison.

In the vision I was standing on a hillside, I looked around and noticed large letters that read Hollywood on another hill across from us. I was in Hollywood California, and Kelly was with me. I followed the direction of Kelly's frantically pointing arm and saw a giant humanoid creature trampling the city down below, he was on the same scale as the Kraken—I mean huge! I looked over at Kelly and asked her why the police or military wasn't doing anything, and she explained that they can't see the truth. To them, it was a tornado, or possibly a hurricane. That's when I snapped back to the present.

I looked Alicia in the eyes, she was trembling. I guess that some of the oracles energy was still left inside me. Honestly, I hoped it be the last time I ever had a vision, as I was not a fan of glimpsing future or past events. Some things were better left unknown because once you know something, it's not like you can just forget about it, and that can cause all kinds of problems.

"So—what did you see in the vision?" I asked.

Kelly stood in a trance like state for a moment. "A giant monster was destroying Hollywood; you were there Davis!" She blurted.

Just then Apollo came over and insisted it was time for me to go. He explained that Alicia needed to start her training right away so that he could help her sort out this newest vision. Apollo wrapped his arm around Alicia's shoulders and ushered her off. She still seemed dazed and confused as she walked away, I figured visions must have affected mortals on a deeper level than demigods.

I said goodbye to everyone and Kelly joined me. Leah seemed a bit sad to see me go, but she was too tuff of a chick to admit it or even say a proper good-bye.

Leah waved at me, "Keep out of trouble Davis," she said with a wide grin. "Them mortals are a fragile bunch be gentle with them."

I laughed. "I'll try my best!"

Zeus walked over to Kelly and I. "So, where would you like to go?" He said, "I can send you anywhere you desire."

It didn't take me more than a second to choose my destination. Apparently, it been in the back of my mind and I been so busy with everything going on in my life that I didn't even realize it.

"There is only one place I wish to go," I said. "My Aunt Lisa's in Pennsylvania."

Zeus then focused his gaze on Kelly, "And you my dear where would you desire to be?"

Kelly froze as if she had nowhere to go. So I grabbed her hand and said, "She is coming with me."

Zeus gave me a grin and wink, I figured that was his way of saying smooth move kiddo.

"I set the hearth to your requested location," he grinned. "Don't worry about all the details, you left your grandparent's house with your Aunt about a week ago, to the best of her knowledge you are in the backyard playing with a friend right now."

My jaw dropped at the thought. Then it hit me what about Alicia so I said, "What should I tell Alicia's mom?"

Zeus let out a hearty laugh, "Ahh I forget sometimes you were raised by mortals," he said. "She is having dinner with her mother as we speak, in good time she will replace the current Alicia when all is safe and the time is right."

"Good to know."

Kelly and I walked over to the hearth, we both stopped and looked back at everyone. Then we stepped through the flames, oddly enough they just felt warm. Then, in a blinding flash of light we were standing in Aunt Lisa's backyard, even Waffles. Until now, it never clicked in my head how homesick I truly was, I missed my Aunt Lisa more than I'd like to admit. But—apparently, I've been here for a week, so I couldn't just run up to her getting all emotional.

I could see the love in Kelly's eyes as she looked at me. I felt kind of guilty for not picking, which girl I wanted to be with. After all, both of them were equally amazing. At this point I really didn't want to pick, I enjoyed having them both around as friends. But what Aphrodite told me about Kelly being my soulmate tugged at the back of my mind. I would take some time to sort my feelings eventually, but for now, I had bigger things to worry about like Zeus seeking blood for tribute and Cronus awakening in Tartarus. Like I seriously did not want to see my final vision come to pass, it takes an army of gods and demigods to battle Cronus. Typical kids my age worried about simple things like school, a part-time job, getting their first car, you know what I mean. Like, don't get me wrong...I still wanted these things too, but they now seemed like a pipedream—like any day Zeus would be sending Hermes to fetch me, and I was uncertain what he had in store for me next, but his emphasis on big plans did not settle well with me.

Being back at Aunt Lisa's brought back memories. Like why I ran away and the feeling of the survivor's guilt. Apparently, I came full circle with those feelings. I now knew the answers to these questions and honestly felt happy to be alive for a change. I now had a sense of purpose and was excited to head back to Mount Olympus in a few days and see my new friends and Alicia. And see what the plan was for stopping Cronus.

I locked eyes with Kelly. "Whatever you do, please be honest with me from now on," I said. "No matter what it's about."

"I will Davis," she smiled. "Oh, and by the way thanks for rescuing me."

Kelly kept staring at me dreamily; I guess no other guy ever went to the Underworld and back for her before.

Kelly's big emerald green eyes studied me like she was searching for answers. "I guess I'm due back on Mars, I don't have anywhere to stay here. Don't worry though we can keep in touch, and I'll see if I can convince my father to make peace with Zeus."

I grabbed her by the hand. "You're already home if you will stay that is?"

She smiled from ear to ear. "I thought you'd never ask!"

Kelly smiled. "So do you think your Aunt will mind you bringing a girl home?"

"Don't you mean two girls?" I said. "We can't forget Wawa!"

Kelly laughed. "Nah we wouldn't wanna do that."

I looked over at Kelly. "How I see it—I'm going to be sixteen in a few weeks, so I don't think she can say too much about it. If she doesn't approve I guess, we can both stay on Mars!"

The look on Kelly's face said more than enough, she was glowing. I could tell that the thought of me following her through the universe made her giddy.

I glanced at both Kelly and Waffles. "Let's go home, girls, I'm sure Aunt Lisa will be excited to see us!"

Kelly snaked her arm around my waist and together the three of us walked toward the house. My gaze lingered on the tract of trees in front of Alicia's house, I guess I was curious to see what her shade looked like, but she was not out in the yard.

I smelled fried chicken as we reached the house, it was mouthwatering. I loved Aunt Lisa's fried chicken, I hoped she made enough for all of us, as even Waffles was drooling.

"I say we take a few days off from this whole saving the world gig," I suggested while turning the doorknob.

"Besides I'm starving, let's grab some of Aunt Lisa's famous fried chicken—and discuss a few things, like how we can stop Zeus from spilling the blood of the innocent."

Thunder boomed above leaving us looking skyward.

DON'T MISS THE NEXT EXCITING
ADVENTURE IN THE
THE GUARDIANS OF OLYMPUS
SERIES

THE
BLOOD
OF THE
INNOCENT

www.ingramcontent.com/pod-product-compliance
Lightning Source LLC
Chambersburg PA
CBHW030548180626
46816CB00005B/1458